CHRISTMAS AT THE AMISH MARKET

NEW YORK TIMES BESTSELLING AUTHOR

SHELLEY SHEPARD GRAY

Print ISBN 978-1-952210-77-8

www.hallmarkpublishing.com

My beloved speaks and says to me: Arise, my love, my beautiful one, and come away, for behold, the winter is past, the rain is over and gone.

Song of Solomon 2: 10–11 (ESV)

The blessing of sharing outweighs the blessing of having.

Amish Proverb

Chapter One

It was business as usual at Raber's, the sprawling Amish market. Well, business as usual for a Thursday afternoon in December. Customers crowded the aisles packed with candles, jars of jam, wooden trains, woven baskets, and red and green quilts. The deli, bakery, and furniture sections all had long lines. The scents of balsam, peppermint, and cranberry filled the air—a constant reminder the big day was under twenty-five days away.

Lots of Walden locals were coming in, of course, but so were a great number of folks from nearby towns. And quite a few English tourists, too, from all over Ohio and even beyond. Their arms were filled with items, and their hands were clutching wooden baskets with fresh bread and cheese.

It was all enough to make even the most curmudgeonly shopkeepers smile in anticipation of tallying the days' sales.

Unless, of course, the shopkeeper happened to be feeling overwhelmed and extremely shorthanded.

Which Wesley Raber was...and had been for the last ten days.

What a time it had been. First, his father had almost had a heart attack, which had sent the whole family into a tailspin. Soon after, the doctors scheduled a procedure to put in a stent and prescribed a full month of rest. Within a day, his brother Paul and his wife in Crittenden County had offered to help take care of *Daed* and *Mamm*. His sisters Frannie and Marianne, along with their husbands, had helped *Mamm* and *Daed* travel to Paul and Jenna's.

Once they'd gotten there, *Daed* had been a handful, and *Mamm* had been ex*haus*ted. So his three siblings had called to let him know they would be there for a spell, leaving Wesley to run Raber's Amish Market on his own until December thirty-first.

It wasn't as though Frannie and Marianne worked in the store, anyway. Neither lived all that close. Unlike Wesley, they were both married; they had their own lives to concentrate on. But Wesley had always worked alongside his parents. He'd never been in charge of the entire store on his own.

As scary as that responsibility was, it was nothing compared to how worried he was about his father. He'd always imagined his father as invincible. This health scare had proved that he definitely was not.

Every time Wesley allowed himself to think about what could have happened, he broke out into a cold sweat.

"Excuse me, young man!" the *Englisch* tourist called out from the back of the line. Two people in line groaned.

"Young man, here I am," she singsonged. "Over here."

A mite bit annoyed by the summons, Wesley

looked up from the pile of Trail bologna he'd just sliced. "*Jah?*" he said.

A sea of faces stared back at him. Most looked resigned, but a few looked both impatient and irritated. He still had no idea who'd just yelled at him.

"Yes?" he repeated, this time in English instead of Pennsylvania Dutch.

A bejeweled hand rose, signaling for him to come out from the other side of the deli counter. "Oh good. You found me. At last." The hand was attached to a slim woman with bright-red hair. When he met her gaze, she raised her chin. "Young man, I need some assistance, please. I really have a lot to do today."

Saul Freeman, whose bologna Wesley had just wrapped, pursed his lips. He kept quiet, but his opinion was loud and clear. He was peeved.

Wesley knew this, because he felt exactly the same way. It was on the tip of his tongue to tell the woman to wait her turn and stop being so pushy.

Instead of giving into that impulse, Wesley worked on keeping a blank expression. It was a skill he'd perfected over the years. There was always someone who didn't care to stand in line.

"Here you go, Saul," he said with a tight smile. "When you're ready to check out, Ernie can help ya over at the counter."

The older man's white, bushy eyebrows rose up to near his hairline. "You really won't take *mei* money right now? The line to check out is four people deep."

"I'm sorry, but I cannot. I don't have a cash register."

Saul harrumphed as he turned and walked away.

Immediately, Flora Miller stepped up to the counter and pulled out a list from her pocketbook. The ties on her white kapp flew a bit with the motion. "Here ya go, Wesley."

"*Danke*, Flora." Scanning the list, he inwardly groaned. Flora asked for ten slices from no less than six different types of meat and cheese. Her order would take some time. "I'll get to it right now."

She folded her hands over the black apron covering her dark-gray dress. "I hope so. I've been waiting for a while now. At least ten minutes."

"I'm sorry for your wait, but we're shorthanded today."

"I noticed." Craning her neck, Flora looked around the store. "Where are your parents, Wesley?"

"In Kentucky." He placed ten slices of Muenster cheese in a plastic bag.

"Really? Where?"

Glancing at the list again, Wesley pulled out the smoked turkey breast he'd cooked a week before. "Crittenden County."

"My word. Ain't that where your *bruder* lives? I hope he's all right." She gazed at him with a hopeful expression, obviously eager for a bit of gossip to pass along at the next coffee.

"Excuse me!" the bejeweled woman called out again. "Did you hear me?" When he continued to only work on Flora's order, the woman turned to one of the other tourists in line. "I don't understand why I'm being ignored. Does that Amish man understand English or only whatever language they talk?"

"I'm pretty sure he understands English, Shirl. I think he's just kind of busy now."

"Well—"

"Calm down," her friend said. "You're being rude."

And so it continued. For the next hour, Wesley packaged deli meat, helped customers, asked Ernie to forgo his usual break, and apologized over and over again to everyone who was waiting in line.

When the last customer left at half past five—a full thirty minutes later than he was supposed to be open—Wesley locked the door with a snap and turned the sign over to *Closed.*

He'd done it. Or, rather, he and Ernie had.

Wesley grinned over at his father's fifty-year-old friend. "What a day, huh? And to think, it's only December fourth!"

Ernie did not return his smile. Instead, he untied the black apron from around his waist and handed it to Wesley with something akin to a snap. "Something is gonna need to be done, Wesley. I ain't of a mind to work like this every day."

"Excuse me?"

"When I said I'd fill in to help out your parents, your father told me I wouldn't be on my feet all day, but I am." His pale-blue eyes flashed in irritation. "Furthermore, you said I would get at least three breaks during my six-hour shift. Today I only got lunch."

Wesley felt his cheeks heat with embarrassment. He actually had said that. Maybe he'd been a little too eager to say whatever he could to convince Ernie to work thirty hours a week during the month of December.

"I'm sorry you only got to have lunch today, but you saw how busy the store was."

"It was busy, that is true. But a man my age needs

to sit down from time to time. I barely had time to eat my sandwich, Wesley. Why haven't you rehired one of those teenagers your father brought in last year? Emma and Ben were good'uns. You need to see if at least one of them is available."

"Ben has another job, and Emma wasn't all that good." He wasn't trying to be mean, but it was true. "She needed help doing just about everything."

"Well, you still need to do something. With the way things are going, I'm going to be too tired to enjoy the season."

Wesley hadn't had time to eat at all, and his parents, who were older than Ernie, always worked hard on their feet for hours on end. It was to be expected in December. He kept that bit of information to himself, though; he was pretty sure Ernie wouldn't care.

"I'll figure something out," he said.

"I hope you do. My bunions are hurtin' me something awful. I'm gonna have to soak 'em good in Epsom salts, too." Looking even more perturbed, Ernie threw a hand up in the air. "Don't know why I'm telling you all this anyway. Things won't change. They never do."

Things never change? "What do you think needs to change?"

"If you have to ask me, it's obvious that it ain't gonna happen." Ernie made a great show of rubbing his lower back. "I'm heading home."

"Thank you again for your help."

Ernie waved off his thanks as he walked to the back to get his coat and lunch pail.

Alone now, Wesley needed a burst of energy. He had a whole store to clean, a cash register to close out, and three boxes of fresh stock to unpack and display. He was going to be here another two hours, and that was if he was lucky.

Which, of course, meant Ernie wasn't going to be the only person upset with him today. Liesl was going to be madder than a wet hen. Leaning against the counter, Wesley said a quick prayer for strength.

Usually, he would've taken everything in stride. He wasn't a child, after all; he was twenty-six years old. Moreover, he'd been essentially managing the store for the last several years.

But his parents really were the heart and soul of the Amish Market, and there were a great number of customers who didn't like working with anyone but Able Raber. Some of them even acted as if Wesley was still trying to get the hang of things, even after all this time.

When the door opened, he jumped to his feet, realizing that he'd forgotten to lock the door behind Ernie's departure.

"I'm sorry, but the store is—oh, hiya, Liesl." He smiled at the pretty sight she made.

"Hi to you as well," she said as she wandered inside. She had on a dark-navy dress that made her green eyes appear almost the color of jade. Her neatly pressed white *kapp* was placed perfectly over carefully arranged honey-colored locks. Not a strand of hair was out of place. As usual, her confident manner and pleasing features commanded his attention and practically made him tongue-tied.

It had always been that way, too. From the first time they'd exchanged words when she'd entered the store, he'd been smitten, and when she was seventeen and he was twenty-one, they'd started courting.

Now that he'd been courting her for some time, though, he feared she was losing patience. She'd become more demanding of his time of late...and had been hinting that she desired only one thing for Christmas.

He suspected that thing was him getting down on one k*nee*. Actually, he reckoned most everyone was waiting for that...but something was still stopping him from committing to her for the rest of his life.

Maybe it was just his cold feet, but he didn't think so. Instead, he kept battling the persistent feeling that something was missing from their relationship. All his life he'd watched his parents be true helpmates. His brother and sister-in-law seemed to act the same way. That sense of belonging seemed to be absent from him and Liesl.

Or perhaps it was just missing from him? He didn't know.

When she got to his side, her smile dimmed. "What's going on?"

"Nothing too much. Ernie just left."

"Oh. Well, are you ready?"

"For what?"

The last of her smile faded from sight. "For our outing. Don't you remember? We've had plans to go to the Pinery tonight."

His stomach sank.

The Pinery was a quirky place on the outskirts of Walden. For eleven months out of the year, it was a garden center and nursery, but during the month of December, it became an enchanted place. The employees decorated every bit of it to the hilt and even designed a maze of Christmas trees, each one adorned with lights and ornaments.

A dozen or so vendors with brightly painted carts sold hot chocolate, warm pretzels, and freshly baked sugar cookies that they somehow managed to keep warm. Carolers wandered about singing songs, craftsmen sold their wares, reindeer frolicked in the petting zoo, and children could even go skating when the pond froze solid.

The whole town loved the event. It was a cornerstone of Walden's Christmas season, and visitors came from all over. In fact, it had become so well-known and loved that the Pinery had resorted to selling advance tickets. They charged a pretty penny, too, but still sold out fast.

Several weeks ago, Liesl had purchased two tickets for that evening.

And between his father's heart attack, the store, and his constant worries about not letting his family down, Wesley had forgotten all about it.

And on top of that, he was going to have to tell her that he couldn't go.

He felt terrible about it. But what could he do? He'd promised his whole family that he wouldn't let them down. Every day and evening in December was important to the store's success. Even one day of mediocre sales or poor service could ruin a store's reputation. If he did anything to jeopardize that, he'd never be able to forgive himself.

He hoped Liesl would understand...but he doubted it. To say that she was going to be disappointed was a terrible understatement.

Chapter Two

Liesl stared at Wesley in shock. There he was, looking so handsome in his Raber's standard dark-blue shirt, gray pants, and black apron. His sleeves were slightly rolled up, showing off the muscles in his forearms. Unfortunately, the wary expression in his hazel eyes gave him away.

He had forgotten. He'd forgotten their special plans yet again.

She'd arranged her whole week around their date. Last night she'd worked late on the dress she'd promised to sew for Mrs. Beachy's five-year-old, so it would be done ahead of time, and she wouldn't have to worry about it. Moreoever, she'd made a new dress for *herself* for the occasion.

She'd washed her hair and taken extra time to fix it, and even had traded chores with her sister Emma for the evening—no small feat, since Emma hated sweeping the kitchen floor.

But the worst part was that she'd told everyone she knew that Wesley Raber was escorting her to the Pinery. More than one girlfriend had said she'd look for them there.

At times Liesl had almost even made it seem like the whole event had been her handsome beau's idea. While that was technically a lie, she didn't think the Lord would be too upset with her about taking that liberty. After all, Liesl knew Wesley would've arranged it, and called for reservations, too, if he hadn't been so preoccupied with the store.

He was always preoccupied with the store.

Seeing the look of regret on Wesley's face hurt. She knew he was sincerely sorry that he'd forgotten all about their big plans. Unfortunately, it didn't mean that he would leave the store and fulfill his promise.

She realized now that putting her wishes first simply didn't occur to him. When they'd first met, Wesley had been completely attentive and had gazed at her like she was the sun and the moon.

Now?

Well, unfortunately, he sometimes seemed to forget she existed. It stung her pride, and that was the truth.

"Wesley, what is going on?"

"I'm sorry, Liesl. The shop was so crowded, I fear that tonight's outing slipped my mind."

She'd be sad about that later, when she was home alone in her room. For now, though, it was up to her to save the evening's plans. Maybe he would prove her wrong and take her out, after all.

Summoning a chipper tone, she smiled. "I wish you would've remembered, but I'm here now. All you have to do is put on a sweater and coat and we'll be ready in no time."

Wesley's eyes widened. "You still want to go?"

Obviously. "I'd like to. We have reservations." Reservations that had been very hard to get.

He sighed. "Well, now. About that..."

"Yes?"

He looked down at the floor. Rubbed at a stain on the wood floor with the toe of his brown boot. "I'm afraid there's a problem."

Usually Liesl had lots of patience for everyone, but his beating around the bush was becoming a bit aggravating. No, it had been aggravating since she'd walked in the door. "Wesley, please just tell me the truth. Do you intend to go to the Pinery tonight?"

"*Nee.* I'm sorry, but I cannot go." When she stared at him, he looked at her directly in the eye. Unlike in years past, his stare didn't melt her heart or encourage her to forgive him for anything. They were playing the same game they always did—just on a different day.

"You cannot, or you will not?"

"I cannot. Because of the store." He waved a hand. "I mean, look around."

She gave the area a cursory glance, but in truth it was all she could do to not roll her eyes. She was tired of thinking about this market. "Everything looks like it always does, Wesley."

"It's not. Everything is a cluttered mess. I need to clean the floors and bathrooms, unpack the new merchandise, and settle the accounts. It has to be me, too. There isn't anyone else, since my parents are in Kentucky."

"I see."

She knew about his father, of course. She felt sorry for the whole Raber family, too.

But she didn't like being forgotten.

"Do you?" He actually brightened.

"What I see is that you didn't ever plan to go out this evening. I see that you don't want to put off anything until tomorrow. I see that you forgot about our date."

Wesley stared at her like she was suggesting he pull someone off the street. "This is *mei* family's store, Liesl. If I mess everything up, I'll cause my father even more stress. Don't you understand? I have no choice but to stay here."

He wasn't going to change his mind—no matter how upset she was. "*Jah.* I understand completely."

He reached for her hand. "I know you are disappointed, but life is full of unexpected twists and turns. This is one of those times, don't you think?"

Looking down at their linked hands, Liesl realized that his warm grip didn't feel comforting or special. It didn't feel like much at all.

She sighed. "Wesley, I know the Lord is working in His own ways. You know how concerned I've been about your father. I am glad the doctors discovered his problem and he is getting better. I'm thankful, too, that your mother and brother's family are taking care of him. That's a blessing. But…I also must admit that I'm disappointed. I was looking forward to spending time together this evening. I miss seeing you."

"I miss you, too, Liesl."

"Truly?"

"Of course. You know how special you are to me. I promise, I didn't forget because I don't care about ya. I'm just overwhelmed. That's all."

His gaze was warm and caring. Maybe she was being too harsh. He really was a wonderful man. Everyone thought so.

As if he sensed that her anger had ebbed, he smiled tentatively. "Hey, I have an idea."

Hope filled her heart again. "Yes?"

"How about you stay here with me?" His smile widened, like he'd just thought of the best idea in the world. "If you help me work here at the store, we can spend lots of time together."

"Wesley, are you truly asking me to spend the evening helping you clean this store instead of going to the Pinery?"

"It won't be so bad." He winked. "I won't make you clean the bathrooms. I'll do that. You can sweep and dust."

"You'd like me to sweep and dust," she murmured.

"Come on. I mean, you help all sorts of people clean from time to time, ain't so? I know you go over to Roland Hochstetler's house and straighten things, right?"

She stiffened. "Roland is a widower with a little four-year-old girl. He needs help."

"I do, too, Liesl. Come on, it won't be so bad."

He was serious. There was a new, hopeful tone in his voice. It sounded a lot like he was proposing a trip to Disneyland.

Or to the Pinery to see the lit Christmas trees, sip hot chocolate, and eat warm pretzels. Sweeping floors in her new dress was most definitely not the same.

Looking a little shamefaced, he added, "I feel terrible about spoiling our plans. But maybe after we finish here, I could take you out for hot chocolate and maybe even a cookie or two? I would enjoy that."

She knew he was trying, but hot chocolate and two cookies weren't going to improve her mood.

Not wanting to sound peevish, Liesl thought quickly...

And came up with the perfect thing to say.

She folded her hands primly in front of her waist and did her best to look regretful. "I'm not sure if working here at the store would be all right with my parents, Wesley."

"Why not?"

"We'd be here alone." Looking her best to sound mildly shocked, she continued. "The store is dimly lit, and we'd be together in here without a chaperone in sight. Why, anything could happen."

That wasn't exactly a falsehood. Her parents would not be pleased to find out that the two of them had spent the evening in the building all alone. Not all *that* displeased, because it was Wesley, known as the most perfect man in Walden. And he was perfect, too. With his blond hair, firm jaw, and gentle, strong demeanor, he'd caught pretty much every girl's eye at one time or another. Not to mention, he was now running one of the most successful businesses in Walden. A woman on his arm would never have to worry about doing without. Finally, he was fundamentally good. He didn't lie or cheat or gossip or bully.

Or do things he wasn't supposed to...which was why being completely alone together for hours wasn't exactly a good thing. Wesley was not the type of person to shrug off a good reputation. Especially not hers.

Unless, maybe, there was a bit of fire under all that goodness? Her nerve endings started to tingle.

There. She'd put it out for him to take the bait. In her mind, she imagined that he was now thinking of pulling her into his arms and kissing her passionately—just because he could.

But instead, her plan completely backfired. He took a step backward and raised his hands in protest. "Of course I would never do anything like that. I would never disrespect you or take advantage of the situation."

It seemed as if things were now going from bad to worse. She needed to go and figure something out. "Even so, it is probably best that I get on my way."

"Shall I walk you back?"

"I'm just three blocks away. I'll be fine."

"All right." He walked her to the door. "I am sorry about this evening. I know you're disappointed, but I don't know what else to do." He sighed. "I need some help, and not a teenager, either. I need someone responsible who could step right in and work with customers and the dozen other things I can't seem to get done. But that ain't gonna happen, is it?"

"I'll pray that the Lord will work with you on this."

"I'll pray, too." He smiled at her. "I best get to work or I'll be here all night."

"Good night," she said, lingering. Waiting for him to change his mind.

He held the door open for her. "Good night. Be careful going home."

Realizing that he wasn't even going to kiss her on the cheek, she walked out and promptly heard the door click shut and lock behind her.

Luckily, the street was decorated in its Christmas finery. The streetlights were lit, brightly colored red and green lights decorated planters in storefronts, and there were many people out and about.

Taking her time walking home, Liesl did some thinking about Wesley, her dreams of him finally kissing her, and the frustrating situation they were now in the middle of. She'd liked him for so long. Honestly, she'd dreamed of him courting her for a whole year before he'd made a move. The evening he'd shown up, hat in one hand and flowers in the other…why, she'd thought the Lord had finally answered her prayers and they would have a smooth and perfect courtship.

But it hadn't exactly been that way. She'd soon found out that while Wesley was kind and sweet to her, he didn't exactly have as much passion for life—or for her—as she might have imagined. He was more the steady, plow horse type of man. He *clip-clopped* along at a steady pace but never exactly did anything flashy.

He was dutiful, not spontaneous. That was a *wonderful-gut* quality in a husband, but not so much in a suitor.

But maybe it wasn't his fault? Maybe what he needed was some time to be spontaneous. He needed some good help.

A person like…her aunt Jenny!

Jenny would be perfect! She was hardworking and fun. She was always looking for a little extra money, too. Maybe if she was at the store, Wesley would be able to breathe a little more easily.

Liesel picked up her pace and rushed through the front door, almost knocking down the evergreen wreath. Inside, the living room was an oasis of calm. A pine-scented candle was burning on top of the bookshelf. A fire was crackling in the fireplace. Like every year, the many Christmas cards they received hung on a red ribbon like laundry on a line.

Her mother looked up from a puzzle, startled. *Daed* blinked as though he'd been woken up from a nap in the rocking chair.

"Liesl? What happened?" *Mamm* asked.

"Wesley had to clean the store tonight and couldn't get away."

"He is a hardworking man," *Daed* said. "Hard-working and respectable."

Liesl sighed inwardly, but she only nodded. "He is those things, for sure and for certain."

Her mother studied her from head to toe. "As much as we're all proud of Wesley for working so hard, I'm sure you are disappointed about not going to the Pinery tonight."

"I am, but I'll get over it. *Mamm*, I had an idea. See, Wesley needs some Christmas help. He's over-whelmed right now."

"It's a bit too late to put out a Help Wanted sign, ain't so?" *Daed* asked.

"It is, which is why I'm so glad I thought of some-one who might be able to make his life easier."

"Who is that?" *Mamm* asked.

"Aunt Jenny."

"*Mamm*'s youngest sister Jenny?" *Daed* frowned.

Liesl nodded. "*Mamm*, weren't you just saying that Jenny was worried because she was at loose ends un-til January?"

"I did say that." She looked in her father's direc-tion. "I'd love to see her, too. What do you think, Ar-mor?"

He rubbed his chin. "I think that idea has promise. Jenny has always seemed like an independent girl to me. She likes making money and doesn't like sitting around and being bored. It's worth calling her."

Her mother still looked worried. "What do you think I should say?"

"Just explain to her about Wesley and his father's heart problems and the store," Liesl said impatiently. "I'm sure she'll want to help him."

"It might work out. We have lots of space..." *Mamm* mused.

"Jenny would love to spend time here. Even though you're the oldest of eight and she's the youngest, you two have always gotten along." Getting even more excited about the prospect, she added, "Plus, you know how close we are. She's practically another sister to me."

"Indeed, since she's twenty-six to your twenty-two years," *Mamm* pointed out. "I suppose if she wants to work at the market, it would certainly help out Wesley."

Liesl smiled. "See? This will all work out perfectly. Jenny could stay here, walk to work, help Wesley, and make some money." And she would have more time with Wesley, and they'd find that spark they'd been missing.

"It does sound ideal," her father mused.

"*Mamm*, will you call and leave a message now?"

She tossed down the puzzle piece she was holding. "Liesl Fisher, I'm not gonna walk down to the phone shanty in the dark."

"I'll walk with you. We could take a flashlight."

"Not so fast, Liesl," her father said. "Your mother and I are going to need to talk about it."

"I understand. But hurry, would you? Poor Wesley is going to wear himself out from working so hard. Plus, he needs to have some fun, too, don'tcha think? Everyone needs to take a break from work every now and then."

"We'll talk and decide what to do later," her mother said. "Now, since you're home, would you like to do the puzzle with me?"

"*Danke*, but I'm going to head upstairs. I have a book to read."

"You are such a good girl, daughter. Always thinking of others."

A burst of guilt flooded her face, but she didn't refute the compliment. After all, if Jenny did say yes and came to Walden, then it certainly would help her out. And give Wesley a much-needed extra hand.

And...if this plan just happened to help herself as well? Well, there was nothing wrong with that.

After all, the Lord must have thought it was a good idea or He wouldn't have encouraged her to think of it.

Almost believing that, she slowly walked up the stairs, carefully changed into a much older, softer dress, and sat on the top of her bed with two library books.

If everything went well, a year from now she'd be planning her wedding to Wesley. She'd always fancied a Christmas wedding. Snow on the ground, red and green ribbons, mistletoe...leaving for their wedding night in a shiny black sleigh.

Liesl sighed. Their wedding day was going to be beautiful, indeed.

Chapter Three

THE KITCHEN SMELLED LIKE GINGER and cloves, spiced apples, and brown sugar. The hardwood floors shined, the white walls were clean and bare of any decoration, and the circular rag rug in the center of the space was as finely made as ones in any store.

Jenny Kurtz loved the time she spent in her mother's kitchen. Loved all the things that went hand in hand with her vacations from the Anderson family.

Well, she loved everything about coming home... except when her mother was in the mood to tell her grown daughter what to do.

Jenny didn't love that much at all.

"I think you should think twice about heading over to Walden," her mother said. "There's no reason on earth for you to work at the Amish Market. Why, you've been working all year!"

Her busy work schedule was a common complaint of her mother's. "I know how much I've been working, *Mamm*. There's no need to remind me."

"Well, how about this? There are at least a good handful of reasons to stay. Plus, you could spend some time with me and your father. We would like that."

Jenny knew her mother didn't say *handful* by chance. Actually, it was with great purpose—because she had a good five men in mind for Jenny to possibly marry.

What her mother neglected to understand, however, was that those five men hadn't interested her when she was fifteen, twenty-one, or even now at twenty-six. None of the men in their large district in Middlefield had ever interested her all that much.

Well, not since Jeremiah had nearly broken her heart in two.

"*Mamm*, as much as I love being with you and *Daed*, I have no interest in those other 'reasons.' I'm far too old to attend the singings and such that the younger ones are planning."

"They're gatherings for single men and women, which is what you are," her mother said.

"*Mamm*..."

On a roll, her mother continued. "Besides, the only reason so many of them are so much younger is because most of the eligible young men around your age have already been taken."

They'd had this conversation so many times, it was practically a well-known dance. Jenny loved her mother dearly, but she simply couldn't go through these steps again.

She sat down and neatly folded her hands on her lap. "Mother, you know why I want to go to Walden for a couple of weeks, and it has nothing to do with any men—whether they're eligible or not. I want to spend some time with Liesl."

"I see." She sighed. "To be sure, Liesl is a lovely girl, but—"

"*Nee, Mamm,*" Jenny said quickly. "I don't want to hear you speak poorly of Liesl. She's a lot of fun and so sweet."

"She's also a girl who likes to get what she wants."

"There's nothing wrong with that," Jenny said. "Besides, it isn't as if Liesl makes her wishes a secret."

"It's not very ladylike."

"I, for one, am starting to feel like keeping one's wishes to oneself is overrated. Besides, the thing that Liesl really wants is to spend more time with her boyfriend, Wesley. I think that's sweet."

"It is sweet...but her method to do that isn't all that admirable." Her mother folded her arms across her chest and harrumphed. "She's asked you to work in the store!"

"I had written her that the Andersons were going to be gone the month of December. They gave me the month off. Paid."

"They are a kind English family, for sure. And I know that you do love their *kinner*, too."

"I do." She was nanny to six-year-old Annabeth and four-year-old Parker. They were good children, and she adored the job.

"They are also very wealthy and pay you well."

"Both points are true." She couldn't think of another nanny who got to have a whole paid month to go home to see her family while the employers went to their ski chalet outside of Lake Tahoe.

"Well, my point is that you are not doing anything for yourself, dear." Her mother leaned slightly forward. "For eleven months of the year, your days revolve around Mr. and Mrs. Anderson's schedules and their children's needs."

"You make me sound like their burdened servant. That isn't how it is at all. They treat me like a member of the family. I get days off, too."

"*Jah*, but what do you do then?" she waved an impatient hand before Jenny could speak. "Oh, I know you attend church, walk, and attend to your chores, but that ain't spending time with girlfriends or getting to know eligible men." She took a deep breath. "And now? Now, when you at last have a whole month to relax and give some of the men around here a chance? All you want to do is go help your silly niece and her boyfriend."

"You're not being fair."

"Jenny—"

"*Mamm*, I've made up my mind. I already told Liesl yes and I'm leaving on the bus tomorrow morning."

"So, you won't be home for Christmas."

"Armor and Laura May invited you and *Daed* to spend Christmas with them, *Mamm*. I think you should, too." She quickly continued before her mother pushed away the idea yet again. "You two could ask a driver to drop you off on Christmas Eve. It would be *wunderbar*. We'd all be together."

For once she hoped her mother would accept Armor and Laura May's offer. Then, her mother could actually get to know Liesl and just how nice of a girl she was. Maybe, too, she'd stop being so judgmental about her sister's family.

"First of all, as much as we would love to be with our eldest daughter, we've already made plans with four of your siblings and their families to be here." *Mamm* sent her a sideways glance. "They were all counting on seeing you, by the way." She took a deep breath. "Secondly, even though I would be near you—it wouldn't be that wonderful, because you would have to work part of Christmas Eve and on the twenty-sixth."

"I'll be working because I said I would, not because I have to. I promised."

"I know."

"I still wish you'd consider going to Walden." How long had it been since *Mamm* had visited?

"I cannot."

Jenny folded her arms across her chest. "Mother, one day you are going to have to realize that Laura May and Armor do not run a different type of household."

"It's different enough, child."

Jenny knew where her mother was going. "Their church district might be more open and progressive, but their values are still the same. They're all Old Order Amish like us."

"Their ways are much more open. Why, I do believe the girls are allowed to ride bicycles."

It was all Jenny could do not to roll her eyes. "We mustn't judge, *Mamm*."

"Fine." *Mamm* lifted her chin. "All I'm saying is that you might regret your choice. No matter how nice Liesl is or how much money you make, or how well you get along with your sister and her husband... Spending Christmas in Walden won't be the same as being here."

Jenny couldn't dispute that. Her mother was a

good cook and her Christmas meal was always wonderful. Being with lots of her other siblings would be *wonderful-gut*, too.

But it would also feel awkward. Either *Mamm* or one of her siblings would point out Jenny's single status and ask too many questions. She would end up feeling embarrassed about being the only one out of eight siblings who still wasn't married.

Plus, no matter how hard she tried, Jenny doubted she'd ever live down the time everyone met Jeremiah.

Jenny had been so proud to bring him...and then he'd been rude and pompous. Within an hour, it was obvious that all of her friends and family were doing their best to avoid him.

And, maybe her, too?

Somehow, his know-it-all attitude had ended up reflecting on her, as if no woman would pick Jeremiah if they could have attracted someone better.

Since he'd broken her heart, she'd felt even worse about herself.

Standing up, she smoothed her hands down the sides of her dark-blue wool dress. "I need to pack, *Mamm*. I'll help you with supper in a little bit."

"Fine." She turned on the faucet and washed her hands...almost as though she were washing her hands of the whole situation. Each movement she made practically screamed her irritation.

Jenny turned and walked out of the room.

She should've handled her news about Christmas better. *Mamm* was disappointed that she wasn't going to be around all month, and who could blame her? All fall, Jenny had written that she was looking forward to spending more time at home.

However, some time ago, she'd realized that she could no longer put her parents' wishes ahead of hers all the time. Being only a good daughter didn't provide all that much consolation—especially not in the middle of the night when she couldn't sleep.

Thinking back to her relationship with Jeremiah, she winced. He'd courted her with an enthusiasm that had been flattering. For over a year, he'd been attentive.

Then, *bam.* Whether it was because she hadn't been what he expected or the new woman he'd met had been hard to forget—or maybe it had something to do with the fact there had been a really full moon and a particularly rainy summer—he'd left.

Well, he hadn't technically *left.* It had been more like he had come over one evening, ignored both the perfectly arranged chocolate whoopie pies on a plate, and the new way she'd pulled back her hair...

And had succinctly broken up with her.

I found someone else, Jenny, he'd said. She'd gaped. Waited for an explanation. He'd waited barely five minutes before standing up and saying that he needed to leave.

If she allowed herself to do it, she could still feel the needles of disappointment pricking her skin as she'd sat alone in the parlor. Trying to wrap her mind around the fact that he'd left her so easily. He'd let himself out, closing the door behind him. Never once had he actually looked her in the eye.

Or at those stupid whoopie pies that had taken her forever to make.

Three months later, Jeremiah's engagement had been announced. One of her best friends from school had thrown him a party—just as if Jenny's heartache hadn't even been noticed.

Another month went by. Then two. When Jenny still moped around the house, her parents had comforted her. But after another two, *Mamm* had begun hinting that Jenny was taking things too hard and should go to another singing and smile more. She'd even hinted that all the good men would be snapped up soon and that she couldn't afford to be so picky. Like she was an old maid with nothing else to live for.

It had felt like a slap in the face. That was when she'd realized that staying home and being obedient was only going to make her more miserable. The very next day, she applied to a nanny service. Within a week, she'd met the Anderson family, had heard they would like her to travel to Colorado with them on vacation, and had accepted the job immediately. She'd never looked back.

Now, she was doing things for herself. Going to Walden would keep her busy, give her time with her favorite niece, and even allow her to make a little bit of money to put into her savings account. Besides, working in a busy market at Christmastime sounded like fun.

And, if it happened to give her a break from her mother's meddling, that was a bonus.

Maybe it was the best bonus of all.

It was freezing when she got off the bus. Wishing she'd brought a thicker scarf to wear around her neck, Jenny made do by fastening the toggle on her black wool cape and arranging the black bonnet over her kapp more securely.

"You got everything, miss?" the gray-haired bus driver asked.

"*Jah.*" She pointed to the two navy suitcases in the open baggage compartment. "Those bags are mine."

He reached in and pulled them out easily. "Here you go. You got someone coming for ya? It's cold out."

"*Jah*—ah, there's my niece." She waved a hand. "Liesl!"

"Jenny!" Liesl called out as she ran toward her. "I'm so glad to see you!"

Jenny hugged her tight before holding Liesl at arm's length so she could get a good look at her. Liesl wasn't wearing a bonnet, and her black wool cape hung open, almost as if Liesl had only tossed it on as a fashion statement.

Whatever the reason, the open black cloak set off Liesl's wool dress. "Look at you in a beautiful yellow dress. You look as pretty as ever."

"*Danke*, but it's just a plain dress."

"Yes, but the fabric is so soft, it feels wonderful." Though the dress was Plain, Liesl's talented workmanship shone. The unexpected buttercream color of the wool dress was as surprising as it was becoming. It also set off Liesl's dark-blond hair and perfect features. "You are quite the seamstress."

She shrugged. "I like to sew."

"I've missed you. It's been too long."

"That's because you have your exciting job with your fancy family," Liesl teased. "Aunt Jenny, how are you?"

Jenny chuckled at her niece calling her *aunt.* It had long been a source of amusement for them. Liesl's mother Laura May was the oldest in a family of eight children. Jenny was the youngest. In addition, Laura May had married early and had Liesl that very year, which was just a few years after Jenny had been born. Therefore, they were technically aunt and niece, though they'd usually considered each other to be cousins.

"I'm well," she said as she reached for one of her suitcases while Liesl took hold of the other. Then, while the last few passengers said goodbye to the driver, they started walking across the parking lot toward Liesl's buggy.

"How are your parents? Are they coming for Christmas?"

Jenny winced inwardly. "*Mei* parents are fine, too. I'm sorry, but I don't know if they are coming this way for Christmas or not."

"They haven't made up their mind yet? But it's just a few weeks away."

"They're not ones for traveling at Christmas."

Sympathy shone in Liesl's eyes. "I'm sorry about that."

"Me, too."

As Liesl clicked her tongue and gently snapped the reins, Jenny smiled at Liesl. "Please don't worry about them. I hope they'll come, but if they choose not to, I'll still be here. And I'll be happy to spend the holiday with you."

Liesl brightened as she continued to guide her horse down the road. "I feel the same way." Looking hesitant for a moment, she added, "I've missed you, too, Jenny. It's been so long since we've spent more than a few hours together."

"I've been thinking the same thing. And now we'll get to spend the whole month in each other's company. I'm looking forward to it."

"Me, too. I really hope you don't think the only reason I'm glad you're here is to help out at Wesley's store."

Jenny had always loved Liesl's honesty. For her to bring that up was her niece to a T. She was such a sweetie. "I didn't think that at all, dear."

"Wesley is so overwhelmed, you see. He's so pleased and grateful for the help...Why, you are practically his Christmas present."

Well, that was a little awkward. Part of Jenny wanted to protest. To say that there was more about her than just being a good worker...but she didn't dare. She wouldn't risk hurting Liesl's feelings like that. Besides, she had accepted the opportunity. She could very well have told her no and stayed at home.

"I hope not!" she said at last. "An old maid like me wouldn't be anyone's Christmas present."

"Don't be silly. You aren't an old maid at all. Why, I bet you still have plenty of good years left."

"*Danke.*" Jenny chuckled. Oh, but she'd missed this girl and the way she blurted whatever was on her mind. Jenny had always wished for even a little bit of Liesl's forthrightness because she tended to suppress much of what she was thinking in order to not cause any waves.

Jeremiah's visit to the parlor and his easy, bare breakup had been an example of that. She'd just taken it and let him leave. What would he have done if she'd gotten mad and told him how she felt? How would he have reacted if she'd started yelling at him? She reckoned he probably wouldn't have done anything differently, but maybe she wouldn't be still thinking about it after all this time.

"Tell me about your beau," she said.

"Oh, Jenny. He's handsome. He's kind, too."

Jenny had heard that much. "What else?"

"Hmm?" She paused. "Well, he is a hard worker. Everyone likes him, too. I'm so blessed that he is courting me."

Again, Jenny felt as if the descriptors were less than inspiring. She'd thought Liesl was in love. Liesl should be describing every little thing about him. That was the Liesl she knew."When am I going to get to meet this Wesley Raber?" she asked as Liesl expertly guided the horse to the right and right again to her family's broad driveway.

"Unfortunately, probably not until tomorrow. I invited him over for supper tonight, but he had plans with one of his neighbors. You'll get to meet him at the store tomorrow."

"What time will we go?"

Liesl's brow creased. "Well, I was going to take you over in the morning, but now I'm afraid I cannot. I have a sewing customer who asked me to help her repair a dress she messed up. I'm so sorry, but I can't see her later. If I did that, it would throw the rest of my schedule off. You see, I promised Roland Hochstetler and his daughter that I'd stop by as well."

"I understand."

"Do you?" She bit her lip. "Elizabeth is a really *gut*

customer. But she never wants to simply pay me to sew her a dress; she always has to give it a try first."

Jenny couldn't help but giggle at the idea. "And let me guess—she never does too good a job with it?"

"Every once in a blue moon she does. But most of the time, she doesn't." As she reined in her horse and set the buggy's brake, she said, "I really am sorry that I won't be able to walk you over. I hope you don't mind meeting Wesley on your own. Well, not mind too much."

That was another thing about her favorite niece. Liesl looked and seemed at first meeting like an angelic silly girl, but in actuality, she was extremely capable. She could drive a horse as well as any man, chat with most anyone, and sew better than most seamstresses with twice as much experience.

She also did all of these things with so much confidence that most people might forget she did anything at all. Liesl just did things well and moved on.

Jenny pressed a hand on Liesl's arm. "I'm not mad. Not at all. I'm sure Wesley and I will get along just fine." After all, she was going to be doing him a big favor.

Looking relieved, Liesl smiled. "I know you will. Wesley is wonderful. He's a hard worker, understanding, and so handsome."

Jenny didn't point out that Liesl had already said these things. "He sounds too good to be true."

Liesl chuckled. "He's not like that. He just happens to be the best man I've ever met. You're going to love him."

"Since he likes you so much, I'm certain I shall. After all, he must have good taste."

As Liesl blushed, Jenny felt another burst of warmth flow through her. It really was so nice to see someone so happily in love. Though she doubted Wesley was even half the things Liesl claimed him to be, Jenny didn't much care. If he was good to her niece, anything else hardly mattered at all.

Chapter Four

WESLEY PRIDED HIMSELF ON BEING an optimist, and also on never getting too flustered, but he knew he was failing on both counts that morning.

All he'd been able to think about was his new worker, Liesl's maiden aunt. He'd been hoping at the very least Liesl would stay for a few hours and help her Aunt Jenny get situated, but then she'd told him at church that she had other plans on Monday morning.

Aunt Jenny was simply going to show up on her own.

Hearing that news had rubbed him wrong. He didn't understand how she could simply throw the two of them together like that. It seemed rather rude, especially when one considered that her aunt was an older woman and no doubt still trying to get the lay of the land in Walden. This Jenny was probably going to be a bundle of nerves when she showed up at the store. If she even got there.

Liesl was likely not even aware of how dismayed he felt. Just like he had many, many times, he'd merely nodded and said he understood. There was something about Liesl that made even the most annoying action seem adorable while it was happening. It was only later, when he was navigating the consequences of whatever had happened, that he felt differently.

Time and again, he'd forgiven her for forgetting moments that were special for him...and for acting a little less than concerned when he'd told her about his father's heart attack. Even when she'd said she didn't have time to go with him to the hospital because she had plans with her sister, he'd understood. He'd even defended her to his mother when she had acted as if Liesl should've dropped her plans. That simply wasn't his girlfriend's way of doing things.

Of course, in Liesl's defense, this mysterious Aunt Jenny wouldn't have even come to Walden to help him if not for Liesl.

No doubt, Liesl assumed that her part in the whole situation was finished.

Maybe she was right about that, too.

Over the past few days, he'd struggled to decide which chores Jenny could do while he waited on customers. He'd finally decided on dusting and straightening items on shelves. Christmas season did a number on the customary neat appearance of the store. People were constantly picking up things and placing them back in the wrong spots. This, of course, made it difficult to help people find things. But it also took away from the usually orderly way his parents had run the store. New visitors often commented on how neat, clean, and well-run the store was.

"Hiya, Wesley," old Samuel Schrock called out just seconds after Wesley had changed the Closed sign to Open. "Are ya open for customers yet?"

It was a quarter to nine. He opened the store at half past nine most of the year and at nine in December. But time and again, the clock's numbers did little to stop him helping his customers. "*Jah*, come on in."

"*Danke. Mei* Mary has a long list of things for me to be doing today. She made me promise to shop here first."

"Do you need some help?"

"*Nee.* I don't need anything from the deli today. Just some jams and pickles." Looking concerned, Samuel turned to Wesley. "You still have your spicy sweet pickles, yes?"

"Lots of 'em. Get what you need," he said as an English couple came inside, bundled up well enough to be living in Alaska. They gazed around the space in something akin to awe.

"May I help ya?" he said as he walked around the counter.

"Maybe, but I'm not sure," the woman said. "My sister told me to come in here for peanut butter and honey. Oh, and a jigsaw puzzle."

Wesley pointed in the direction that Samuel had trotted off. "Peanut butter and honey are down that way. Puzzles are over by the windows."

"Thanks," the man said as he picked up a basket. "You've been real helpful."

"I aim to please," Wesley answered…just as a group of women who were friends with his mother entered the store like a gaggle of geese.

"Morning, Wesley!" one said. "How are you doing?"

"I'm *gut. Danke.*"

"And your father? How is he doing?"

The reminder of his father's health shook him up

a bit, but he was glad for the concern. "*Daed* seems to be doing better," he said, managing a smile. "*Mamm* is trying to get him to relax more."

"I'm glad to hear that. We'll keep praying."

"Thank you. I'll tell *mei* parents you asked about them." Inserting a more professional tone, he added, "Is there anything special you need today?"

"We just came in to look around."

"Take your time."

He was about to add something else when yet another woman entered, this one making him take a second glance. She had light-brown hair, rosy cheeks, hazel eyes, and was wearing a purple long-sleeved dress. Just as he was about to greet her, Samuel called out.

"Wesley, come help me carry these pickles, would-ja?"

"Certainly." Rushing to the older man's side, he grabbed the three jars he was pointing to and set them on the countertop. "Anything else?" he asked when Samuel reached the counter.

"*Nee.* Just this and then I'll be on my way."

Wesley rang him up and placed everything in one of the empty boxes he'd stacked to the left of the register. Then he glanced at the clock. It was now five after the hour and Liesl's aunt hadn't shown up yet. Still worried about Liesl not making time to introduce the two of them, he frowned. "Samuel, I fear I'm on my own right now. If you give me a moment, I'll run this box out to your buggy for ya."

"I'll be glad to help you, sir," the English man said. "Autumn, you pay and I'll be right back."

"This is real kind of you," Samuel said.

"It's no trouble at all."

As the pair left, as another couple entered—but no maiden-looking aunt. Wesley struggled to keep his countenance relaxed as he rang up the purchases. "Fifty-four dollars."

"Here you are." The woman slid a credit card across the counter.

As Wesley ran the card in the machine, he noticed that the pretty woman in purple was now chatting with the group of older women and even pointing out some of the merchandise on the bottom shelves. "Do you need anything, ladies?" he called out.

"*Danke*, but we are good," one of them said and gestured to the pretty woman.

Wesley wondered what she'd meant by that but didn't have time to spare another thought about it as several more people entered the shop.

And so it continued for the next hour. He multi-tasked, rang up customers, chatted about the store, his parents, and Christmas...and privately seethed as the hands on the clock continued to move and there was still no sign of Liesl's wayward aunt.

He wasn't sure whether to put the blame on the aunt or on her niece. Liesl could have neglected to give her aunt Jenny good directions; the poor woman might have been wandering around the town in the cold. Or Liesl could have very well taken her aunt out to breakfast, where they'd lost track of time. That had certainly happened more than once when Liesl was out with her friends.

Or there was also the possibility that Aunt Jenny simply wasn't the sort to care about timetables or responsibilities. Just the thought of that being the case was aggravating. So far, having this new helper was going to be worse than being on his own.

After ringing out the latest customer and seeing that the store was almost quiet, he decided to make a quick inspection, just to be sure nothing was in too much of a disarray.

But the shelves holding pickles and jams and other foodstuffs were surprisingly clean and neat. So was the area of toys. Why, someone had even sorted some of the carved wooden animals and organized them in a pleasing way.

Who on earth would have done that?

"I hope you don't mind that I took it upon myself to do a bit of cleaning and organizing."

He turned...and found the young woman in the purple dress. "You're still here?"

Her head tilted to one side. "Was I not supposed to be?"

"It's not that. It's just...well, I noticed you enter, but I then I lost track of time and assumed you'd left." He felt his cheeks heat a bit. Boy, he hoped he didn't sound like he'd been eyeing her too closely.

She stared at him for a moment, and then her expression cleared. "I'm sorry. I think we're at cross purposes. I've...well, I wanted to stay out of your hair while you were so busy with all the customers, so I tried to be useful while I waited." She held out her hand. "I'm assuming you're Wesley. I'm Jenny."

Her shook her hand but was still trying to process her words. "Who did you say you were?"

She pulled her hand from his. "I'm Jenny Kurtz. You know, Liesl's aunt?" When he still gaped at her, trying to connect the name with the pretty young woman in front of him, a faint line formed between her brows. "Forgive me, but have I misunderstood something? Liesl led me to believe that you needed help this Christmas. Is that not the case?"

"I thought you were old."

Her hazel eyes narrowed. "Excuse me?"

He'd offended her with his clumsy manners. "What I meant to say was that I thought because you were Liesl's aunt, you would be middle-aged. Older. You know, her maiden aunt."

Confusion gave way to amusement. "We get that all the time. Jenny likes to refer to me as her aunt—which is true, of course. But as you can see, she and I are almost the same age."

He was still having a difficult time matching his expectations with the fresh-faced woman standing in front of him. "How old are you?" As soon as he asked, he felt his cheeks heat. If his mother had been nearby, she would've given him a talking-to. "Hey, forget I just asked that. It ain't none of my business."

"I'm not the kind of girl who gets offended by mentioning my age. For the record, I'm twenty-six." Before he could say anything about how twenty-six was absolutely nowhere near maiden aunt territory, she cleared her throat. "Perhaps we should start over again?"

Now he was thoroughly embarrassed, both by his rudeness and the fact that she'd put herself to work without him doing so much as saying hello.

"*Jah.* I mean, yes, of course. Please forgive my rudeness." He held out his hand. "Let's try this again. It's nice to meet you, Jenny. I'm Wesley Raber, and

I run my family's market. Thank you for helping me out this December. I appreciate it."

Her smile widened as she slipped her hand into his. "I'm glad to help. Now, before you get swamped again, perhaps you could tell me what you'd like me to do?"

Wesley grasped her hand carefully, much the way he always held Liesl's. What he noticed right away, however, was that she had a firmer grip than her niece—and that holding her hand felt comfortable. Not awkward at all.

Startled by the train of his thoughts, he released her hand quickly. Then he got his head straight. At long last. "First, you see that door in the back? That's to the back room. The bathrooms are there. There's my office, too."

"Good to know. *Danke.*"

"I mean, there is a small refrigerator in my office. You can put your lunch there. Or get some water or something."

"*Danke*, but I'll be fine."

Seeing another group who had just entered the store, he added, "Feel free to join me behind the counter. We can discuss things more while we're ringing people up."

Some of the distance in her expression eased. "I'd like that, Wesley. After I take another walkabout, I'll join you there. I'm sure we'll get along just fine."

Watching her walk away, Wesley couldn't help but agree. This Jenny Kurtz was more than he'd expected. Far more.

Chapter Five

JENNY HAD BEEN AN EMPLOYEE of the Amish Market for five hours. Five, crazy, stressful, exhilarating hours. Though she'd often thought that taking care of the Anderson *kinner* had been tiring, they'd had nothing on working the Amish Market in December.

The customers came in waves, pouring into the store, buying gifts and deli items, then flowing out—just as another wave of people parked outside and entered. When she'd asked Wesley when he took breaks, he'd just laughed and told her that he and Ernie took them whenever they felt they couldn't wait any longer. Waiting for a lull was a futile exercise.

That was why when the market started to fill again, Jenny knew it was time to take a break. When the newest customers waved off her offer for help and instead scattered throughout the store like a bag full of marbles, Jenny knew she could no longer wait to gather herself together.

It might not have been the best choice to make, given that Wesley would likely need assistance, but Jenny felt she owed it to herself to take a quiet minute or two. The store had been so busy that she'd barely taken time to eat a quick lunch.

But though the store had been busy and she wasn't used to being on her feet so much, the thing that really had her rattled was how she'd felt around Wesley. She seemed to be aware of every move that he made.

It was unnerving.

The truth was that Wesley Raber was so much more than she'd imagined. So much more than Liesl had conveyed. Maybe it was because Liesl had focused on Wesley's good looks. And it was true, he was handsome.

But there had been something in his countenance when he'd suddenly realized how wrong he'd been about her that had been adorable. She'd known too many men who didn't like to be wrong. Men who, even when they'd known they were wrong, hadn't wanted her to be right. Wesley's easy acceptance of his mistake and ability to switch gears had been as much of a surprise as a source of relief. Liesl was so smitten, Jenny would have hated to not feel that he was worthy of her regard.

But what was giving her fits was that she'd also felt a spark of attraction. It had been sudden and unexpected.

It also embarrassed her. Though of course she would never act on such a thing, Jenny had always considered herself to be a giving sort of person. The type of woman who put others' needs before her own. She wasn't one to be selfish. She surely wasn't the type of woman to covet her niece's boyfriend!

That was another reason she took a small break.

After using the restroom and eating half a sandwich, she went back to the store. But instead of heading back to Wesley's side, she veered down an empty aisle and hurriedly began to organize a row of candles. She gave herself a talking-to while she did it, as well.

There's nothing wrong with being human. But there is something wrong with doing anything other than pushing those thoughts out of your head.

Less than five minutes later, she stood straighter and admired her handiwork. The candles were nicely organized once again, both by scent and size.

"Hello, miss?" said a middle-aged man in a dark-brown coat. "Do you work here?"

"I do. I'm brand-new, but I'll be glad to help you if I can."

"I was just wondering if you have a favorite candle." He smiled sheepishly. "My wife loves flowery-scented ones, but she's particular. If something is too sweet, she finds it off-putting."

"I've felt the same way at times."

"See, the problem is that I find all of them too sweet so I can't make a decision."

Jenny smiled at him. It was cute how he was approaching this selection like it was a matter of great importance. Though, perhaps it was? Wanting to please someone one loved always mattered. At least, she'd thought that was the case.

She picked up the pale-yellow candle with the jaunty purple gingham ribbon wrapped around it. "I've always been a fan of lemon-scented candles. They make a room smell fresh but not cloyingly sweet."

His eyes lit up. "I'll take two of those. Any others?"

She scanned the selection again, then picked up an ornate candle with a crisp green ribbon. "What about cranberry? It's perfect for the Christmas season."

"I'll take two of those, too."

Seeing that he already had his hands full, she said, "How about I walk these to the counter for you?"

"I think that's a great idea. The way my day has been going, I'd likely drop them on the ground."

She laughed softly as they walked side by side to Wesley behind the counter. "I've had days like that myself."

"I'm sure glad I found you. My Annie is going to be so pleased."

"I'm glad I could help," she said simply as she set the candles on the counter. "Here you go, Wesley," she said when she realized he'd been watching her.

"*Danke.*"

"Your employee here was a great help," the man said.

"That's good to hear." Wesley smiled at her.

Noticing that a couple more customers stood in line behind the man, Jenny asked, "Would you like me to stay here and help wrap up and bag items?"

Wesley's eyes widened before nodding. "Sure. That would be real helpful."

Jenny wondered why he was acting as if she had a novel idea but figured it didn't matter. All that mattered was that the Lord was giving her work to both occupy her hands and her time. Both were good to her spirit. Anything was better than to be dwelling on either her past relationships...or her unsettling awareness of Wesley.

As she carefully wrapped each candle in tissue paper and placed it in the tote bag, she reminded herself to be thankful. It was much better to concentrate on working instead of anything else.

After the man left after sharing another word of thanks to her, Wesley smiled at her. "You did a *gut* job with him."

"I was only helpful. It was nothing."

"Still...I think you're gonna work out just fine. You seem to have a natural knack for customer service."

The compliment felt good. "I hope you'll feel the same way when I leave today," she joked.

He grinned but merely moved on to the next customer.

The rest of the day seemed to fly by, mainly because there was always so much to do. Jenny wrapped up items, chatted with customers, and every so often walked around and straightened the shelves and merchandise. When the store got quiet, Wesley took a short lunch break, then quickly sent her to the back to finish her sandwich and rest her feet.

When the sun started its downhill descent, he competently shooed the last of the customers out the door and then finally locked it. Then he turned to her and grinned. "We did it."

"We sure did. I canna believe how fast the day passed."

"To be honest, I was surprised, too. I had worried that the crowds might get you frazzled. It can do that to the best employee."

"Everyone was pretty nice. They just wanted what they came in for."

"Sometimes that's easier said than done. I usually

feel like I'm always running two steps behind. Your company made my day go much easier, to be sure."

She had a feeling he wasn't just saying the words to be nice. "I'm glad I could help." She looked up at him—and was startled to see that he was already staring at her intently. For a split second she could swear she saw a spark in his gaze. A spark similar to the ones she'd used to feel around Jeremiah—back when she was sure he was as in love with her as she'd been with him.

Whatever it was, she thought it might be a match to the way she'd been feeling about Wesley. Comfortable, happy...and perhaps stunned by their easy compatibility.

She cleared her throat. "Um, what should we do now?"

"Now?"

She waved a hand. "Would you like me to sweep the floors? Maybe clean the toilet?"

The mention of the toilet seemed to be all he'd needed to come back to reality. "*Nee*. I'll clean that. If you could sweep the floor and dust a bit, I'd appreciate it."

"Are you sure?"

He flushed. "Of course. Let's get on with it now. I'm sure Liesl is going to worry if I keep you here too long."

Liesl! Though Jenny hadn't forgotten her dear niece, the mention felt like a splash of cold water. And even though Jenny had a feeling that Liesl was not going to be worried about her or count the hours until she returned, she did reckon that her niece would be full of questions about her first day.

And would be wondering how she and Wesley had been getting along. And why wouldn't she be curious? After all, Liesl and Wesley were practically engaged.

"I'll go get the broom," she murmured. "It's in the storage room, *jah*?"

He nodded. "While you do that, I'll ah, go clean the bathroom."

They went their separate ways. If neither of them smiled or exchanged friendly banter again, Jenny figured there was no worries about that.

After all, they'd both had a very long day.

Chapter Six

Wesley had offered to walk Jenny home, but she'd refused, saying it was but a short way and the weather was brisk but not frigid. He would've argued the point, but she'd looked so determined to walk by herself, he'd decided not to press.

Therefore, when he put on his overcoat and heavy boots at half past six, he'd felt a bit at a loss of what to do. For the first time in weeks, he wasn't ex*haus*ted. It was also the first time in weeks that he'd gotten out of the store before suppertime.

Walking down the sidewalk, accompanied by the first twinkling lights of the evening, Wesley decided to stop at Bruno's for spaghetti. The meal would be filling and warm, and he wouldn't have to tackle either cooking or washing dishes when he got home.

As he walked toward the well-lit restaurant with the green and red neon sign on the front—a mainstay in Walden for years—he could already hear the faint lilting notes of the violin and the laughter no doubt spurred by the joking and teasing of Bruno himself. The man had a larger-than-life personality and was a favorite of many, whether the people were Amish, Mennonite, or English.

The scent of garlic, pasta sauce, and fresh bread filled the air when he walked inside. The stone fireplace was lit, and the flames' pretty glow cast bands of warmth into the main dining room. The entryway was decorated with tiny white lights for the holidays. At least a dozen bright red, pink, and white poinsettias graced two tables nearby. Wesley stood for a moment and simply admired another proprietor's hard work. Making a place so inviting took a lot of work and effort. Bruno and his staff had done an outstanding job.

"Hello, Wesley. Long time, no see."

Turning, he noticed that the middle-aged hostess was eyeing him with an amused expression. "Hiya, Karen. You're right. It's been too long. Any chance you've got a table open?"

She looked down at the laminated seating chart on the hostess table. "For how many?"

"Just one."

She looked up at him in surprise, then skimmed a fingernail along the chart. "Would you mind sitting at a small table near the kitchen?"

"Not at all. If I can sit down and get a plate of spaghetti, I'll be a happy man."

"We can surely take care of that." Grabbing a menu, she smiled at him. "Come this way."

Mouth already watering, Wesley followed Karen through the maze of tables and chairs. The dining room was filled except for the one small table next to the swinging door leading toward the kitchen. About the only thing the table had going for it was that it was empty. Other than that, there was no ambiance, and no view of either the outside or the rest of the dining room. It looked to be about one foot away from having a plate of pasta accidentally spilled on it.

Karen looked at it doubtfully. "Believe it or not, this is Bruno's favorite spot, but no one else's."

"If it's good enough for Bruno, it's good enough for me."

And it turned out that his spot actually was a good place to dine. He enjoyed overhearing the faint calls, jokes, and complaints from the staff in the kitchen. He liked watching the servers hustle in and out of the kitchens. His day was done but the workers at Bruno's were just starting their shift. He felt a camaraderie with them. They might have very different jobs, but they, like him, were serving the community and hoping to bring a smile or two.

Ten minutes later his teenaged server brought a plate of spaghetti, a side plate of two meatballs, a bowl of salad, and three pieces of garlic bread. It was a feast, to be sure.

"It's *gut* I'm hungry," he said.

His server grinned. "I always tell people to expect to bring home leftovers."

Just as he'd finished a good half of his meal, Bruno himself walked over and took a chair across from him. "Wesley Raber, I just got word that you were here. I came over as soon as I could. Thanks for coming in."

Wesley reached over and shook the proprietor's hand. "I'm glad to be here. Sorry if I took your usual table, though."

"No worries. I'm gonna be here for a while tonight."

He cocked his head. "I'm surprised to see you here on your own. Where are your parents?"

"My father had a spell with his heart and had to get a procedure done at the hospital." He was pleased that he was able to speak about that so easily. At Bruno's look of concern, he added, "He's gonna be all right, but he's supposed to rest for a bit. They're over at *mei bruder's haus* until the New Year."

"I'm sorry."

"Thank you. I'll pass your good wishes on to them next time we talk."

"How's business then?"

"Busy. Really busy. But that's what we hope and pray for, you know. A busy Christmas season helps get one through a slow January."

Looking around at the dining room, Bruno nodded. "I often think the same thing. I'm grateful to our loyal customers."

"It's good to see you. Thanks for saying hello."

"You should come back again soon with your girl. What's her name again?"

"Liesl. Liesl Fisher."

"Yes, that's it. She's such a lovely girl. Bring her," he said as he stood up. "If you make a reservation, we'll make sure you get one of the best tables in the house. Right in front of the fireplace." He winked. "It's everyone's favorite spot. Romantic, yet warm and cozy. She'll think you hung the moon."

Wesley chuckled at the expression but couldn't help but think that Bruno was right. Liesl would be mighty pleased if he treated her to a romantic night out. He certainly owed her a few nights like that, too. "I'll keep that in mind."

After dinner, Wesley went home. After he put his plastic tote bag of leftovers in the refrigerator, took a long shower, and then relaxed for a spell before heading to bed, he felt at a loss. He wasn't sure why that was, either. Jenny had been a great help to him, and the day had gone well.

But maybe that was the problem. It had gone so well that he'd started to imagine what it would be like if she were nearby and working with him after the New Year. Of course, that wasn't going to happen.

Shaking his head, he decided to shrug on his coat, walk to the phone shanty at the end of the street, and leave a message for his parents and his brother Paul. At least they would feel assured that the store was taken care of.

He grabbed a flashlight, walked outside, and gazed up at the stars, imagining one day staring up at them with Liesl by his side. The thought caused him to smile.

Knowing her, she'd grab his hand and say that next time he wanted to take her out in a field, they should plan a romantic picnic. That, of course, would make him wish he'd planned something romantic in the first place.

That was their life together, he reckoned. His Liesl was always making plans and moving two steps ahead while he tried to keep up and make her happy. Life with her would never be boring, for sure and for certain.

Smiling again, he felt at peace. *Jah*, that was what he'd needed. A reminder that he might appreciate Jenny's work ethic and pleasant demeanor, but there was nothing else between them.

Not one thing at all.

Chapter Seven

FROM THE MOMENT JENNY HAD stepped into the Fishers' home, she'd been surrounded by Liesl's good spirits and her parents' kind words. They'd had a "special" supper waiting for her: spaghetti and meatballs with a fresh salad and garlic bread. It had been followed with her favorite Christmastime treat—ice-cream sundaes with hot fudge and peppermint stick crumbles.

"This is all so lovely." She smiled at her sister. "*Danke*, Laura May."

"You are welcome, but I canna take much credit, Jenny."

"Oh?" She stared at the meal in confusion.

"It was Liesl's idea," Armor said.

She turned to Liesl. "You sure didn't have to go to so much trouble."

"I wanted you to know how much I appreciate you jumping in to work at the shop." Liesl smiled.

"I already knew you appreciated it, silly."

"That might be true, but now you're gonna be working all the time and on your feet. I didn't think a simple thank-you was enough."

Jenny noticed that Liesl looked almost embarrassed. “It was enough. There was no need for you to ever worry that I expected something more.”

“You are too good to me, Jenny.”

Just as she was about to shrug off the praise, Laura May jumped in. “This thank-you is from all of us. We think the world of Wesley, but we have a feeling he might be hard to work for.”

“How so?”

“He has high expectations for how the store should be run,” Liesl said. Looking like she was weighing her words carefully, she added, “I fear he might be a bit difficult from time to time.”

Jenny was surprised. “I didn’t find Wesley to be that way at all. He was very helpful and patient with me.”

“Truly? Every time I’ve seen him working at the market, he’s seemed to only have one purpose—to serve the customers.”

Jenny had gotten the feeling that he did take his customers’ wishes seriously, but she would’ve been surprised if he hadn’t. “The store was busy but Wesley was fine. I actually enjoyed my day at the store.”

Looking relieved, her niece smiled. “I hope he stays that way.”

Jenny was starting to get confused, too. Liesl was almost acting as if she didn’t like Wesley’s dedication to the store. Surely she didn’t think that would change if they got married one day. Did she?

Feeling uncomfortable about both the fancy meal and the conversation, she cleared her throat. “What did you do today, Liesl? I’m sure you were busy with your sewing projects.”

"I was. I had a fitting and then helped out Roland and Lilly for two hours."

"Who are they?"

"Roland is a widower and Lilly is his adorable little girl." Smiling softly, she added, "Lilly is four years old and just the sweetest thing."

"It's very kind of you to help them so much."

"Liesl helps them quite a bit," Laura May said in a far less enthusiastic tone.

"I enjoy it. When I got back home, I worked on some small items that people have ordered to give as gifts. In between, I made supper."

"You sound like you're almost as busy as Wesley!" Jenny teased.

"I promise, I'm never that busy."

Laura May looked at her daughter fondly. "You know how Liesl is, Jenny. She's always doing two things at the same time."

Jenny grinned. Even when she was little, her niece would do two things at once. "I've never known how you were able to do that."

Armor laughed. "No one has. But what can ya do? She's not the type of girl to sit still for long. Sometimes I thought Liesl would try to manage this *haus* when she was just four or five." With a wink, he added, "I reckon she could have done a good job of it, too."

Looking a little shamefaced, she retorted, "I wasn't that bad, *Daed*."

"Only a little bit." He shrugged. "That ain't a bad thing, though."

Knowing the teasing was all in fun, Jenny said, "I remember one time when you wanted to play school with me and my siblings."

Liesl pressed a palm over her eyes. "I knew this was where you all were going. Please stop."

"Come now, you didn't do anything bad. All you did was tell us what to do." She waited a few beats. "For hours."

Laura May chuckled. "Poor Jenny here had to do so many math problems I thought her hand was gonna get a blister."

Liesl covered her eyes with one hand. "I was a handful. I know."

"It was actually kind of funny," Jenny said. "I ended up being the fastest at my times tables that year. My brothers all swore up and down it was because of your bossy ways." A flutter of disappointment settled inside her. Of course, all that was back when their mother hadn't got a bee in her bonnet about Walden's "fancy" Amish community.

"Glad I could help."

And so the silly conversation continued. They chatted about old times when Laura May still lived at home. Jenny told stories about being a nanny and even Armor shared a story or two about when he was a young man during his *rumspringa*.

Later, after they all did the dishes, Jenny went to her room and changed and pulled out one of her favorite books she'd been reading.

"Knock, knock," Liesl called out from the other side of the door. "May I come in?"

"Of course."

Liesl was in a beautiful light-pink nightgown with a fluffy pink robe over it. On her feet were pink slippers. In comparison, Jenny's five-year-old flannel nightgown seemed rather old and worn in comparison. Why had she never noticed that when she had been home?

"You look pretty," she said. "That pink color looks good on you."

Liesl glanced at her gown in surprise. "This? Thank you. I decided to make a new nightgown last month. I had some extra material after a job."

Liesl studied Jenny's nightgown. No doubt she was noticing the faded trees and reindeer print that Jenny had once thought looked cute but now seemed more than a little forlorn and silly on a woman her age. "I'll make you one if you'd like."

"Though I don't want to make more work for you, I'll take you up on it. I'd never pass up something you make."

"I'm glad to do it. It won't take long. Plus, it might be time to retire that gown."

Liesl might be a mess of contradictions, but she spoke her mind, and that was a fact. "I was just thinking the same thing. So, how are you?"

"I'm fine." She ran a hand along the quilt on Jenny's bed. "I just wanted to see if you needed anything."

"I'm fine. I'm always fine, dear."

"Do you think all those stories my parents shared were signs that I really am too bossy by nature?" Looking genuinely distressed, she added, "I like to think of myself as confident, but perhaps I come across as more rude and opinionated than anything else."

"I think the stories prove that there are some things one just can't help. One of them just happens to be the way the Lord made us. Everyone needs a

Liesl in their life. You make sure that things get done and get done well."

"I hope Wesley doesn't hate that about me."

"Liesl, I'm sure he doesn't. I don't know him well yet, but I do know that he thinks the world of you."

She visibly relaxed. "I guess I'm just being silly."

"No, you want him to be happy. There's nothing wrong with that. It's commendable."

Liesl smiled softly. "I hope so. I'm sure he's the one for me."

"It's good you know."

"It's too bad that Jeremiah wasn't the man for you."

"To be honest, I've often wished things had turned out differently. I wanted Jeremiah to be the one, but I think the Lord had other plans."

"Do you think the Lord really had a say in your love life?"

Thinking about Jeremiah—and how she'd heard that he was now happily married with a babe on the way—Jenny nodded. "I hope so. I mean, if He doesn't, then I don't know who to depend on." She smiled again, hoping Liesl would understand that she didn't need her niece to feel sorry for her, but just to understand.

But instead of smiling in return, the other woman just stared back at her—almost as if Jenny had said something earth-shattering.

Though, she had no idea what that could be. After all, Liesl had a charmed life. A loving attentive family, a wonderful boyfriend, and even the blessing of a wonderful skill that she could use all her life. There was likely nothing else in the world she could ever want.

"I think I'd better get to bed," Liesl said as she headed to the door. "Tomorrow starts early."

"Always," Jenny said softly.

But later, as she drifted off to sleep, her mind kept reflecting back to the way Liesl had looked at her. Maybe something else was on the girl's mind. Something more than just counting her blessings.

Chapter Eight

The next morning dawned bright and sunny. It had snowed a few inches overnight, making the fields around their house look sparkly. Almost like something Elsa in Frozen would enjoy, Liesl decided with a small smile. She'd gotten to watch a bunch of Disney movies with a few of her friends during their *rumspringa*.

She remembered that one of the girls who'd chosen not to be baptized Amish had thought their choice of movies to be mighty tame. Liesl hadn't cared what she'd thought; she'd been entranced by the cartoons, romances, and catchy songs.

Roland's little daughter, Lilly, would no doubt love watching *Frozen* as much as she did. Bemused by her train of thought, Liesl wondered what types of shows the little girl would want to watch when she entered her "running-around" years.

It would be nice if they had that in common...

"Liesl? Liesl, are you with me, child?"

"Hmm?" She turned to see her mother standing by her side, studying her with a perplexed expression. "Oh! Sorry, *Mamm*. I was just looking at the snow."

"It sure seemed like you were further away than that."

Looking around the kitchen, with the sparkling stainless stove with its gas burners, the arrangement of pottery on the shelves, and the forest-green rag rug she and her *mamm* had made together under their feet, Liesl tried to get her bearings. Her mother wasn't wrong. For a moment, she had been someplace different. She'd been in Roland's extremely plain and sparse kitchen...and doing her best to brighten up Lilly's day.

Her mother craned her neck, obviously trying to see if there was anything of interest in the backyard. "I'm glad to see that no more snow has fallen. I told Jenny to walk with care this morning."

"I heard you." She also had shared a smile with Jenny. Jenny took care of two children for a living. She likely didn't need to be reminded to watch out for slick spots on the road. "I'm sure Jenny got to work just fine."

"I hope so. As much as I enjoy seeing her, I do worry about her working too much."

"Jenny reminded me that she's perfectly capable of speaking her mind. If she didn't want to be here, she would have told me so."

"I suppose you're right." Her *mamm* walked back over to the mixing bowl and continued working on the cake for the evening's supper. "Well, what are your plans today, daughter?"

"I'm going over to Roland Hochstetler's *haus*."

"Again?" Her mother put down the measuring cup she was holding. "You were there just last week."

"I know that." She'd also been at Roland's yesterday. And two days before that. It was a blessing her mother had forgotten.

"I'm uncertain why you would be going over there again."

Her mother said is as a statement, but it was a question, clear as day.

"Roland needs a new coat and I sew." Liesl rolled her eyes, just to put on a good show, but the fact was that although she was going over to measure him for a new coat, that was far from the only reason.

Unfortunately, her mother didn't look like she was buying Liesl's act one bit. She folded her arms over her chest and peered at Liesl from over the top of her glasses. "Do you think it's wise to go over there so much?"

"Mamm, he needs help. You know his sweet wife went to Jesus."

"It's not your place to help him."

"Of course it is. Roland isn't the type of man to ask everyone in the community to help him straighten his kitchen or play with his daughter." Realizing that she was sounding a bit too involved, she added, "Anyway, it's not like I go over there all that often."

"People might talk."

"How many times have you told me that listening to gossip is no good for anyone?" She smiled. "Remember, *Mamm*, 'A narrow mind and wide mouth often go together.'"

Her mother harrumphed. "And here I thought you ignored all my advice!"

"I listened." She hadn't exactly wanted to follow her mother's advice, but she had surely heard the words. Even though she thought in this case her mother might have a good point, Liesl wasn't going to do anything differently. "Mother, I fail to see why my visits to the Hochstetler *haus* is a problem. Roland is nice and his little girl is adorable."

"Lilly is very special, indeed..." Her mother's voice drifted off, like she was afraid to say what else she was thinking.

This wasn't a new habit of her mother's, but usually she only did it when Liesl had done something she thought wasn't right. Like when she'd been seven and got caught sneaking a piece of chocolate from the grocery store bin and then lied about it. "Mother, I canna read your mind. If you have a problem with Roland, you need to tell me."

"There is no problem with him. He is well respected."

"I think the same."

"I just wonder if spending so much time at his house is appropriate, given that you are both single."

"I supposed that is true, technically."

"It is true, *literally*. Neither of you is married."

"*Mamm*, when Roland's wife was so ill three years ago, I went over there at least once a week to help. No one ever told me that I shouldn't."

"Your help truly was a blessing. I'm sure Roland, Lilly, and Tricia's family were grateful for your assistance, too. I am proud of you."

Feeling frustrated with the conversation, Liesl shook her head. "*Nee, Mamm.* I wasn't looking for a pat on the back. I'm just saying that I spent a lot of time there, and during most of it poor Tricia was sleeping. Roland was a gentleman, and I did nothing for you to be ashamed about. I mopped floors and washed dishes. Now, I make Lilly dresses and play with her for a spell. She and I have a good time together, and Roland needs all the help he can get. That's all there is to it."

"I suppose..."

"*Mamm*, I promise. There's nothing to worry about."

That was the truth, too. While it was true that she had noticed that Roland was handsome, and that his body looked very strong since he farmed, she didn't care about any of that. What really mattered was that he was kind and his daughter was sweet.

But that didn't mean anything was going to happen between them. After all, she had Wesley—and everyone believed they were perfect together.

Her mother studied her intently for another moment before chuckling. "You're right." She stirred the cake batter with a little more gusto. "Forget I brought it up."

Liesl was happy to do that—especially since she had no idea what her mother was pretending to laugh about. "What about you? What are you going to do today?"

"I thought I'd stop by the market to see how Jenny is doing."

That was surprising. "Why wouldn't she be doing well?"

"I'm sure she is. I just want to see it for myself. She is my little sister, you know."

Their differences in ages were so wide—her mother was forty-two, while Jenny was twenty-six—that Liesl sometimes forgot that they were siblings. Thinking of how busy Raber's Market was going to be, she warned, "It's gonna be crowded, know. And since Wesley is coming over tonight, you could ask them both then."

"That may be true, but I want to see how things are with my own eyes. It's sometimes amazing how much one can notice...if one takes the time to notice what is right in front of one's eyes."

Fearing that her mother was going to start spouting more cryptic words of wisdom, she glanced at the kitchen clock. "I better gather my things together. I'll need to leave soon." She sure didn't want Roland to wonder where she was.

Roland's white clapboard *haus* was a little more than two miles from Liesl's. His barn was whitewashed, with a dark-green metal roof, and everything about the land and yard was neat and well-cared for. Even in the middle of December.

When she knocked on Roland's shiny black front door, Liesl was struck again at how different the inside of the house looked compared to the outside. It smelled musty and forgotten.

He answered almost immediately. "*Gut matin*, Liesl."

"Good morning to you." Noticing that he was frowning slightly, she stepped inside. "What is going on? Is everything all right?" She pulled off her mittens, eager to get to work.

"I noticed that you walked here. Yet again." He closed the door behind him.

If he noticed that, then it meant he'd been watching for her out the window...and knowing that gave her a little tremor of happiness. Ignoring it, she smiled at him softly. "*Jah*, I did. But why are you acting like that is a problem?"

"I worry about you walking alone. It's cold out."

"Not that cold."

"And a woman walking alone. A pretty woman like you..." His voice drifted off.

Her heart went out to him. Roland really was such a considerate man. "There is no need for you to worry about me. Not for a single moment."

"Of course I'm going to worry about you." His cheeks flushed. "I mean, you've done so much for me and Lilly, I would hate it if you twisted your ankle or something when walking through the snow."

"I'm used to walking or riding my bike wherever I need to be."

"I'll be happy to hook up the buggy and take you home. It might be safer, ain't so?"

If her mother thought the gossips would be wagging about her visiting Roland, it would be nothing compared to the talk if everyone in Walden saw him driving her around in his buggy!

"Roland, *danke*, but *nee*. I'm fine." Seeing Lilly peeking out from the doorway, she led the way in. "Let's go in and get your jacket measured. I want to see Lilly, too."

"Of course." He waved a hand forward. "I have to tell ya, I know someone who couldn't wait to see you today."

"Really? Who?" she teased as she pretended to peek around the room. When she spied the edge of Lilly's bright-blue dress, followed by a little girl squeak, Liesl frowned.

"Roland, I hope you aren't going to tell me that the mice have been eager to see me."

Roland ran a hand along his short beard—the evidence that he'd once been married. "Hmm. The mice might be eager...if you are carrying cheese?"

Liesl pretended to pat down her dress for hidden pieces of cheese. "I don't think I'm carrying any blocks of cheese. Hmm. If it wasn't mice, what could be making that squeak?"

"It wasn't a mouse. It was me!" Lilly cried out as she hurried to stand in front of Liesl.

"Oh my stars! I didn't see you there. Hiya, Lilly." Bending down, she gave the little four-year-old girl a hug. "I missed you."

"I missed you, too. *Daed* said you would be here soon." She smiled brightly. "He said you would come over soon and you did!"

"Your *Daed* is always right. Ain't so?" she teased with a smile in his direction.

"Not always, but every once in a while, the Lord is good," Roland murmured.

"Liesl?" Lilly pulled on her apron. "You gonna make me another dress?"

"Lilly, that ain't nice to ask," Roland said.

Liesl hadn't planned on making one, but she certainly couldn't say no. She could never say no to the sweet little girl. Thinking of her stash of fabric, she said, "I have some pretty yellow fabric. Would you like a yellow dress, dear?"

Roland cleared his throat. "As much as Lilly might

like a new yellow dress, she has plenty of others to wear."

Lilly looked crestfallen but didn't say a word. And that, of course, made Liesl feel even more tender toward the girl. "I would love to make a yellow dress for you."

"That ain't necessary," Roland said.

From her crouched position, she smiled at him. "I know, Roland, but that's the good thing about gifts, yes? They're freely given."

For the briefest of moments, Roland stared back. His dark eyes seemed to take in every part of her... and that he wasn't finding anything to be lacking, either.

Liesl felt her heart quicken. It had been so long since she'd felt so much approval. Usually she was aware of her parents feeling slightly disappointed in her actions. Or Wesley treating her to a smile...but even then it always felt a little distant. More like a smile that one might show to a wayward child or cute pet.

But with Roland? He stared at her with appreciation in his eyes. And happiness. It was as if she was finally doing something right. She felt at peace and confident and happy.

It would be wonderful. *Wonderful-gut*...if he was Wesley.

But he was not.

As the moment between them stretched into two, Liesl knew something had to be done.

Getting to her feet, she brushed her hands against the skirt of her dress and cleared her throat. "I suppose we'd better get started or I'll be here all day."

Roland blinked, then stepped back. The warmth in his eyes cooled. "Yes, of course. We canna have that."

Liesl wondered if he believed that any more than she did.

Chapter Nine

LIESL FISHER HAD SAVED HIM. Roland knew that without a doubt.

The first time Liesl had come over, he'd been ex*haus*ted and discouraged. Tricia had been in the last, painful stage of her cancer fight and had been suffering so much. He'd been out of ideas of how to help her heal...and even out of ideas of how to make her life bearable. He'd been in a very dark place.

Tricia's disease had not only changed her body, but her personality as well. His normally patient and kind wife had practically become a stranger to him during the last few months of her illness. Things that had used to make her happy only made her irritable. She'd begun to criticize him often—and much of the time, he'd felt so helpless he'd believed he'd deserved the harsh words. Soon it seemed as if he could do nothing right.

And then she'd even started losing her temper with Lilly.

Roland had been so confused by her changes, he'd gone to visit with her doctor on his own. The doctor had been sympathetic, to be sure. He'd told Roland that Tricia's cancer had affected her brain and that she couldn't help herself.

That had been hard to hear.

But even worse had been the awful news that while they weren't going to give up and that Jesus absolutely did gift others with miracles, things weren't looking too good.

Dr. Cronan had even suggested that Roland start preparing himself for the worst. He'd cried the whole way home from that appointment and hadn't even cared that the driver had witnessed him do so. Learning that he'd already lost the Tricia he'd fallen in love with had been heartbreaking. Realizing that Tricia's chances of living more than two more months were very slim had been even harder.

But after a long night of prayer, he'd accepted the Lord's will. He hadn't stopped yearning for a miracle or given up hope that one day his sweet wife would start acting like she used to, but Roland had also made himself start accepting his new reality.

Tricia might not ever get better, the house wasn't going to clean itself, and he couldn't work forty hours a week, be both mother and father to Lilly, be the only caretaker for Tricia and remain on his feet.

After that day, many things had changed around the house. He'd asked Tricia's nurse to work another eight hours a week, he'd cut back his hours at work, and he'd begun the terrible, awkward dance of trying to make Tricia's days as good as possible. That included him sometimes giving Tricia space so she could rely on the nurse to take care of her. And him getting Lilly out of the house a bit every day so she wouldn't be surrounded by her mother's illness and bad temper.

Just when he'd thought he couldn't do anything more, Liesl had come into his life.

The first time she'd arrived in order to make him four new shirts, he'd tried to shoo her back out the door. He didn't want anyone to see what terrible shape Tricia was in. Or himself.

Or even the house.

But Liesl, all five foot three inches of practicality that she was, had somehow talked her way inside, surmised the situation within a minute, and announced that she was going to help him. She'd beamed when she'd said it, too. Just like she was glad to take on the new burden.

He'd been so stunned, he'd only nodded...but had been secretly expecting her to never come back.

But she had. Sometimes only once a week. Sometimes almost every day. Always with a smile and a joke and her hugs for his daughter.

Now, she came over several days a week, helped with laundry, played with Lilly, and did a little bit of dusting and mopping the floors.

Before long, he and Lilly weren't looking forward to Liesl's visits for her help but for her sunny smiles and good attitude. She'd been a bright ray of sun in some of the darkest days of his life.

When Tricia had gone up to heaven just three months after Roland's private conversation with the doctor, Roland had mourned her terribly. But he hadn't fallen apart, and for that he would always be grateful.

Now that a full year had passed since Tricia's

death, he and Lilly had settled into a routine of sorts. Lilly now spent two days a week with her grandparents, sometimes had a neighbor watch her, and sometimes even went to work with him.

But her favorite days, without a doubt, were the ones when Liesl came to visit. When Liesl came over, Lilly seemed like her old self. She would giggle and smile and chatter with Liesl like a magpie.

Now that Lilly was older, Roland knew they needed to tell Liesl that she no longer needed to devote so much time to him and Lilly. She was a lovely, vibrant young woman and had a steady beau as well.

He just wished that he wasn't dreading the conversation so much.

After she'd measured him for his jacket and a neighbor girl had come over to help Lilly with her chores in the barn, Roland knew it was time to have the talk that was so needed. He felt like he was about to get a tooth pulled.

"Liesl, before you go, may I speak with you for a moment?"

"Of course." She put her canvas tote bag back on the kitchen counter and looked at him expectantly. "What do you need?"

"Uh...to speak with you." He'd already said that, hadn't he? Feeling like a dolt, he cleared his throat. "Would you mind if we sat down in the living room?"

"Of course not."

No doubt she was wondering why he was sounding so awkward and stiff. Just once, he wished the Lord had gifted him a bit more with the manner that He had given young Wesley, Liesl's beau. Every time Roland shopped at the market, he'd noticed the easy way Wesley was with everyone who visited. It was a cliché, but the customers really did often leave like friends.

He sat down on the couch and waited until Liesl sat down primly on the opposite end. As usual, she was as lovely as a picture. Her white *kapp* was pristine, her golden hair neatly fashioned in a bun, and her dark cranberry–colored dress gave her skin a lovely glow.

"Roland?"

There was nothing to do but forge ahead.

"Liesl, I want to tell you how grateful I am for your help the last year. You helped so much when Tricia was sick, cleaned our house when I could barely seem to be able to get out of bed, and became a true friend to Lilly. Through it all, you never even took a dime from me. We will always be grateful for everything you've done."

A faint line formed in between her brows. "I was happy to help you, Roland. I love being here." Looking a little flustered, she added, "I mean...I love seeing Lilly, and coming here didn't feel like work at all."

"You helped us both more than you will ever know. I'm very grateful."

"Roland, you've told me all of this before. Why are you bringing it up now?"

"Because I've been doing some thinking, and I feel like we've begun to take advantage of your good nature." Feeling guilty because all he wanted to do was beg her to stay, he added, "You will not need to come over here any longer."

Her faint smile faded. "You are firing me?"

"I would have had to hire you in order to fire you,

right?" He smiled even though he was grimacing inside. "All I'm doing is giving you back your time."

She continued to stare at him. "But I liked coming over here. I enjoyed it." She shook her head. "I mean, I do enjoy coming over. I look forward to it."

He liked having her over as well. Perhaps too much. *Nee*, definitely too much. After all, everyone knew that Wesley had been courting Liesl for some time. He was far more suitable, too. He was younger, handsome, so personable, and was from a warm and loving family. They were a good match. A perfect match.

Looking away, he continued his speech. "That is why Wesley Raber has to be one of the most blessed men in Walden. You are truly one of the kindest people I've ever known, Liesl." Hating that he was about two seconds from taking back his offer and begging her to keep coming over, Roland got to his feet. "Now, I had better let you get on your way."

Liesl got to her feet and walked to the kitchen without another word. "I should go tell Lilly."

"You may if you would like. However, my neighbor Rebecca is over in the barn with her."

"Do you think Lilly will understand why I stop coming over?"

He was sure she would be upset. But he would rather take the brunt of his little girl's disappointment than place it on Liesl's shoulders. "*Jah.* I think she will understand well enough."

"I see." Picking up her canvas bag, Liesl glanced at the kitchen door. The back door where she'd begun to just knock on twice before heading inside. "I guess it's time I went, then."

"I think that is best." When she didn't move, he forced himself to open the door for her. "Enjoy your afternoon."

She nodded. "*Danke*, Roland. You, too." She turned and walked outside. He stood and watched her leave, hating that he'd no longer half hope for rain so he'd have a reason to spend more time with her.

But that in itself was more than enough reason for him to break things off.

Because he knew he wasn't doing this just for Liesl's benefit; it was for his, too. He was embarrassed, but the sad, awful truth was that he had started to care for Liesl. Care for her in a way that had nothing to do with gratitude or babysitting.

No, it had everything to do with his heart and her smile...and the way he sometimes had even been thinking about kissing her and one day even calling her his own.

Chapter Ten

Jenny's laughter cut through the buzz of conversation in the store, causing more than one person to smile. Wesley, who was in the middle of helping Curtis, couldn't help but peek over at her. Just to see what she was up to. Jenny, wearing a burgundy dress under her black apron, giggled again. She was standing near the bakery, restocking trays of cookies. And laughing with none other than Ernie.

Wesley hadn't known that Ernie knew how to laugh.

"Ernie, *nee*! I am not going to fall for another one of your knock-knock jokes."

"Come on, Jenny. This one is a good'un. I promise. Knock, knock."

Wesley could practically feel the entire crowd in the store lean in to hear the rest of it.

"Fine. Who's there?"

"Eve."

"Eve who?"

"Christmas Eve!" Ernie exclaimed, looking pretty pleased with himself.

Jenny clapped her hands. "You're right. That

might be your best one yet." When Ernie walked away, she smiled at the young woman in line. "May I help you?"

"Yes, please, Jenny. Could I have two dozen of the frosted stars?"

"Of course, Pattie. It's my pleasure."

"I knew waiting in line for your help was worth my time."

Though Jenny had only worked at the store a full week, it was quickly becoming apparent that she was as popular as the trays of Christmas cookies in the bakery.

"I would tell ya that good help is hard to find, but you got yourself the best employee the Amish market has ever had," Curtis said as he watched Wesley wrap his order of smoked turkey breast in wax paper.

Wesley smiled at the eightysomething English man, all dressed up in his jeans, cashmere sweater, and Bean boots. "I'm guessing you're speaking of Jenny?"

"Of course, Jenny! She's not only kind enough to help an old goat like me, but she also is efficient. She knew exactly what table I've had my eye on and said she knew of the perfect pair of young lads to deliver it to my house later this afternoon."

Everyone knew which pine dining table the man had his eye on. He'd been gazing at it for over a year. Wesley had spoken about it with him at least a dozen times. So had his father. So had Ernie.

However, none of them had considered asking why Curtis was hesitating to make the purchase. Wesley had assumed that the older man was concerned about the price. He'd never guessed that Curtis had been most worried about getting it delivered. Apparently, Jenny had figured that out after one brief conversation, and she'd already arranged the delivery.

"I'm happy for ya, Curtis. I'm sure you're gonna be mighty happy to have it in your own home instead of just admiring it here."

"Now that I know it's coming, I can't hardly wait."

After Curtis paid for his items and left, Jenny walked over to Wesley's side. "He's a character, isn't he?"

"He sure is. Underneath all his jokes and such, he's a *gut* man. A mighty good one. Hardworking and solid and kind." Not wanting to gossip, but also not wanting to keep a well-known detail about Curtis from Jenny, he added, "He's just...well, I'd describe him as a bit of a lost puppy. He lost his oldest son in a car accident several years ago. Since then, he's never seemed the same. Some days are better than others, but it's obvious that he's never bounced completely back."

"Oh my. That's very sad."

"It is, but that's love for you, I reckon. Whether it's of a romantic nature or a familial one, it takes your heart and holds on tight."

Looking reflective, Jenny nodded. "I think that's true. Even when your head tells you one thing, your heart doesn't always want to get on board. In fact, sometimes, all it seems to want to do is kick and scream and argue."

He liked the colorful way she put things. "That sounds a bit like a heart attack, wouldn't you say?"

She smiled, but it wasn't full-fledged. Instead, it looked sad and close to being melancholy. "I guess so, only this time, it's not muscles and arteries that get into trouble, it's emotions and hope."

Wesley studied her closely. "Someone really hurt you, didn't he?" he asked more quietly. "You know about heartache because you've experienced it."

"I have."

"What happened?"

"It's not something I care to talk about."

She sounded dejected. She was usually so positive, it took him by surprise and tugged at his heartstrings. So much so, he was tempted to pull her into his arms, just to give her comfort.

Or...maybe not just for comfort?

Taken aback by his train of thought, he cleared his throat. "Of course. I'm sorry for prying." Glancing at the big clock on the wall, Wesley added, "Would you stay near the counter and check the remaining customers out? Now that I'm not needed at the deli counter, I think I'll take a walk through the store."

"Of course. Take your time."

Walking away, he forced himself not to apologize again. They were getting to know each other, and one didn't get to know another person well without talking about things that mattered.

Plus, if everything went well with Liesl, Jenny and he would be family. Family supported each other. He just wondered when Jenny was going to actually feel like Liesl's maiden aunt. Or if it would ever be possible to only think of her as a distant relative.

But that wouldn't do, of course. He vowed to keep her at more of a distance. It would be best to keep things a bit more professional. After all, Jenny would be out of his life again in just a few short weeks.

Honestly, he should be wondering how the shop was going to survive in January. What were they all going to do without her laughter? Wesley was pretty sure Ernie wasn't going to go around telling him knock-knock jokes.

Two hours later, Wesley was walking next to Jenny, headed to the Fishers' home. It was just beginning to snow. Some of the downtown shops in Walden were lined in tiny white lights, and almost every one of them had either a Christmas wreath or garland on the door.

The candy shop at the end of his block played soft Christmas music on an outdoor speaker, and the windows were decorated with antique Christmas tins and silly stuffed reindeer.

Jenny stopped and pointed to one wearing a cardboard cutout sign that read Vixin. "It looks like this poor reindeer is not only a vixen, but her owner can't spell."

He chuckled. "I think you're right about that." He pointed to a playful-looking handwritten sign on the back that read Help Wanted: Contact Santa. "That's cute."

"It's adorable. Some people don't care for these silly Christmas characters, but I think they make the season even more fun." She pointed to two more reindeer who were sipping hot chocolate in mugs topped with a tower of marshmallows. "Poor Santa has his hands full with this lot."

"I reckon so." He grinned as he noticed a whimsical cuckoo clock on the wall. The face of it was painted with hearts and the bottom of it was bordered with the words "my own true love." "I've walked by this shop at least twenty times but never stopped to peek inside."

"Truly?"

He nodded. "I was always in too much of a hurry, I guess."

"Well, that's a shame. The owner has put so much care and thought into the window displays. They make one smile just looking inside."

It was kind of the way Jenny made everyone smile—just by being in her presence. Appalled by the direction of his thoughts, he cleared his throat. "Indeed they do."

When they started walking again, she said, "What are the chocolates like?"

"I couldn't tell ya. I've never had any."

"Is the store new?"

"*Nee*. I...well, I guess I never had the occasion to go inside."

"Oh."

Jenny seemed disappointed by his comment, which made him wonder why he never had taken the time to go into the store...or at the very least, looked at the Christmas window display. Had he really been that busy?

Just as he was about to suggest that they turn around and go inside, Jenny spoke again. "I'm sorry, Wesley. Here I was, sounding like you aren't romantic, but of course you wouldn't have needed to buy any sweets. Liesl isn't much of a chocolate fan."

She wasn't? Struggling to remember what dessert Liesl had eaten the last time they'd dined together, he said, "I think she likes apple pie."

Jenny laughed. "She does at that, Wesley."

He knew there was another joke in her words somewhere, but for the life of him, he couldn't figure out what that was, either.

Suddenly, he felt more awkward and foolish than he had been at his first Sunday singing when he was fourteen, when he would stare at all the girls and blush every time one of them met his gaze.

"It sure is snowing now," he said.

"It is, indeed."

They said nothing more the rest of the way to the Fishers' house.

Chapter Eleven

Jenny had known that Wesley visited her sister's house a few times a month. The Fishers and the Rabers had grown close, so he was practically part of the family. Of course, she was also well aware that Wesley was Liesl's beau and that her niece was practically counting the days until he would propose.

Even though she'd known all that, Jenny had still experienced more than a few moments of dread about Wesley's upcoming visit. Getting a front seat to the couple's romance might bring back memories of some especially sweet moments she'd shared with Jeremiah. To her shame, she'd even wondered if she would feel jealous.

The truth was that she was starting to notice things about Wesley. He was a handsome man, tall and sturdy, and so capable. And his hazel eyes were mesmerizing. She was sure that once she'd counted at least five different shades of green and brown in them. A good man, too. Though she would never act on her feelings, she couldn't seem to help wishing that she had found a man like him instead of Jeremiah.

So she'd been prepared to be a tad bit uncomfortable during Wesley's visit. It turned out that his visit was far different than what she'd imagined. Truth be told, she'd found Wesley and Liesl's relationship to be confusing.

First of all, though Liesl and Wesley had smiled at each other when he'd entered the living room, neither had so much as crossed the room to say hello. Then, instead of sitting next to her, Wesley had sat on Armor's right. The two men talked business during most of the meal.

To Jenny's surprise, Liesl didn't act as if this was either surprising or a disappointment. Instead, she talked about a recent visit to Roland's house. In fact, Liesl had lit up like a Christmas tree when she'd talked about playing outside with Roland's four-year-old daughter, Lilly.

If Wesley had thought it strange that his girlfriend seemed to enjoy spending so much time at another man's house, he didn't act like it. Actually, he didn't seem to mind it at all.

As the meal continued, Jenny continued to watch the two of them interact. Kept waiting for Wesley to look across the table and grin, like they were sharing a private joke. Kind of the way she and Wesley had shared glances when Ernie told one of his knock-knock jokes. So far, she hadn't seen anything like that.

She waited to see him gaze at Liesl with longing in his eyes. Or even happiness. Or even a simple appreciation of her beauty.

But that didn't happen.

Actually, the only time she'd witnessed Liesl and Wesley exchange words directly to each other was when one of them asked the other to pass a dish.

Jenny supposed there was nothing wrong with any of this. All couples had their own dynamics. It just didn't seem to fit either Wesley or Liesl. The Liesl she knew was needy. She loved affection, talking, and attention.

The Wesley she was coming to know had certainly been chatty at work. Whenever they'd had a free moment, he'd asked her all sorts of things about her life and interests.

Why wasn't he asking his intended a heap of questions, or at the very least, looking like he wanted to spend a few moments alone with her? Surely Laura May and Armor weren't that strict with them.

"Jenny, is everything all right?" Laura May asked.

"Of course. Why?"

"Well, you've hardly touched your food, and you look like you're staring into space." She frowned slightly. "Oh no. Are you ex*haus*ted? Was work too taxing for you?" She turned to Wesley. "Are you allowing my little sister to have breaks or are you working her to the bone?"

"Laura May, don't be so silly," Jenny said. "I'm a grown woman, you know."

"I know...but I'm still asking."

Wesley looked like a cornered animal. "I've given her breaks. At least, I thought I had." Sounding even more worried, he added, "Jenny, have I been asking too much of you? Have I not helped you enough?"

Aware of the entire family staring at her, Jenny shook her head. "I have gotten breaks, and you are not asking too much of me, Wesley. I promise." Hating that everyone was focused on her, she shrugged. "If I'm quiet, it's because I'm used to eating on my own, you see. Most times, the Andersons eat with their *kin-*

ner and give me the evenings off. I guess I've become a quiet diner."

Liesl gazed at her fondly. "Of course you are, Aunt Jenny. I should've remembered that."

"What does that mean?" Wesley asked.

"Only that Jenny here doesn't need a lot of attention," Liesl explained. "She's always been easygoing and keeps to herself."

Jenny knew Liesl's description of her wasn't exactly accurate, but she did keep that to herself.

Armor frowned. "I don't believe I've ever noticed that you are quiet at mealtimes. Are you finding so much conversation to be taxing? Do you want to eat alone while you're here, dear?"

Ack, but this was awful. "*Nee*, I do not." She chuckled, though it sounded forced and awkward. "You all need to stop worrying about me. I am perfectly fine and enjoying this meal very much. No doubt I'll be chatting like a magpie soon enough."

"You don't have to do anything special for any of us, dear," Laura May murmured. "Just like when you were a little girl and you skipped instead of walking, I've always liked you, just the way you are."

And now her face was flushed and she felt foolish. "*Danke*." Eager to say anything to move the conversation along, she added, "Wesley showed me the chocolate shop windows on the way home. The reindeer in the windows made me laugh."

"I like the one sipping hot chocolate," Liesl said. "Nancy, the owner, is gifted. She decorates the windows for every holiday."

"She goes all out at Valentine's Day," Laura May added. "Last year, she had stuffed teddy bears having a party. It was adorable. Everyone I know enjoyed looking at it."

"They are silly scenes, to be sure, but I think well worth her efforts," Armor added. "After all, it gets me inside every year." Smiling at her softly, he added, "*Mei* Laura May does love Nancy's chocolates."

"I'll have to go inside soon," Jenny said. "I'm eager to try the hot chocolate."

"You should. It's *wunderbar*," Laura May said.

"Liesl, it's a shame you don't like chocolate," Wesley blurted.

"You don't like chocolate?" Laura May asked. "Since when?"

Liesl blushed. "I like it well enough. I have gotten a couple of candies there from time to time."

"You have?" Wesley asked.

"Like I said, chocolate has never been my favorite treat." Smiling at Jenny, she said, "Now, dear Aunt Jenny, on the other hand, is chocolate crazy."

Realizing that that description was rather accurate, Jenny giggled. "I do love chocolate."

"Remember when we walked two miles just so you could get a hot fudge sundae?"

Now she felt like a glutton, indeed. "It was a hot day, Liesl. Besides, you had said you wanted some exercise. It was a tasty treat after an hour's walk."

"I had plain vanilla ice cream and loved every bite." She smiled at Wesley. "One day you and I should visit the candy store just so you can try a chocolate or two yourself."

"Oh. Of course, Liesl. Whenever you want."

Jenny glanced at him through her lowered eyelashes. His voice had come out rather stilted, but then when he met Liesl's gaze, he looked enchanted... didn't he?

Of course he did. And who could blame him? Liesl was a lovely girl and she loved Wesley so much.

Obviously, she'd been misreading their whole relationship. If she had, it would've served her right, too. She was only there for a short amount of time; she had no reason to judge or guess how they were.

In addition, she was the one with a failed relationship. Not them. She obviously had a lot to learn about love.

"It's mighty kind of you to help me with the dishes, but it wasn't needed," Laura May said to Jenny as she passed her a plate to dry an hour later. "I don't mind doing dishes on my own."

"I was surprised Liesl left them for you."

"As you know, she doesn't usually. It's just when Wesley comes calling, she wants everything to be perfect for him. She told me once that if she did dishes, he'd likely volunteer to help, too." Laura May chuckled. "That, I suppose, means she doesn't want him to have to put his hands in soapy water."

"Wesley washes lots of things at work. He never stops to take a break when he's there." Inwardly, Jenny groaned. She was sounding like Wesley's number one fan, which was more than a little odd. "I mean, from what I noticed," she added weakly.

"All the more reason to let the two of them relax, *jah*?"

"Of course." After setting the dish on the counter, she reached for a casserole dish out of the drainer.

Laura May smiled and scrubbed another pot. "So, now that we're alone, tell me the truth. How is working at the market? I'm sure it's mighty different than looking after *kinner.*"

"It is different, for sure and for certain. But I wouldn't say it's completely dissimilar. After all, I usually spend most of my days making sure someone in the Anderson family is happy. Now I just do that in smaller spurts of time for a greater number of people."

"I never thought about it that way." She handed her three forks. "And how is Wesley as a boss? Hopefully not too hard on you. I have worried about that."

Jenny chuckled before she could stop herself. "He is the opposite of being difficult or demanding."

"Oh?"

"He's been nothing but patient and kind."

Laura May looked a bit taken aback. "Goodness. I never imagined that."

"The store is so busy, I would've thought Wesley would have been less patient with me, but he's been very understanding. I think he hasn't forgotten that I only came out because Liesl asked me to."

"She probably asked a bit much of you. Perhaps I did, too?"

"Never."

Her sister shrugged as she rinsed another handful of silverware. "There's no sense worrying about it now. What's done is done."

"Working at the Amish Market isn't a hardship. I'm enjoying meeting all the customers. I like doing a good job, too. The customers notice, which in turn makes Wesley happy. He cares a lot about the store."

"If he does, I think it's because he cares about his family. He doesn't want to let them down." Pausing a moment, Laura May looked out the kitchen window. It was dark outside, the short winter days encouraging the sun to set by five.

"I'm sure he cares about Liesl, too."

"*Jah.* I know that he does." She frowned. "It's just that...well, I sometimes wonder if they might have jumped into things a bit too quickly."

Jenny was tempted to ask what her sister meant but decided not to pry. Jenny adored Liesl, but she also knew that for most of their lives, she herself had never pushed too hard or asked Leisl too many difficult questions. She certainly wasn't going to start doing that when she and Wesley were so close to becoming engaged!

After checking to make sure the coast was clear, she whispered, "Do you expect a Christmas proposal?"

"Liesl does, but I'm not so certain it's forthcoming." Laura May paused. "I don't think Wesley would do anything so important without his parents being nearby. And who can blame him? He's so worried about his father and his responsibilities at the store."

"That makes sense," Jenny said. But as the minutes passed, she wondered if maybe Laura May had thought there was another reason.

With effort, she pushed that thought away. One mustn't go looking for trouble, she decided.

Even when one wasn't exactly sure what that trouble was.

Chapter Twelve

Liesl's favorite place in her family's sprawling house was the four-season room located in the back, just beyond the kitchen and family room. One could find a measure of privacy there that wasn't possible in the rest of the house. It was also extremely comfortable.

In the summer her *daed* exchanged the screens with glass and switched the usual wicker furniture with two cozy small sofas. There was a small propane gas fireplace in the corner. When the fireplace was on, a few candles were burning, and the snow was blustery and cold, she was sure there was no better place in all of Walden.

Usually, her parents relaxed there in the evenings after supper. Her father liked to gaze out the window and identify both individual stars and his favorite constellations. Her mother simply liked to relax. More often than not, she fell asleep on the couch.

However, on nights when Wesley visited, her parents allowed them to have the best room in the house. Oh, it hadn't been granted readily. It wasn't until Wesley had called on Liesl for almost a year that they were allowed so much privacy.

Not that she and Wesley did anything inappropriate. Ever.

Her sister, Emma, had found that amusing. More than once she'd said that Liesl and Wesley having the room to themselves was something of a waste.

"If I had a beau and *Mamm* and *Daed* allowed us to sit by ourselves in the four-season room, we would not be playing cards," she'd declared last month.

Liesl had privately thought their card games did seem rather unromantic—though she would never admit that to her sister. "I like playing cards with Wesley."

"You don't want to do anything else?" Emma had waggled her eyebrows. "You know, something where you two are a whole lot closer?"

The question might have been shocking if Liesl weren't twenty-two and Wesley weren't twenty-six. Or if they hadn't been courting for such a long time. Or if she hadn't begun to wonder why Wesley hadn't been wanting to pull her into his arms. She'd even begun to wonder if something was wrong with her. More than one girlfriend had whispered stories about becoming breathless after a particularly heated make-out session on a living room couch. Each time, her friend had blushed and giggled and given Liesl a knowing glance. It had been obvious that everyone, besides Emma, thought that Wesley was amorous in private. He was not.

Again she deflected Emma's inquiry. "You shouldn't even be thinking about kissing."

"Oh, please. *Everyone* thinks about kissing."

"Well, I don't." Yes, she was lying, but what could she do?

At that, Emma had looked at her with an expression very close to pity. "Liesl, I'm not an expert on relationships, but I canna help but think that if you only like playing cards with Wesley Raber, you should do some thinking about why that is."

Emma's words had hurt, but Liesl supposed they most likely weren't wrong. Though she knew that the Lord considered affection and commonalities and kindness to be wonderful gifts upon which to base a marriage, there had been times—not that she would tell the Lord this—when she'd been secretly hoping for something more between them.

Something more...meaningful. Something with a spark.

Or perhaps even two sparks. Firecrackers, even.

But tonight was different, because Wesley was acting different. For once, he wasn't trying to get her to play cards or talking about the store. Instead, he was attentive and affectionate. He was touching her a lot, too. So far, he'd brushed a strand of hair off her cheek, rubbed her forearm, and had even placed his hand on the small of her back when they were walking. None of it was noteworthy—at least not for a courting couple.

For them, though? Well, it was rather disconcerting.

"Are you comfortable here on the couch?" she asked.

"Very much so. I like sitting here next to you and watching the snow fall." He smiled as he reached out and ran his thumb along her cheek.

She was so surprised, she flinched. "Do I have something on *mei bokka?*"

"Not at all. I, um, felt like feeling your skin."

"Oh."

He frowned as he leaned closer. "Liesl, are you all right? You seem kind of tense."

"I'm not tense at all." But of course she was. It was like the Wesley she knew had been replaced with his amorous counterpart. She had no idea if she was supposed to be enjoying his touches or fending him off. She really should've asked her girlfriends for more details.

She smiled weakly.

After another moment, Wesley scooted closer. Close enough so their thighs touched. Then, in what was rather an unpracticed move, he slipped his arm around her shoulders. His hand curved around her shoulder. She was practically pinned to his side.

He was warm and smelled of clean cotton and fresh soap. Glancing at his profile, she noticed once again how perfect his jaw was. How smooth his cheeks were. He must have shaved before coming over. Did he usually do that? She racked her brain, trying to remember if his cheeks had always looked so baby-soft when they'd been playing Uno.

Unfortunately, she couldn't remember.

"I've always liked this room, Liesl," he murmured.

She shifted. "*Jah.* It's, um, everyone's favorite."

Wesley pulled away a bit so he could see her face. "Including yours?"

"Oh, *jah.*" Trying to ignore the fact that his hand was now rubbing her back, she swallowed hard. "I like sitting here and watching the world go by."

He looked down at her with a fond expression. "The world? All you can see from here is the woods, Liesl. Well, the woods and the stars."

"That's the world I'm talking about." When he looked at her in a puzzled manner, she shrugged. "It's the only world that matters to me on most days."

"I didn't know you felt that way. I thought you always had one eye looking out toward the big world." When she frowned, he added, "You know, the outside world."

Liesl wasn't sure why, but it felt as if the conversation was an important one. She chose her words with care. "It is true that I'm interested in all sorts of things, and I don't see why the fact I wear a bonnet means I shouldn't care about anything else. But I really am happiest at home. I like baking a cake that turns out well and tastes good. Making clothes out of fabrics that are pretty. Sitting in a warm room when the weather is bad outside. I like being here in Walden."

"I see."

Did he? Did he really? "What about you? Is that how you feel?"

"Well now, I have to admit that I'm not rightly sure." With the arm that was not around her shoulders, he pulled on the snug collar of his white shirt. "Of late, all I've been thinking about is getting through Christmas."

She was disappointed that he hadn't told her more but chastised herself. Of course he wouldn't be thinking of only her—not when he had so many other, more important things to worry about.

"I'm sure your father's heart and health have been weighing heavy on your mind."

He didn't answer for a long moment. "It has. I...I guess I always just thought *Daed* was invincible. That no matter how many years passed or how many hours he worked, he was always going to be the same. His heart scare was not only a wake-up call for him, but for me, too. I want to take care of him—but also take care of me." Gazing at her intently, he added, "Obviously, I'm struggling a bit. Thinking about myself is something new. Usually all I think about is the store...especially at this time of year."

"I'm glad you're thinking about yourself more. That's a good thing, don't you think?"

"I hope so." He pulled his arm away, giving her more space, yet leaving her feeling chilled, too. "Of course, if we don't have good sales numbers this Christmas season, it will be all my fault. I'll know that I shouldn't have spent so much time thinking about myself."

The tension in the room deflated...or maybe it was just her expectations. "I see." Liesl felt flat, like all the air had been taken out of the moment, and all she was left with was a deep longing for things to be different.

She loved Christmas. It wasn't just because of the presents or festivities; it was the feeling of hope that surrounded the season.

In December, more people seemed to be kinder. They tried harder to listen. Tried harder to be considerate. Everyone planned things; they made gifts. They took the time to let people know that they were important.

Which, she realized with a sense of dismay, she'd been waiting for Wesley to do. To say the words about love that she'd been longing to hear.

"I know my focus on the store upsets you, Liesl. However, I don't have much choice. With my parents out of town, the store's success is dependent on me. And I'm afraid if I mess things up, it's only going to add more stress to my father's heart."

"I know, Wesley," she said. She did feel for him, too. However, he'd also worked nonstop last December. And all the years before that.

"I can't neglect my responsibilities."

"I realize that."

"Do you?" His eyes clouded with questions. "I'm sorry, but I have a feeling that all of my working upsets you."

"It doesn't. I mean, it doesn't exactly."

He turned to face her. "I'd rather you didn't lie."

"I'm not lying." She sighed. "All right. Yes, I suppose I am disappointed that you are consumed by the store, but that ain't your fault. You don't feel that you have a choice." Yes, she'd chosen her words with care, too. He did have some choices...He just didn't want to make different ones.

Wesley stared at her for a long moment. "You know what? How about if I close the shop early one day this week and we go do something fun?"

"Would you really do that?"

He smiled at her fondly. "I really would."

"What about your parents? Are you worried about what they'll say?"

"They aren't going to say anything disparaging. I know they realize that a lot fell in my lap and that I've been doing the best I can. They'll understand that I need a night off with my girl."

She was his girl. Of course, she'd heard him say that before, but not for a very long time. Feeling reassured, she smiled up at him. She'd been acting silly. It was obvious that Wesley cared about her. She mattered to him. Mattered more than the shop or Christmas season.

"Tell me a date and I'll be ready."

"Let's plan on Thursday."

Her heart felt so full. "Thursday it is." She looked up at him again. Noticed that his gaze flickered to her lips. Felt a new spark burn between them. He was going to kiss her. At last, he was going to pull her against him, kiss her passionately—and for just a few minutes, they were going to forget that there was anyone else in the house.

Like there was no one on earth but the two of them.

Wesley cracked his knuckles, breaking the moment.

She blinked, trying to catch up...then realized that her fantasy wasn't going to come true after all.

Looking like he had just completed a difficult assignment, he wrapped his arm around her again and leaned back on the cushion. "You're right, Liesl. This is nice out here. *Nee*, better than that. *Wunderbar.*"

She smiled as she leaned into his side. It was comfortable, sitting next to him. Relaxing. Almost as wonderful as everything she'd dreamed about.

Chapter Thirteen

THE KNOCK ON THE FRONT door came just as Wesley had sat down at his family's circular oak kitchen table with a steaming bowl of chili. Hoping it was only a package being delivered, he ignored it. It might have been rude, but as usual, it had been a long day at the Market. All he wanted to do was sit down, eat something warm, and relax.

He'd barely taken the first bite when someone knocked at the door again.

"Wesley, open up!"

He knew that bold voice well—it could only belong to his sister Frannie. Their father had often said Frannie should be an auctioneer. She was that loud.

Pushing back his chair, he strode to the front door. "Coming, Fran!"

When he opened the door at last, he grinned. "Uh-oh. It must be my unlucky day." The teasing statement was a familiar one. He and his brother Paul often muttered it whenever both of their nosy, meddling sisters showed up at the same time.

Just as they were that evening. Both Frannie and Marianne were wearing black cloaks, black bonnets over their white *kapps*, and black boots. Frannie was sporting thick pink mittens on her hands, while Marianne had on serviceable dark-green gloves. He loved their differences as much as he loved how steady each was.

"Come in, you two."

"Glad you opened the door, brother," Frannie said as she barreled in, practically bringing in her own brand of sunshine with her. "For a moment there I feared you wouldn't be home."

"I'm home and glad to see you, Fran," he said as he hugged her—a little awkwardly, because her baby bump had grown quite a bit since last time he'd seen her. "You, too, dear Marianne. I didn't expect to see you for several months, though. I thought you were going to stay in Kentucky until Christmas."

"Gideon and I were ready to return. As were Frannie and Caleb." Marianne, so slim and with blond hair like his, stood up on her tiptoes and kissed his cheek.

"Paul and Jenna were okay with that?"

"Oh, *jah.* Too many cooks and all that. It turns out that *Daed* does better with only one of his *kinner* telling him what to do."

He could see how that could be. "I'm glad you made it back safely."

Marianne looked him over. "I am, too...though you're looking old and tired, dear brother."

"We all canna be twenty-one," he teased. He held out his hands for their cloaks. "I was about to sit down and eat my supper. Would either of you care for some chili?"

Frannie wrinkled her nose as she pulled off her mittens and then untied the strings on her black bonnet, revealing her white kapp underneath. Immediately, her complexion brightened. Frannie's dark-red hair always gave her cheeks of color.

"Is it real chili or Cincinnati chili?"

"Real." Everyone knew that Liesl's family ate Cincinnati-style chili on Christmas Eve. No one was a fan of the concoction, which involved serving the dish with cheese and onions and spaghetti noodles.

"Well, at least there's that. *Danke*, but I don't think the babe will care for chili tonight."

"I have saltines if you'd like them instead." When she just shrugged, he turned to their younger sister. "Mar?"

Marianne had already neatly removed her gloves, bonnet, and boots. She'd also set the boots neatly by the door and placed her gloves and bonnet on the table in their family's worn and well-loved living room. "*Danke*, but I don't care for any chili, either. We only came by to see you and make sure you weren't working yourself to the bone."

"I'm all right." His sisters exchanged glances.

"Come sit down and finish your supper, Wes. We'll sit and pester you with questions while your mouth is too full to answer," Marianne added as she led the way into the kitchen.

Frannie circled her hands around his arm as they followed. "Don't you wonder what we'd all be like if Marianne had been born first instead of last?"

"I reckon we'd all be tired of being managed," he said with a laugh. "Paul and I have often said the Lord sure knew what He was about, bringing Marianne into our lives when He did."

"I heard that," Marianne said.

"I had no doubt you did, dear," Frannie murmured as she joined her sister. "Eat, Wesley."

Maybe another day he might have been reluctant to dive back in, but he really was too hungry to adhere to good manners. Uncaring that they were watching him, Wesley shoveled in chili and saltines like his bowl was in danger of being pulled away.

"Do you want some more, dear brother?" Frannie asked once he'd finished. "There's nary a crumb left."

"Not yet." He stood up and put his dish in the sink. "Now, what brings you both here? And, more importantly, who brought you here?" He hadn't seen the buggy or one of their horses.

"Caleb and Gideon dropped us off. They went over to English Doug's *haus*. Do you remember meeting him? Doug lives on the other side of town, you know." Gideon and his best friend Doug had been fierce hockey players on the pond near their houses when they were kids. Doug, being English, had gone on to play hockey in high school. Everyone had wondered if Gideon would jump the fence—not because he longed for a different faith, but because the bishop wasn't real pleased about men in their community playing hockey.

"Oh, I know. What's going on? What are they doing?"

"Watching hockey on the television." Marianne smiled. "We told our husbands to have a good time."

"Besides, we wanted to check on you."

"As you can see, I am fine."

Frannie shook her head. "Unfortunately, I disagree. You're looking kind of sallow. Are you getting enough sleep?"

"You know I am."

"I don't know anything of the sort. All I do know is that *Mamm* and *Daed* are with Paul and Jenna in Kentucky and you are working nonstop at the store."

"It's December, Fran. You know as well as I do that working long hours comes with the month."

"I know." She sighed. "I told Caleb that he should've let me work with you."

"What? Not only would you have had to hire a driver to take you back and forth every day, but you are six months along. Of course you canna be on your feet all day." He turned to Marianne. "And before you start, *nee*."

"I'm not that bad of a worker."

"You are a mighty *gut* sister, a wonderful woman to be in charge of auctions, mud sales, and a dozen other activities. Working with me at the store? *Nee*." Looking at her fondly, he added, "We both know that we'd butt heads. You like to do things your way, and I like to do them my way."

Marianne looked taken aback by his summation, but it was obvious that she didn't disagree.

Frannie chuckled. "Sorry, sister, but not even *Mamm* nor *Daed* thought you working at the shop with Wesley was a good idea."

"It don't matter anyway," he reminded them. "I have a temporary worker."

"We heard. Her name is Jenny, yes?" Frannie asked.

"*Jah*. She's doing great, too."

"From what I've heard, everyone seems to like her. I canna believe she's Liesl's aunt."

"It's disconcerting since Jenny and her sister are

so far apart in age, but what can one expect? There are eight children in their family."

"I wasn't referring to Liesl's age, Wesley."

"What are you referring to?"

"Only that Liesl had no trouble asking her aunt to help you in the store..."

Wesley blinked, wondering if Frannie meant something by the comment. "They are close," he murmured.

His sisters exchanged looks.

That was too bad. For as many years as he'd courted Liesl, his sisters had never seemed to be completely on board with the relationship.

"You know, if you just gave Liesl a chance, I think you'll realize that you two have been judging her too harshly."

"I'm not judging her at all," Marianne said quickly.

Though he usually let their unspoken disapproval slide, he was still feeling guilty about how he hadn't been terribly attentive to his girlfriend of late. So, against his better instincts, he went on the defensive.

"What, exactly, do you not like about her?"

Marianne shifted uncomfortably. "Wes, as you might recall, I haven't said anything disparaging."

"And I haven't said a single thing," Frannie said with a pious expression.

Which could only mean one thing: trouble.

"It's everything you didn't say that I noticed." Facing them both, he added, "This ain't the first time I've noticed your silence, either. If I promise not to get mad, will you two finally tell me what it is about Liesl Fisher that you two don't like?"

Marianne stayed silent. Frannie swallowed.

"Please tell me."

"You have it all wrong," Frannie said at last. "We like her fine."

"We really do," Marianne added. "It's just..."

Wesley raised an eyebrow. "Just..."

"It's just that she don't seem like a good match for you," Frannie finally admitted. "I'm sorry, but she never has. At least, not to me. She's rather direct, you know. And she doesn't seem interested in the store."

"That's it?" he asked, his voice filled with sarcasm. "That is why you two have been noticeably chilly toward her all this time?"

"It hasn't been the whole time," Marianne countered. "As I've said, we do like her. I also think she's a talented seamstress. But it's obvious she's not the best mate for you. Even Gideon has thought this."

He was becoming annoyed. "Mar, you are only twenty-one."

"I don't see how that makes a difference. I'm married. You are not."

Wesley paused, waiting for Frannie to point out that she was married as well. But to his surprise, she didn't say a word. Her silence made him realize that she was very bothered by the conversation. Usually Frannie had something to say about everything.

Choosing his words with care, he said, "I'll have you know that I like Caleb and Gideon verra much."

Marianne nodded. "You should. They are good men."

"But neither of them are perfect. And, I'm sorry to say, there have even been times when I wondered if they were the best choices for each of you. However,

I always have treated both of your husbands with respect."

Marianne folded her arms across her chest. "I have never disrespected Liesl."

Frannie stood up and walked over to the sink. She turned on the faucet and squirted some soap in the sink. "We didn't come over here to discuss Liesl Fisher."

"Are you sure? Because it seems that way. And don't wash my dishes."

"Settle down. I cannot sit here and watch those dishes get dried-up and gross in the sink."

If he hadn't been so tired and annoyed, he might have argued a little more. But because he was, he let Frannie's need to do something slide.

Besides, he had something more important to say.

"I intend to ask Liesl to marry me soon." He knew it was time. She expected it. And after all, a man couldn't just keep courting someone forever.

He got to his feet as well as he glared at them both. "And when I do, I hope you will be her new sisters. I hope you'll not only treat her with respect, but also make her feel welcome."

Marianne swallowed. "We'll do our best, I am sure."

Wesley shook his head. "Forgive me, but that ain't good enough."

"You're right." Straightening her shoulders, Marianne faced him. "I promise, dear brother, that I will be nothing but welcoming and respectful of your future wife."

"Frannie?"

"I will do the same," she said. "I am grateful for

you for the reminder, Wesley. From this point on, you—and Liesl—will feel nothing but acceptance and grace from me."

"*Gut.*"

"Now, may we please talk about something else?" Frannie asked.

"Of course. Tell me what each of you is giving our parents for Christmas."

Marianne brightened right up and began to eagerly chat about some needlework project she'd been working on for six months.

Frannie glanced his way and winked. The smile they shared was familiar. Walking over to the sink, he picked up a dish towel and started drying the dishes his sister had just kindly washed. This was familiar, too.

He only hoped that one day, when he was doing such chores with Liesl, it would feel just as natural and easy.

Privately, he wasn't sure if that would ever be the case.

Chapter Fourteen

The yank on Roland's pants leg startled him enough to jump. "Lilly, what?" he barked. His child's eyes widened and her bottom lip started to tremble—until he ran his thumb along the apple of her cheek. "Sorry, sweet. I didn't mean to snap. What is it?"

She rose up on her tiptoes. "I canna see out the whole window like you can. Do you see Liesl yet? Is she here?"

He'd been telling himself that his four-year-old daughter wouldn't notice her father gazing out the window like a lovesick fool. Obviously, he'd been wrong. He smiled at how silly he had been. "*Nee*, but she should be here soon."

Two days ago, Taco had gotten a start and knocked down a section of his stall. Roland needed to rebuild it and reinforce the rest of his horse's home. Knowing it was too cold to have Lilly out there with him, he'd asked a number of people for help.

When no one was available, he'd reached out to Liesl. She'd agreed immediately to come over today.

Lilly walked over to her little chair by her coloring table. "You said that last time I asked."

"Because you asked me the same question only five minutes ago. You need to learn to be patient, *jah*?" That was something he needed to remind himself about, too.

She sighed. "Being patient is hard work."

"It is indeed." It took a bit of effort, but he didn't crack a smile. Lilly often spouted statements like they were pulled straight out of the Scriptures. He'd learned that teasing her about them only hurt her feelings.

Noticing that she had her pack of crayons opened and a picture started, he turned to face her. "What are you working on?"

"A Christmas present."

"You are? Is it for me?" He smiled.

She shook her head. "*Nee.* I told Liesl I was gonna make her a pretty picture for Christmas."

He walked over to her and bent down slightly. His father had built Lilly the tiny desk, and she loved having something in the kitchen that was just her size. "I am sure she'll love it. Any picture you make is a *wonderful-gut* gift." Their refrigerator was covered with her latest efforts. Seeing them first thing every morning never failed to make him smile.

Still looking serious, Lilly nodded. "I was worried that I was supposed to keep my gift a secret, but she said that Christmas gifts didn't have to be secrets. She said all gifts are nice to receive—even when someone knows about them."

"I would have to agree with that."

"Does that mean you're gonna tell me what you got me for Christmas?"

Her eyes were so full of hope, Roland was almost tempted. But the best part of gift giving was anticipating the recipient's reaction. It might be selfish, but he wasn't going to give that up."*Nee.*"

"But—"

"Just because we want something, it doesn't mean it's gonna happen. You're going to have to wait until Christmas morning to discover your gift from me."

Little Lilly, all three and a half feet of her, seemed to consider that for a long moment, then turned back to the window. "Do you see her yet?"

He looked again but didn't see a single sign of Liesl's buggy. "*Nee.*"

She sighed in her dramatic way. "I'm gonna go potty."

Roland smiled as he watched her trot down the hall. It wasn't so very long ago that he had to go with her. At least, it didn't feel like that long ago.

He sat on the window seat and attempted to get himself together. It was time to face the facts. His daughter wasn't the only one of them to be eagerly awaiting their guest. It also wasn't the first time he'd gazed out the window in hopes of seeing her.

To his shame and embarrassment, he was looking forward to seeing Liesl as well.

When Liesl was there, everything in the house was bright again. It was that simple.

He didn't know how he was going to handle it when Wesley Raber finally proposed. Liesl would be overjoyed, and he would have to pretend to be happy for her.

And maybe he would be. He wanted nothing more than for Liesl to be happy. But it would be a very hard adjustment for him and Lilly, without a doubt.

He would have to come to terms with the fact that she would never be his, since marriage was forever.

Almost as painful would be the fact that it would no longer be proper for Liesl to spend as much time with him and Lilly. He'd tried to end her visits, yet here he and Lilly were, waiting to see her again. Yes, when Wesley finally made his move, they'd feel her absence like the loss of a limb. It was going to be difficult to handle, for sure and for certain.

But handle it he would. After all, he'd handled far more difficult things from the Lord. He would survive this, too.

"Knock, knock," Liesl called out in her bright, cheerful voice.

"Liesl! Hey," he said, opening up the screen door. "Come in."

She was looking even prettier than usual, with a bright-red wool dress, soft-looking mittens, and a scarf around her neck. But what was most appealing was her sunny expression.

"What were you doing, standing at the window?" she asked. "I waved when I walked up but you didn't seem to see me."

"Lilly and I were standing here looking for ya. She suddenly had to go potty, and I guess my mind went walking."

Her eyes were bright with merriment. "She suddenly had to go potty?"

He could feel his cheeks and neck heat. "When I say things like that I realize that I'm officially a father twenty-four seven now. There's no escaping it."

"Not that you'd want to, right?"

He smiled at her. "Of course, right. I'd be lost without my little girl."

A slight frown marred her perfect features as she looked down the hall. “Is Lilly all right? Do you think I should check on her?”

Come to think of it, the child had been gone for a while. “Of course not. I’ll go.”

Lilly’s laughter stopped him in his tracks. “Surprise!” she said around a giggle. “I was hiding.”

“And perhaps spying?” Roland asked.

“*Nee.*” When he gave her a long look, she looked guilty. “Well, maybe a little bit.”

“Lillian.”

After tossing her gloves on the kitchen counter, Liesl walked over to her side and reached for her hands. “Why were you spying on us, dear one?” she asked.

To his surprise, his little girl turned bright red. “Umm.”

“Good girls speak the truth, even when it’s hard,” Liesl said. “What were you hoping to see?”

“That *mei daed* would kiss you.”

Roland just about fell off his feet. “Lilly, what a naughty thing to say.”

“I’m sorry.”

Again, Liesl took the lead. “Were you thinking of some of your friends’ parents?”

“*Jah.* Bethy says her parents kiss each other hello and goodbye every day.”

“That is nice. My parents do that, too.” She winked. “But only when they think they’re alone.”

Lilly brightened. “You and *mei daed* should kiss hello, too. Right?”

Seeing that Liesl was blushing, Roland rushed to put an end to the subject. “Wrong, daughter. You are being impertinent.”

Lilly looked crushed. "Why?"

Still wearing her cloak, Liesl knelt down in front of her. "Because husbands and wives kiss, but your father and I are only friends. Friends don't kiss. There's a difference, right?"

"I don't want there to be."

Ack, but this conversation was becoming more awkward by the second. "Lilly, you know better than to say such things to Liesl and me. You ain't a *boppli.*"

"I know." She looked from one of them to the other. "But I can still hope, right? I want Liesl to be my Christmas wish."

Liesl looked puzzled. "What is a Christmas wish?"

"You hope and pray for something, but it canna be a present. It has to be something to happen."

"Who in the world told you that?" Roland asked.

"Bethy's *mamm.*"

Roland exchanged a look with Liesl. It was obvious that maybe Bethy's *mamm* shouldn't be so free with her emotions—or maybe even her kisses—when his daughter was around.

Liesl, on the other hand, didn't look angry. Instead, she looked like she was doing her best to follow his young daughter's train of thought. With care, she unfastened the grommet holding together her cloak, then tossed it over the back of one of the kitchen chairs. "So, if I understand correctly, according to Bethy's mother, everyone gets to make one special wish and your wish involves me?"

"*Jah.* I want you to come over for supper one night."

And that took the bluster right out of him. "Before Lilly's *Mamm* got so sick, my Tricia would always insist that we have supper together, even if I lost track of time in the summer and came in late."

"Mommy said that sharing supper together is a good way to end the day because it says we care about each other."

"And you care about me," Liesl stated.

Lilly nodded her head with such force, it almost looked as if a ventriloquist was moving it. "*Jah*!"

Feeling like he was walking on a tightrope, Roland said, "Lilly, while I agree that we both ah, value Liesl, and that Mommy was very wise, we have to understand that—"

"I would love to," Liesl interrupted.

He gaped at her. "Liesl, what did you say?"

She raised her eyebrows at him, letting him know that she knew he'd heard her plain as day. "I said that I would love to have supper with you both one evening before Christmas."

Lilly's face transformed into a wealth of smiles. She honestly looked like she was close to expiring on the wood floor, she was so excited.

And for him, well, Roland couldn't deny that he would look forward to sharing a meal with Liesl as well.

It wasn't right. It was likely selfish, too.

But it couldn't be helped. After all, he was a man who was filled with flaws.

Finally stepping away, Liesl said, "Roland, I know you're going to be out in the barn for several hours, but before I leave today, let's decide what day to have our supper. "Lilly, you and I could even work on something together."

"You'd let me help?"

"Of course. I would like that."

"Me, too." Lilly clapped her hands.

Roland felt his heart give a little leap, too. Having Liesl over to share a meal would be wonderful. Then, he'd take her home in his buggy. Lilly would no doubt fall asleep, and the two of them would be alone. It would be so sweet.

Almost as if he was hers.

But he surely wasn't.

"Ah, would you being over here for supper be all right with Wesley?"

Liesl blinked. "Wesley?"

"*Jah.* I mean, will you being over here in the evening upset him?"

Lilly's brow wrinkled. "Who's Wesley?"

"He's...well...I'm not sure what he is anymore." She looked at Roland. "Or what he would think about me being here for supper." Looking even more confused, she murmured, "I don't know at all."

Stunned, Roland stared at her. Now what in the world did that mean?

Chapter Fifteen

"You are so blessed," Emma said to Liesel not more than two minutes after Roland and Lilly had dropped her off at home. Grabbing Liesl's hand, she gave a little yank. "Come see what Wesley Raber brought you!"

She was having a hard time keeping up. "Wesley brought me something?"

Emma grinned. "*Jah*, and it is *wunderbar*!"

Speechless, Liesl followed her younger sister through the kitchen and to the dining room. And there, in the center of the table, was a bouquet of red roses in a stoneware vase. A small index card with her name written in Wesley's distinctive handwriting was next to it. She picked it up.

Emma giggled.

Realizing that her sister looked a little too excited, Liesl turned to look at her. "Did you already read my note?"

A guilty look appeared in her eyes. "Um, I didn't mean to. Go ahead and read it."

No way was Emma going to get out of that so easily. "Is that how you know that it was Wesley who gave me flowers?"

"Wesley delivered the flowers himself. It weren't hard to figure that out, sister."

"I'm sure he didn't hand you the envelope and invite you to read my personal message, though. That doesn't sound like something Wesley would do."

Looking guiltier, Emma wrinkled her nose. "Well, that is true. He didn't. Besides, it weren't like his message was all that personal."

She sighed, turned her back to Emma, and then read the short note.

These roses reminded me of you, Liesl. I hope you like them. Wesley.

As romantic notes went, it had a lot to be desired. But given that it was from Wesley, it was huge. Colossal, even.

"Emma, don't read my notes from Wesley anymore."

"I don't see why you're so upset. It weren't like he had all that much to say—or that Wesley brings you flowers all the time."

Liesl felt her cheeks heat, because Emma wasn't wrong. "You know what I'm talking about. Don't do it." She shook her finger at Emma, too. Just like she was scolding Lilly for being naughty.

Still acting mighty full of herself, Emma folded her arms over her chest. "I won't do it again. I promise. But if you had been home like you were supposed to, you would've seen Wesley." Her voice lowered. "He did ask where you were, sister."

"What did you tell him I was doing?"

"I told him the truth, of course." When Liesl continued to stare at her, Emma's voice turned weaker. "I told him you were delivering sewing projects. Isn't that what you were doing?"

"Well, yes." And she had delivered an item to a customer. But of course, she'd also spent the majority of her time with Lilly and Roland. "*Danke* for telling Wesley that. I mean, thanks for telling him the truth."

"Why would I have lied about it?"

"No reason. I mean, of course you wouldn't have lied." And...now she was sounding tongue-tied and maybe like a liar, too.

"Liesl, why on earth are you acting so strange? You should be happy. You received a bouquet of flowers. Of roses, which is really special. That's a whole lot more than I've gotten this whole year."

Liesl felt for her sister; she really did. Emma was fifteen, struggling to adjust to being home and having neither the structure of the English school she attended nor all her friends near every day.

She was also in the middle of an awkward stage. Her skin had spots, her body was still developing, and she was in a bit of a fight with their parents about her desire for braces. Which she kind of really did need.

On top of that, she was desperate to do all the things her older sister was doing. Emma wanted to flirt with boys, or to at least have one to seem interested in her. So far, that hadn't been the case...but her best friend Rachel was already becoming very popular.

Gentling her voice, she said, "I've told you that everything takes time, Emma. You need to believe that."

"It's hard to take your advice when you had Wesley when you were my age."

The comment, while true, felt a bit jarring. Even though at first all she and Wesley had done was talk during the singings on Sundays, he'd always made it known that she was the girl he liked the most.

Since then, they'd had their ups and downs. But no matter what, Wesley had been a solid fixture in her life for years...so much so that she'd begun to take him for granted.

Was that why she had started looking forward to spending time with Roland and Lilly so much? Because Roland was something new?

If that was the case, what was wrong with her? She should know better. No, she should be better!

Emma popped a hand on her hip. "Is that all you have to say about how different our lives are? Nothing?"

"Just because I wanted to think about my response, you shouldn't be so pushy."

"It feels like you don't care about what I'm going through."

Liesl simply didn't have the energy for her sister's drama right at that minute. "I suggest we speak later, when you aren't feeling quite so emotional."

"Fine." Emma turned on her heel and stormed off, no doubt to stomp around the house until their mother noticed and stepped in.

Usually, Liesl would do just about anything to avoid that confrontation, but now she just didn't care. She had other things to worry about.

Mainly herself.

Leaning down, she inhaled the familiar fragrance of the roses in bloom. As she'd expected, the scent was as perfect as each bloom was.

Maybe as perfect as Wesley was for her.

The comparison brought her up short. Was Wesley perfect for her, though? *Was he, really?*

Completely confused, she sat down at the table and continued to stare at the flowers. They really were beautiful. She was excited to receive them, too. But she was also a little confused about why he'd picked today of all days to deliver them.

A horrible thought settled in. Was today a special day she didn't remember?

"Is the coast clear?" *Daed* asked as he poked his head into the dining room.

"Clear from whom?"

"Our Emma, of course. She's in yet another snit, I fear."

She smiled at her father. "I believe today's snit is my fault. I...well, I wasn't as understanding as I usually try to be."

Sitting down across from her, he asked, "What does she need your understanding about?"

"Being fifteen and not having a beau."

"That ain't a problem, though. It's a blessing!"

She chuckled. "For you, it is. For her, not so much." She shrugged. "*Daed,* lots of girls at fifteen are like ships sailing through bumpy waters. They're feeling tossed about in different directions and aren't sure which way is which."

"Boys go through that, too."

"Really?"

He nodded. "We canna let you girls have all the fun, can we?"

"I guess not."

"I was once fifteen, too. And...I went through *rumspringa* just like she is. Emma likes to forget that."

She smiled at her father. He loved both Emma and her so much. He also tried to be involved and current in their lives—but sometimes was woefully out of his depth. "Don't worry, *Daed*. She'll remember. Like I said, she is missing her school friends and has too much time on her hands. I was blessed to already know that I wanted to sew."

Eyeing the roses, he said, "And you also had Wesley."

"So you really do know what is going on."

"The flowers were a good clue." Glancing at the roses again, he said, "They're pretty, girl."

"I think so, too."

"If he's bringing over fancy flowers, I guess the boy is finally going to make your mother's dreams come true and propose soon."

Her mother's? "*Daed*, don't you mean my dreams?"

He stood back up. "I could be wrong, but *nee*, I didn't misspeak."

All her insecurities and doubts bloomed again. "Why do you say that? Do you not like Wesley?"

"I like him fine. He's a good man." Looking at her intently, he added, "All I'm saying is that perhaps our dear Emma isn't the only person at a crossroads right now."

Liesl gaped at her father as he walked out of the dining room. Though it was tempting to pretend she didn't understand what he meant, she knew she did all too clearly.

The problem was that she wasn't sure what to do next.

Chapter Sixteen

"THANK GOODNESS YOU'RE HERE," LAURA May said as soon as Jenny slipped out of her boots and cloak. "I need someone calm and collected in this kitchen."

It was then she noticed that neither Emma nor Liesl was nearby, Armor was grumbling in the family room, and her usually serene sister was frazzled.

Even though all she'd wanted to do was go take a shower and maybe sit down for an hour, Jenny walked to her side. "What's going on?"

"Everything. Here," she added as she thrust a pitcher of water in her hands. "Go pour water and make sure the table is set. Please?"

"*Jah.* Of course." Feeling a bit dazed, she carried the glass pitcher into the dining room.

And then discovered the source of the Fisher family's mania. Liesl had gotten the roses.

Uh-oh.

*Nee*ding a moment, Jenny took her time filling the glasses, setting out paper napkins, and straightening silverware.

"I guess you've noticed what came today," Emma said as she entered the room.

"I certainly did. The roses are pretty, ain't so?"

"They are." Looking sullen, she plopped down on one of the chairs. "Liesl doesn't even care, though. It's like she's hardly noticed them."

"That doesn't sound like her."

"It's not true, either," her mother called out from the other room. "Emma, come help me and Jenny get supper on the table."

"Fine." She stood up with exaggerated effort, as if she was carrying a gorilla on her back. "How come Liesl doesn't have to help?"

"She will. Now come here and get this plate of carrots."

Jenny followed Emma into the kitchen, taking special care to stay out of the younger woman's way as she headed back to the dining room with a container of delicious-looking roasted carrots in her hands.

"Those carrots look amazing, Laura May."

"*Danke.* I used my special brown sugar, butter, and orange juice glaze on them. They're going to go well with tonight's roast, brussels sprouts, and potatoes."

"She made a cake, too," Emma said as she walked in, grabbed another serving dish from the kitchen's island, and strode right out.

Jenny whistled low. "You must have been cooking all day! What a wonderful meal."

"It's not all day that our eldest's beau finally steps up."

She felt like her stomach had just done a flip. "What are you saying?"

"*Mei frau* is saying she's sure a proposal is imminent," Armor said. Lowering his voice, he said, "I ain't so sure that's the case, though."

"I heard you, Armor. And you don't know everything."

"You might not, either, Laura May."

Oh no. This was awful. Feeling a little sick, she blurted, "Shall I bring the potatoes out now?"

"Yes, dear. Armor, you carry in the roast, please."

"Sorry I'm late," Liesl said, her cheeks pink and her expression glowing. "What can I help with?"

"Whatever's left," her mother said.

And so it continued. Each of them carried serving bowls and serving forks and spoons into the dining room. Through it all, Emma looked aggrieved, Liesl was beaming, and both of their parents seemed to be wrapped up in their own thoughts. Jenny was glad no one was talking...because she knew exactly how those roses had come to be sitting on the Fisher dining room table.

The plain and simple truth was that the roses had come by way of an unfortunate string of events. By all rights, it should have been a beautiful string, but Jenny was learning that when it came to matters of the heart, Wesley Fisher was a bit of a mess.

Earlier that day, one of the vendors dropped off an order and handed Wesley a bouquet of red roses as a Christmas present. Jenny had thought that was a bit of an odd gift until the man explained that he had worked out a trade with a florist in New Philadelphia. She needed some chocolates and stuffed animals and was willing to pay in roses. Which meant that all of

Sam's customers were receiving red roses as Christmas presents this year.

After Wesley thanked Sam and the man left, he'd handed them to Jenny. "Here. Have some flowers."

She'd been shocked. "What are these for?"

"Sam is giving out roses for Christmas this year." After explaining to her the situation, he smiled. "I thought you'd like them."

Jenny hadn't even wanted to hold the beautiful bouquet for even five minutes. "You know you canna go around giving me red roses, Wesley."

He'd shrugged and looked away. "You know I'm just passing them on. Aren't women supposed to enjoy roses?" Look, he said, pointing to the blooms. "There's twelve of them. And there's greenery and white stuff, too."

"That would be baby's breath."

"Whatever. They're nice. You should enjoy them."

"Wesley, you are misunderstanding what I mean. Red roses mean love."

Wesley, being Wesley, had started tallying up the store's receipts while they were speaking. But when she said this, he didn't look up—almost as though he was avoiding her eyes. "Fine. Jenny, I love that you're helping me out this Christmas."

"Wesley Raber, do you really think I can take this bouquet back to the Fisher household and no one is going to think twice about it?" And yes, she'd practically yelled that question.

At last he stilled. "You're worried about what Liesl is gonna think."

"Well, yes!" How could he be so obtuse? "You're Liesl's boyfriend. Of course I'm worried about what she is gonna think. If I show up with roses that you gave me, she's going to burst into tears." Jenny didn't even want to think about how Liesl's mother would react.

Deciding that the last thing Wesley needed was time to think about that, she pointed to the door. "The store is basically empty. Go over there right now and deliver these to her."

He held the stoneware vase of roses in his hands. "Do you think she's gonna like them?"

"She is. Just whatever you do, don't tell her that Sam gave them to you as a good-doing-business-with-you Christmas gift."

"I canna lie."

Honestly, it was like she had to do everything. "Write her a note. Say something sweet." When he winced and opened his mouth, she shook her head. "And, *nee*. I am not going to tell you what to write."

Ten minutes later, he'd trotted off, returning an hour after that with pink cheeks from the cold, a pleased, smug smile, and lots of gratitude for her.

"Did you read the note yet?" Liesl asked while they were setting dishes on the table. "It's right here." She handed it to Jenny. "It's sweet, right?"

"*Jah.* It's mighty sweet." Jenny had to admit that Wesley had not lied. He had thought Liesl would like the flowers.

So everything had worked out well.

Except for the fact that neither Wesley nor she had counted on how everyone was reacting to them. And...that there was no way she could ever divulge how those red roses had come to be in Liesl's possession.

The adage really was true: no good deed ever did go unpunished. Especially, it seemed, when it came to matters of the heart.

After they'd sat down, said their prayers, and passed the dishes around, Laura May said, "Jenny, tell us how Wesley decided to give roses to Liesl on today of all days. We've been wondering if today has special significance to Wesley."

"Special significance?" She gulped. "Well, I couldn't say."

"Come now. Surely you can give us some hint," Laura May prodded.

Liesl sat up straighter. "Is there one? I'm so afraid I forgot something important."

"I think the tale would be better coming from Wesley. Don't you, Liesl?"

"Maybe, but I'd still rather hear about it from you so I'm prepared." Looking increasingly girlish, she said, "I'm going to be so embarrassed if it's to honor our first date or something like that."

"You don't even remember when your first date was?" Emma asked.

"It was a long time ago," Liesl replied. "Which you know."

Oh, but this was horrible.

"The roses showed up today," Jenny said weakly. "Maybe he hadn't known when they would arrive."

"That makes sense," Armor declared. "It is December, after all. Flower shipments are real slow when there's ice and snow involved."

"It didn't snow today," Laura May said with a frown.

"Like I said, it would be best to ask him."

Emma cut off a piece of her roast. "When is he coming calling again, Liesl?"

"I don't know. I don't think we have anything planned."

"Why not?"

"Because it's the holiday season and Wesley is shorthanded. He can't get away." Looking mortified, Liesl coughed. "No offense to you, Jenny."

"None taken. I can vouch for Wesley's schedule, though. The days are real busy at the store. I was ex-*haus*ted when I walked out of the shop today."

"Liesl dear, maybe you should plan something fun instead of waiting on Wesley," her mother said.

"It's okay. I'm not worried. I'm still sewing a lot, and we just all agreed that he's busy."

"What I'm trying to share is that while it isn't roses...I received something special today, too!" Laura May announced. "The Pinery is offering a special holiday in lights night, and I entered a drawing for them. I won ten tickets today! Isn't that something?"

"It's something that you waited until now to tell us about it," Armor said. "We haven't gone in years."

Blushing, Laura May waved a hand. "Oh, posh. You know that the two of us won't be going."

"Why not? I would like to see the lights."

"But it's for young people."

"I don't think so. What do you say, Laura May, would you go to the Pinery with me this weekend?"

Jenny felt her heart fill. It was adorable to see her sister smiling like a young schoolgirl. "I'm glad you two will go. I'm sure it will be a special evening."

Liesl, who was sitting to her right, reached out and clasped her hand. "If *Mamm* has so many tickets, then we should all make a night of it. All five of us should go together. Hopefully Wesley will come, too."

"I want to bring a friend," Emma said.

"I think you should, Em. Now that's seven," Armor declared.

"If there are extra tickets, may I tell Roland and his little girl Lilly about it, too?" Liesl asked. "They've been having a difficult time of it this holiday season."

"Of course," Armor said. "Now we have nine. We need one more."

Laura May clapped her hands. "How about we ask Faith next door? She's a widow now so she might enjoy a night out with all of us."

"That's fine with me." Looking pleased, he grinned at all the women. "There you have it. We'll be going to the Pinery on Saturday night, thanks to my wife."

"I can't wait," Emma said, smiling brightly for the first time all evening.

"Me, neither," Jenny said. "It will be grand."

Liesl nodded but took a gulp of water. Jenny figured she was overwhelmed. She had made plans to go to the Pinery and had received a dozen roses all in one day.

Now all Jenny had to do was hope that Wesley would never tell Liesl the whole story about how he came to deliver the roses.

And that Emma would cheer up and that Laura May would stop planning Liesl's wedding. And, since she was wishing, Jenny hoped that one day very soon she'd stop feeling that little buzz of attraction whenever Wesley smiled at her.

That was all.

It was too bad that nothing ever seemed to go as planned. Not even wishes and dreams at Christmas.

Chapter Seventeen

IT WAS TEN O'CLOCK IN the morning—what Wesley's parents liked to call the "parade" hour. When he was a little boy, Wesley had always been confused by the term. He'd seen a parade, of course, so he understood what the word *parade* meant. But what he hadn't understood was why the sixty minutes between ten o'clock and eleven at the store always made his mother act like she was going into some kind of strange battle.

However, by the time he was nine years old, he'd known exactly what that was all about. No matter what time of year or what day of the week, everything that could possibly happen at the store did...all at the same time. Deliveries arrived. Tourists departed buses and entered the store in a giant wave. Things got broken and children had accidents.

All that was one of the reasons why—just as the store was nearly packed to the gills with frantic Christmas shoppers—he hadn't been surprised when Liesl had entered the shop in need of his attention.

Hardly anyone ever waited until say, three o'clock to arrive.

He was happy to see her, of course. "Hiya, Liesl."

"Hi to you, too." She was smiling like a Cheshire cat as she approached the side of the counter. "I know you're busy, but may we speak in private for a moment?"

He had five groups of customers standing in line, waiting to purchase their items. Jenny was over at the bakery and deli counter helping people as fast as she could. Even Ernie was busy in the back of the store cleaning up a jar of spilled pickles.

"I'm sorry, but I cannot." Looking at Saul Freeman, he said, "That'll be forty-seven dollars and sixty-two cents, Saul."

He dug in his pocket. "Seems kind of high for what I'm purchasing, I'll tell you that," Saul muttered as he tossed a fifty-dollar bill on the counter. "I hope you've got correct change for me."

"I'll do my best," Wesley replied as he opened the cash drawer and started counting out change.

Liesl, looking like an angel in a light-pink long-sleeved dress, stepped a little closer. "Please? It won't take but a minute."

Though Liesl was fetching, and he hated to disappoint her, there was no way he could budge. "Here's your change, Saul." After counting it out, he handed him his bag. "*Danke* for waiting."

Saul nodded before taking his bag.

Just before Flora stepped up in line, Liesl said yet again, "Wesley, please? I have other things I need to do."

Before Wesley could answer, Flora glared at Liesl. "I do, too, Liesl Fisher. More important things than you, no doubt. Wield your charms at him on another day."

Wesley inwardly groaned. "Is this everything, Flora?"

"It is." She harrumphed at Liesl. "Nothing wrong with you learning a spot of patience."

"You're being rather mean, Flora," a woman in line said.

"Maybe so, but time's a'wasting." Flora turned to her with a scowl. "Do you want to wait another ten minutes while young Wesley here focuses on his love life?"

Before things got any worse, Wesley answered Liesl yet again. "Now's not a good time, Liesl. If it's important, come back around four. Store's not as crowded then."

Her green eyes widened. "You want me to wait to talk to you until four? Wesley, that's six hours from now."

He knew that. He absolutely knew that. Ringing up Flora as fast as he could, he asked, "Did you find everything you were looking for?"

"Almost. I came in for some of that red currant jam you sometimes have, but that sweet new employee of yours said you sold the last jar yesterday."

"It's hard to keep in stock. Winnie over in Sugarcreek makes it. It's the best."

Flora rested her elbows on the counter. "Maybe my daughter-in-law bought it for me as a present. Did you happen to see Sarah make that purchase?"

"*Nee*, I'm sorry." He told her the total, then glanced over at Liesl. Hopefully if he got the rest of the folks done, he could chat with her privately in five or ten minutes.

She was no longer standing near the counter.

After Flora handed him her money, he wrapped up her purchase and handed it to her. Then he looked again for Liesl.

"She's gone, Wesley," Flora said.

"Are you sure?"

"Oh, *jah.* You canna ignore a girl like that. Especially not one you intend to marry." She frowned. "Though I'm guessing that advice came too late."

Though Wesley was tempted to tell Flora that she had been part of the problem, he said nothing. However, he feared Flora was right. Though Liesl's important message could've been anything from news about receiving a new sewing order to spotting an especially cute dachshund on the sidewalk, it was important to her.

It wasn't right that he not only ignored her but also pushed off her needs with an audience looking on.

But what could he do? He was currently in between a rock and a hard place with a side of torrential rain added into the mix. It was the holiday season, and he had a slew of customers needing to be served and two parents who were depending on him to not let them down.

"Is this everything?" he asked the next person, who put a wooden basket filled with items on the counter.

"It is."

As Wesley rang up the items, he noticed that the customer—a middle-aged *Englischer* with blue eyes—was looking at him in sympathy. He did his best to ignore it. "That'll be one hundred eighty and seventy-two cents, sir."

"You do take credit cards, right?" the customer asked as he set a Visa card on the counter.

"Of course." Wesley slid the card in the machine and tried not to look as irritated with himself as he was.

Just as the card machine beeped and shot out a receipt, the man said, "Sorry about your girl leaving in a snit."

"Thank you." It would be foolish to pretend it hadn't happened. "I'll try to make it up to her later."

"Flowers help."

"Since I recently gave her some, I fear it won't help too much at the moment. But, ah, thank you for your advice." He took the signed receipt. "Thank you for coming in."

And so it continued. Customers approached, looked at him in sympathy, and bought lots and lots of items. The parade hour of ten o'clock drifted into eleven and then twelve.

Ernie took his break, then Jenny. Wesley told them both he was fine and didn't need any time off.

Since the store was packed with people, both looked like they understood, but Wesley knew the crowd was only half his reason for not stepping away for a few minutes. The real reason was that he feared he wouldn't be able to eat a thing. Liesl had put him between a rock and a hard place. He'd likely chosen the wrong path and she'd never forgive him.

When the crowd finally thinned out around three o'clock, Ernie left and Jenny walked over to the counter. "Go take a break, Wesley."

"I'm fine." Of course, he wasn't. He was standing behind the counter and doing nothing but gazing at the front door of the shop.

Based on Jenny's expression, she wasn't buying his foolishness for a moment. She shook her head. "Everything about you says you are in need of a short break. Why, you've been standing behind that counter for five hours. At the very least, go get something to eat."

"I ain't hungry."

"Wesley, don't be so stubborn."

He was being stubborn, and that was embarrassing, too. Even though Wesley knew Jenny was right, it he felt like if he sat down to take a break, it would be disrespectful to Liesl. After all, how could he take a moment to eat but not for her?

Maybe it hadn't only been about how busy the store was. Maybe part of him had been trying to avoid her. Which made no sense. He was going to marry her, wasn't he?

Jenny was tapping her foot. "Stop acting like one of the *kinner* I nanny. Go relax for a few. I promise, I can take care of anyone who comes in."

"*Danke.*" He still wasn't all that eager to eat, but his body was telling him that it would appreciate sitting down for a spell. Jenny was right, as always. Again, he wondered how he was going to manage once she was gone...and maybe that wasn't just about the store, either.

He pushed the thoughts out of his head. They made no sense. Jenny was Liesl's aunt, and his employee besides.

Just as he was turning away, he noticed that

Jenny was watching him with a look of concern. "I guess you heard about what happened with Liesl?" he asked.

"I did." Looking even more uncomfortable, she added, "I'm afraid the whole store was talking about it."

"I made a mess of things with her, didn't I?" Jenny must think he was a fool.

"Well..." She bit her lip. "I wouldn't exactly call it a mess. But it is Liesl..."

He wanted to ask her to clarify, but that wouldn't be fair to her. Liesl was her niece, and they were too close for him to infringe upon that relationship. So, with that in mind, he settled for being honest.

"I'll try to make things up to her later, but I don't know. She...well, Liesl may not forgive me for a while. Do you know what she wanted?"

"I believe she wanted to let you know that her mother won a set of ten tickets to the Pinery for Saturday night. She would like you to go."

"Yes, of course. I owe her an apology." Realizing he was telling the wrong person, he added, "I'll stop by the house after work and tell her myself."

"All right." Her smile was tight.

"Do you think she'll see me?"

"I couldn't say."

Not wanting to make Jenny say anything more about Liesl, he turned, walked into the break room, and collapsed on the worn couch.

He had no idea how he was going to make things right with Liesl. He needed to do something, though.

His store's phone rang. Someone was calling about an order, probably. He hurried to the desk and grabbed it on the second ring. "Raber's. May I help ya?"

"I should say so, Wesley," his father said. "You haven't called to give me a report on the store in three days."

"I was trying to let you rest. How are you feeling, *Daed*?"

"I'm fine. Now tell me about business. Have you sold much furniture?"

Furniture? "*Nee*, *Daed*. But what have you been doing? Are you still resting? Are you eating better?"

"Wesley, I've already got your mother, Paul, and your sister-in-law fussing over me. I've also had both of your sisters and their husbands watching everything I did, too. I do not need your interference, too." Sounding even crankier, he said, "Now tell me what has been happening. The future of the store is on your shoulders, right? You didn't forget, did ya?"

Slowly, he sat down behind the desk, opened back up the ledger, and picked up a pencil. "*Nee*," he said quietly. "I haven't forgotten."

"*Gut*. Now tell me about yesterday. Did a tourist bus come in?"

He sighed. "*Nee*, but we did sell a lot of the jams and jellies from the Beachys' farm."

"Make a note to call them in January. We'll need to put in an early order."

Realizing that he hadn't done that already, he wrote down a note. "Yes, *Daed*."

Then Wesley mentally prepared himself to take notes for quite a while. His father was depending on him.

Chapter Eighteen

Liesl knew better. Usually, she weighed the pros and cons before discussing with her mother almost anything to do with Wesley. She'd learned years ago that while her mother didn't like to interfere too much when it came to her daughters' love lives, she didn't hesitate to share her opinions when asked.

So, Liesl had known what would happen if she opened that particular Pandora's box. But she'd been so upset, she'd let down her guard and had walked into the house with tears in her eyes.

That little opening had been all *Mamm* had needed to take control of the conversation and start sharing pearls of wisdom. And boy, did she! For the last hour, Liesl had been her captive audience and it was becoming obvious that she wasn't going to be released anytime in the near future.

Liesl loved her mother dearly and usually valued her advice. But it soon had become apparent that the discussion wasn't going to help Liesl's state of mind much. Maybe not at all.

It didn't help that they were speaking in the

kitchen, which meant Emma could eavesdrop. Or that her father had decided to sit in the living room and pretend to read the paper...and interject all of his opinions whenever her mother took a break.

If Liesl hadn't been sure a least a few of the bystanders at the Amish Market would eventually report what they heard back to her mother, she would've kept the whole awful situation to herself...or at least, she would have tried. Instead, she was forcing herself to stand against the kitchen wall and look interested while her mother fussed and offered buckets of free advice.

"Liesl, I think you are making too much of this," her mother said for at least the fifth time in twenty minutes. "Sometimes people just don't have time to chat. Wesley was at work, you know."

Liesl defended herself. Again. "I realize he was. But you don't know how I felt, *Mamm*. Wesley acted as if I was bothering him."

"Daughter, I reckon you were," *Daed* murmured from his easy chair across the room.

"I would've thought you would take my side of this, *Daed*. You know that I don't usually pop into the market just to bother him."

"That is true." With a sigh, her father put down the copy of *The Budget* newspaper. "However, dear daughter, I would've thought you would have been far more understanding and patient with your sweetheart during the busiest time of his year."

"So you're really on Wesley's side."

He got to his feet with a groan, stretched a bit, and then walked over to join them in the kitchen. "Why does there have to be a side? This isn't a case of one of you was right and the other was wrong, you know."

Liesl sat down on a wooden stool. "But it kind of is, don't you think? I needed to see him. I even told Wesley that what I had to speak to him about was important!" Her father looked like he was about to say something, but her mother gave him a nudge. "Everything that happened was so horrible. I stood there, waiting while he continued to ring up Saul."

"Saul was there?" *Daed* asked.

"*Jah*, and he was as grumpy as ever, too. But he's not important. What is, is that all while I was standing there, waiting and waiting...Wesley told me to leave. He practically pushed me aside like a naughty five-year-old!"

Her mother's eyes widened. "He pushed you?"

"Figuratively, he did, *Mamm*."

"Oh."

Her father sighed. "Oh my word."

At last she was receiving some sympathy and understanding! "It was horrible. Maybe even beyond that. Other people witnessed Wesley's poor behavior, too." Realizing her voice was cracking, she took a deep breath. "*Mamm, Flora Miller* was there."

Her mother visibly winced. "That is really too bad, dear."

"See? Now do you understand why I'm so upset?"

Her father moved to the table and sat down next to them. "I do understand, and I'm sorry that you felt embarrassed in front of some members of our community, but that doesn't mean you were in the right and Wesley was wrong."

Daed acting as if Flora Miller was simply just a

member of the community was like saying Christmas was just another holiday.

However, it was obvious that neither of her parents was going to give her the sympathy she was craving. Feeling rather disappointed, Liesl got to her feet. Summoning up the last bit of her pride, she raised her chin. “It is becoming obvious that it was wrong of me to expect your support. I’ll just have to wait for Jenny to come home and speak to her. I’m sure she will be far more understanding.”

Her father exchanged a look with her mother, then spoke. “Daughter, you need to leave your aunt out of this.”

“Why? I have every right to speak to Jenny about whatever I want.”

“You are going to put her in the middle, *jah?*” *Mamm* asked.

But hadn’t they just told her there was no right or wrong? That no one was taking a side? Feeling mentally ex*haus*ted, Liesl said, “I’m going to go to my room for a little bit. Mother, I’ll help you with supper in a half hour.”

“*Danke*, Liesl.”

Feeling completely misunderstood, Liesl walked down the hall. Only when she closed her bedroom door did she let her guard down and release a ragged sigh. How could something that had been supposed to be so good end up being so terrible? She knew everyone was thinking that she was merely being selfish and oblivious to Wesley’s work and schedule. But the truth was that she was very aware of it. Yes, she’d gone to the market to let him know about their upcoming trip to the Pinery. But she'd also wanted to share her news.

One of her customers gave her the biggest order yet. It was for a dozen matching dresses for a wedding, and the total she'd earn was going to be more than she usually made in two or three months. Since he cared so much about business, she'd been sure he would be thrilled about it. Maybe even proud of her. She so wanted him to be proud of her.

She would've told him later—if she'd known he was going to see her later. But she didn't. She never knew when he was going to come calling on her anymore. He hadn't even come over last night after giving her a dozen roses! What kind of man would run cold after making such a heartwarming, romantic gesture?

Wesley's kind, she supposed.

That's why she'd gone to speak to him in the middle of the day. Of course, the whole plan backfired. Now he not only thought she was irritating, but Jenny had witnessed it. As had about thirty other people.

And now her parents, too, were acting as if she didn't have a lick of sense. That was so frustrating. Liesl knew she wasn't the easiest of girlfriends. She was needy and a bit spoiled in a lot of ways. But she wasn't the worst, either. She tried hard, worked hard, and liked making other people happy. Those qualities had to mean she wasn't all bad.

With all that in mind, Liesl made the decision then to keep this new job to herself. It was probably for the best, anyway. A lot of the shine had certainly worn off about it.

And...maybe some of the shine of her relationship with Wesley had, too.

She had no idea if it was even possible to get some of that shine back. It certainly felt tarnished beyond repair.

Chapter Nineteen

"I STILL FEEL SLIGHTLY GUILTY, BUT I think it's the right decision," Wesley told Jenny as they exited the store a little before six at night. "I don't think that visiting Liesl tonight will do much good."

Jenny breathed a sigh of relief. She'd been hoping to hear Wesley say that. "I agree with you a hundred percent."

"It still feels wrong, though. After all, it's been almost two days." Pulling out his key ring from a pocket, he carefully turned the two locks on the door, then jiggled the door to make sure it was secure.

Jenny had watched him do this almost every night without fail. It made her wonder how he could take care of the store so carefully...but treat Liesl with so much less care.

"I can promise you, Liesl still needs time to cool off. Tomorrow evening will be better."

For the last two days, Wesley had acted confused about how to make things right with her. At first, he'd wanted to hurry over to the Fisher house, demand to see Liesl, and then explain to her how busy he was.

Jenny was no relationship expert, but even she knew that would only make matters worse.

Besides, even if he wasn't planning to charge in and state his case, Jenny figured that was probably for the best. To her amazement, the shop had gotten even busier over the last two days. The customers, fueled by busy schedules, and an upcoming snowstorm, and perhaps spurred by the excitement of the season, had been demanding. Wesley had darted back and forth, leaving Jenny to hold her own behind the cash register.

Still standing under the glowing streetlight, Wesley said, "It's starting to snow. Will you be all right getting home? I'd be happy to walk you back if you'd like."

His words were everything proper. But that statement, combined with the feelings that he'd just shared? Well, they made her giggle. "Is that right? You'd feel happy to head over to the Fisher *haus*?"

"*Jah...*" His voice drifted off as he obviously became aware of how silly he sounded. "I guess I do sound a bit contradictory, don't I?"

Even though the air was cold and damp, he took off his hat and ran his fingers through his hair. The motion caused it to stick up this way and that. She couldn't help but stare. Wesley looked discouraged and upset. She was learning that he bottled up a lot of his emotions inside himself. Maybe it was because his father asked so much of him. When he did allow himself to be vulnerable, when he let down all his guards, she could hardly look away from him.

He was the exact opposite of Jeremiah in so many ways. Jeremiah had smiled easily, had flirted easily, and been so glib. She'd thought he'd only been that way with her. But later, she'd realized that he had been that way with everyone. He'd used to tell everyone whatever they wanted to hear.

She would take Wesley's guarded personality over that any day.

Confused by her thoughts, Jenny looked away and tried to concentrate on the snowflakes falling. Or the way the white lights strung on a neighboring street corner twinkled. Or how her stomach had been growling for the last hour.

Honestly, anything—as in anything at all—would be far better for her to dwell on than anything personal about Wesley Raber.

"Did you hear me, Jenny?"

"I'm sorry—I guess I didn't. What did you say?"

He eyed her more intently. "Are you all right?"

"Of course. I'm always all right."

"Somehow, I have the feeling that you say that all the time. Maybe even when you aren't all right." His voice gentled. "Am I...am I causing you too much stress? I know I forget how ex*haus*ting everything can be. Would you like to take tomorrow morning off?"

He was being ridiculous, and that was a fact. "The work has not overwhelmed me, Wesley. And *nee*, you are not causing me too much stress at all. Don't worry so much." She grinned at him. "My line of the family tree is sturdy."

His expression warmed. "I hadn't heard that. You Kurtzes are like sturdy oaks?"

"Exactly." Laughter bubbled forth. "Okay, maybe I'm not exactly treelike...but I'm in no danger of perishing because of a little bit of hard work."

"That's noted, but I do feel bad that I've hardly

given you a day off, Jenny. I would hate to make you sick so close to Christmas."

"I'm in no danger of getting ill. You might be, though, if you don't put back on your hat. Surely your hair is soaking wet by now."

Looking sheepish, he shoved it back on his head. "Perhaps I'm the one who needs to take better care of myself, hmm?"

"I think that would be a good idea. You are liable to run yourself ragged, with all your trotting to and fro. Have a *gut naught*."

"You, too."

She smiled at him before turning away.

"Hey, Jenny?"

"*Jah*?"

"Do you ever wonder what might have happened if things were different?" he asked. "If, you know, maybe you hadn't lived all your life in Middlefield and grew up here instead?"

His expression was vulnerable, more vulnerable than she could recall ever seeing before. "Or if, say, your father had been a farmer instead of a shop owner?"

"*Jah*." His voice was soft, practically begging for her to read his mind—or at least understand.

"Yes," she said at last. Maybe she could have expanded on that answer, but the truth was that she'd been afraid to. What if she inadvertently said too much? That would be a tragedy...much worse than Wesley working so hard that he snapped at Liesl.

Jenny turned and continued walking down the street. Only after a few seconds she heard Wesley start walking as well. With each step, she breathed easier. Yes, this was what she'd needed—to gain some distance from Wesley. And maybe some perspective, too.

Because what they had wasn't a relationship. It wasn't anything like a relationship. They were spending time together because she was his employee. As much as they might enjoy each other's company, it wasn't by choice. Before long, Christmas Day would arrive, Wesley's parents would return home, and the Andersons would need her again. Then, she'd once again be taking care of Annabeth and Parker.

She just wished that thought filled her with joy instead of a feeling of melancholy.

"Oh, Jenny!" Liesl cried out as Jenny walked into the kitchen, no doubt looking like a half-frozen, very wet rat.

In contrast, Liesl was wearing a dark-gray wool dress, a matching apron, her white kapp, and not a hair was out of place. "Oh my stars. You are soaked to the skin. I'll run you a hot bath."

"*Danke.* That would be *wonderful-gut.*"

Leading the way upstairs, Liesl kept eyeing her. "I cannot believe you didn't have on your bonnet. Or that Wesley sent you out off to walk home all by yourself. That wasn't considerate of him at all."

Following her into the bathroom, she sat down on the small bench next to the bathtub. "It wasn't his fault that I forgot to put on my bonnet."

"It might not have been his fault, but he could

have helped you more." She perched on the edge of the tub and turned on the faucet. "He and I might be in a snit, but he's always made sure I was safe and warm."

She knew Liesl was not being uncaring on purpose, but her statement still stung. Perhaps because Jenny knew it was true. While he might not stop working in order to chat, he always looked after Liesl's welfare. Leaning down, Jenny loosed the laces on her black boots. "If you're fussing over me, you must feel better. Do you?"

"Kind of. My parents did their best to get me to settle down. I almost took their advice."

"Relationships are hard."

After pouring in two capfuls of eucalyptus-scented bubble bath, Liesl turned her way again. "I suppose you know that better than most, given what happened with you and Jeremiah."

"I guess I was thinking of him." Standing up, she began pulling out the straight pins on her dress. Each made a tiny *ping* as it joined the others in the container.

"What happened?"

Everything had happened. "That's a long story, I fear."

"He broke your heart."

Jenny inhaled sharply, the soothing eucalyptus scent tingling her senses...but unfortunately it didn't calm or numb the pain that Jeremiah's memory still brought.

Instead, it seemed to magnify the knowledge that while she'd always thought he'd broken her heart, it wasn't in disrepair. Lately she'd begun to realize that it was capable of being mended. The pain she'd taken to wearing like a shield had started to fade, and in its place was the knowledge that while her heart might be bruised, it was still beating.

Maybe even beating stronger than ever.

"Jeremiah hurt me, that is true. But I've started to realize that my heart isn't broken." She slipped off her dress and stockings. Now she was only dressed in her full slip.

Liesl turned off the water. "How come you're feeling better now?" Her eyes widened. "Oh! Did he contact you?"

"*Nee*! I mean, no. I guess what happened is that I started to realize that I am better off without Jeremiah."

"Because?"

"Because Jeremiah wasn't the type of man who appreciated me, Liesl. I didn't want to change myself again and again so he would like me at last. I just wanted him to think that I was enough. And what I realize now is that I am enough. I don't need to be better or different to be worthy of his love."

Her eyes widened. "Like Jesus."

The comparison brought forth a jolt, but she nodded. "'*Jah*. Just like Jesus always teaches us that we are enough to be worthy of His love, I realized that I am worthy enough for both myself and another man. One day I'll meet that man."

"Wouldn't that be something if you've already met him and you didn't even know it?"

Liesl's question stung, especially because Jenny worried it might be true. "It sure would." Standing in front of the tub, she said, "May I take a bath now? I'd like to enjoy the water before the water gets cold."

"Oh! Of course." Stopping at the doorway, Liesl murmured, "*Danke*, Jenny."

She left before Jenny could ask what she was being thanked for. But when she sank into the hot water, she forced herself to stop thinking about Liesl or Jeremiah or even Wesley.

No, all she wanted to think about was the hot, fragrant water warming her limbs. And the way the soothing scent helped to push away her worries.

At least until another day.

Chapter Twenty

Roland's twelve-year-old mare, Star, had been battling a fierce case of colic for two days. So much so, she had gone from acting a bit off to being in visible pain. Worried about her, Roland had gone to his English neighbors and rung up the vet, who had been able to see her within a few hours. After administering both Benamine and Phenylbutazone and then calmly chatting with the horse for an hour, Star had seemed to settle at last.

Naturally, Roland was grateful for the veterinarian's assistance. He was also very thankful that the Lord had helped the animal doctor heal his best plow horse. He was even grateful that little Lilly had understood that the horse's needs had taken him away from her for the best part of two days.

But even though he was grateful for those blessings, he wished the emergency hadn't taken him so far from Lilly for the entire morning. It was getting close to Christmas, and his little girl got bored and lonely easily.

You are also wishing you could've been near Liesl, his conscience whispered in his ear. On another day he'd push that voice away, but he couldn't deny the truth.

Unfortunately, his most joyous moments revolved around Liesl's visits. After he'd called her when he'd needed to rebuild Taco's stall, she'd started coming over again all the time. He hadn't had the nerve—or the desire—to push her away again. When she was nearby, he felt more alive, brighter.

When Liesl was nearby, Roland felt almost like the man he used to be.

After washing up in the barn, he entered the house, presumably to check on Lilly. But of course, to his great shame, it was Liesl's sweet, melodic voice that drew him into the living room.

And there they were, Lilly in her purple dress and Liesl in a cranberry-colored dress, black stockings, and a matching black cardigan over her shoulders. They were sitting together on the couch, Lilly holding a needle and thread in her hand. Though Liesl had told him she likely wasn't going to get to have supper with them until after she finished the dozen bridesmaid dresses she was working on, he was still disappointed. He had allowed himself to imagine sharing a meal with Liesl more than once. And with Liesl sitting with Lilly like that, the very picture of cozy family contentment, it was easy to imagine what it would be like if he shared everything with Liesl.

Which he really shouldn't have been doing.

"Lilly, are you sewing today?" he asked.

Liesl smiled as he approached. "She is, and she's doing a mighty fine job, too."

"I've only gotten pricked one time," Lilly announced as she held up two fingers on her left hand.

Liesl chuckled at his frown. "Don't you worry. The prick didn't draw blood."

"I didn't know Lilly was old enough to sew," he said. "Ain't four years old awfully young to be working with a needle and thread?"

Some of Liesl's bright smile faded. "The needle is one for children. It's sharp but it's bigger and easier to handle. It's the type of needle I first learned on when I was her age."

"Sewing is fun, *Daed*," Lilly exclaimed.

When Roland said nothing, the lines around Liesl's lips and eyes deepened. "I'm sorry if you didn't want her learning such things. I guess I should've asked."

"I didn't say I was." Now he was tongue-tied because he felt mean and too short-tempered.

"It seems that way, though. Are you upset about that? I brought over some fabric remnants that I cut into large squares. I thought we could make a quilt together this winter."

"If Lilly wants to learn, I don't mind. I'm just surprised," he added. "Are you enjoying your lesson, Lilly?"

Lilly nodded. "*Jah*, but I'd rather hear Liesl's stories more."

Roland's gaze returned to Liesl. "What stories are those?"

When Lilly bit her lip—the sure sign that she forgot something—Roland turned to Liesl. "What stories have you been telling Lilly about?"

Looking guarded again, she said, "Nothing bad, I promise. All I've been doing is talking to her about the Pinery."

It took him a minute to figure out what she was

talking about. It had been so long since he'd thought about anything but his daughter or the farm. "You are talking about the Christmas event?"

She nodded. Sounding even more tentative, she added, "It sounds like a lot of fun, *jah*? I thought for sure that Lilly would like to go."

The Pinery was a place where families went, or couples on a date. The thought of going there with only Lilly was painful.

"And you also thought for sure that it was all right for ya to mention it to her without speaking to me first?" When Liesl paled slightly, Roland felt a bolt of shame course through him. He shouldn't have sounded so mean.

"I...I hadn't imagined you would be upset about me telling her about the Pinery. It's um, a mighty popular event."

"I am well aware of that." What he hadn't told Liesl was that he had taken Tricia there soon after they'd gotten engaged. They'd spent the evening bundled up in coats and mittens—and in each other's arms when no one was around to see them. The stars had been out, the sky had been clear, and he'd foolishly believed that the perfect evening had been a sign from the dear Lord Himself that their future was going to be perfect, too.

Not two years later, they'd had Lilly and Tricia was bedridden. She'd only lived a few more months before succumbing to her cancer.

Still staring at him in shock, Liesl bit her lip. "So, I take it that the event is not a favorite of yours?"

"I want to go, *Daed*!" Lilly cried out. "May we go?"

"Lilly, we will discuss this later." He kept his voice

firm, just so she would understand how serious he was being. His decision was not up for discussion.

To his surprise, his normally obedient daughter folded her arms across her chest and stuck out her bottom lip. "*Nee, Daed.* I want to go to the Pinery. Please? Liesl has tickets for us!"

He couldn't believe how much Liesl had taken upon herself. "Is this true?"

She nodded. "*Jah.* You see—"

"You should have asked me first, Liesl."

"I know, but—"

"I don't want to hear your excuses. You've overstepped yourself."

Once again, Liesl showed him that she was as different from Tricia as...as bachelorhood and fatherhood. Which he really should have realized.

Her cheeks flushed with anger. "You need to calm down, Roland. You're acting as if I was suggesting we take Lilly to the movies or the mall or something. All it is, is a bunch of Christmas trees nearby."

Roland was sure there was a dash of sarcasm in there, but he wasn't quite sure where. Just as he was attempting to figure that out, Lilly stomped one tiny foot. "Daddy, I want to go."

Appalled by his daughter's behavior, Roland knew they'd reached the last straw. Obviously, Lilly had picked up some bad habits from Liesl. Habits he'd never realized she'd possessed! It was time to put a stop to it.

"Lilly, you will go sit by yourself in my office."

"*Nee*!" She stomped her foot again. "I don't want to do that. I don't like sitting in my naughty chair."

"Do you want to sit there for a full hour?"

"*Nee.*" Tears filled her eyes.

"Then, you had best listen to me now."

The tears started to fall. She blinked furiously, then turned and walked down the hallway. Still fuming, he watched her open his office door and go inside. Only then did he take a deep breath and turn back to Liesl.

"I believe we need to talk."

She gave a huff of frustration. "Obviously."

It was shocking how bold she was. "Liesl, I think you are forgetting yourself."

"I feel the same way about you, Roland."

"I was going to tell you that not only should you not discuss plans with Lilly without me being there, but you shouldn't encourage Lilly to be so brash."

A hand waved the air. "She is four. Of course Lilly is going to get upset from time to time. Besides, I can hardly blame her."

He folded his arms across his chest. "I think it's time you left."

But instead of turning away in shame, Liesl took a step toward him. "Oh, I'll leave. Don't you worry about that. But first, you are going to stand here and listen to what I have to say."

"I have no desire to—"

"Roland, at the very, *very* least, you owe me this courtesy." She took a deep breath. "First of all, I am *not* your employee. I am not Lilly's babysitter. The only thing I've ever accepted payment for was for the clothes I've made for you both."

To his shock, Roland realized that she was right. "I—"

"Oh, no you don't. I am not finished." She took

another step closer. "Secondly, this Pinery that you seem to find so offensive is a wonderful place. It is full of the Christmas spirit, which is sadly lacking in this home. Christmas spirit and joy are two things that Lilly needs. The reason I mentioned it to her was not because I'm deceitful. It was because my mother won ten free tickets and I wanted to give them to you both." She rolled her eyes. "I was attempting to give you a gift, you...you dummy."

Dummy?

Her words were so explosive, it was difficult to process them all. But he was starting to realize that he'd been very unfair.

"Anything else?" he asked.

"Oh, yes." She held up three fingers. "Thirdly, it is not being disrespectful to give you my opinion. I am not your sweet wife and I have no wish to do whatever you want me to do because you said so. I must add, however, that if you ever do intend to take another wife, you should probably think about that. Just because a woman is Amish doesn't mean she doesn't have a decent brain in her head."

Liesl took another step closer, this time bringing with her the faint, beguiling scent of gardenias. "Finally, I think your office naughty chair idea is stupid."

"Why?" he asked before remembering that he wasn't supposed to care what she thought.

"Because your daughter is lonely, she hates your office, and sitting by herself on a hard wooden chair in a room she hates doesn't make her want to please you, Roland. All it does is make her want to be somewhere else. Or with someone else."

"Like you?"

Liesl waved a hand. "Like a person who smiles from time to time." She turned on her heel and strode toward the front door, grabbing her bonnet and cloak as she did. "Have fun fixing this mess you made, Roland Hochstetler. And...Merry Christmas."

And with that, she opened the door and stormed out, practically slamming it behind her.

Roland stood alone in the room. Stared at the closed door, shocked about the things she'd said.

Then, barely, he heard his daughter crying. He closed his eyes to pray. And then he prayed some more. Liesl had been right in so many ways. He'd not only messed things up with both Lilly and Liesl, but it was going to take many, many days to make things better.

If the Lord hadn't lost patience with him, too.

He turned and walked down the hall. Took a deep breath and at last walked into his office. And found his sweet daughter sitting on her chair crying as if her heart were breaking.

"Oh, Lilly." He crossed the room, knelt beside her, and pulled her into his arms. "I'm sorry I was so cross."

She threw her arms around him and cried even harder. Cried so hard that she couldn't even form words.

Which was his fault.

Making a decision, he picked her up and carried her out. "I'm sorry," he whispered into her ear. "I'm sorry. I was wrong to get so mad. I'll make things better."

But whether she didn't hear or didn't believe him, he didn't know. All she did was continue to cry. Sitting on his favorite chair, he rocked her slowly, felt tears slide down his own cheeks, and finally just sat.

Since Liesl was not there and likely never coming back...There was nothing left to say.

Chapter Twenty-One

NO SNOW HAD FALLEN IN two days. The day was crisp and cold, but the sun, instead of hiding behind the clouds like it often did, cast rays of light in the middle of a robin's-egg-blue sky. It was truly a glorious December day.

Main Street in Walden was looking like a picture postcard. Most of the shopkeepers, himself included, had shoveled the sidewalks around their businesses. Some had arrangements of poinsettias, fanciful snowmen, or Santas next to their front steps.

All in all, the beautiful day was an excellent opportunity to spend some time outdoors. In spite of the Amish Market's crowds, Wesley had encouraged both Jenny and Ernie to take a twenty-minute break that afternoon. They'd agreed—as long as he agreed to take a turn, too.

So that was why he was walking on Main Street at half past two.

And why he just happened to see Liesl, though he'd had to look twice to make sure that the woman walking listlessly in front of him was indeed his girlfriend. His heart started to pound. Guilt and worry, his two new best friends, settled in his heart. He needed to make things right.

"Liesl?" he called out as he strode forward.

She slowed, peeked over her shoulder at him, and at last stopped. "Wesley. Hello."

She wore a dark-gray dress and her usual black cloak and bonnet. The dark colors made her flawless skin look even more perfect, the golden strands that peeked out under the bonnet look even shinier, and her green eyes look even more striking. No matter what she was wearing, Liesl would still be beautiful. She couldn't help that.

However, her outfit and demeanor were so different than her usual bright and pleasing colors and familiar spunky way, he got even more worried. "It's a nice surprise to see you out walking."

"Is it?" One brow arched. "Since when do you go walking in the middle of the day? I thought everything at the store was too important for you to miss a minute." Before he could utter an apology, Liesl continued. "For that matter, when do you ever go for a walk in December? I don't remember the last time you walked to see me. Unless, of course, you are dropping off roses."

He winced at her tone. "I'm sorry. I suppose I deserve that." He'd heard from Jenny that Liesl had gone from looking out the window for his appearance in the evening to going up to her room to read instead. Now he'd messed things up with both his floral delivery...and the way he'd ignored her at the store.

"I don't know if you deserve something or not." She shrugged. "Was there something you needed?"

Ouch. "Not at all." He stepped closer. "Liesl, I didn't call out to you on the street because I needed something. I was happy to see you." When she simply stared at him, he knew he had to apologize. "Listen, I'm sorry about the way I treated you at the store the other day. I know I was rude and that you were upset."

"Oh, I was upset."

"Would you forgive me?"

Barely looking at him, she nodded. "Of course. You are forgiven."

He inwardly winced. The words she said were expected and everything proper, but they were so far from the emotion Liesl usually wore on her sleeve, it made him feel even worse. Deciding he needed to do something, anything, to make amends, he gestured to MiMi's, the coffee shop and café across the street. "What are you doing now? Would you like to go to MiMi's and get some hot chocolate? I heard MiMi decorated the entire interior with sparkly white lights."

"You have time for such things today? I thought it was the Christmas season."

"I've recently started to remember that there are a whole lot of other things to worry about besides the store." Before he could stop himself, he pulled out his watch and glanced at the time. "I bet I could still be gone for another fifteen minutes." Of course, as soon as he heard his words, his cheeks heated.

Liesl blinked, then to his amazement, she started laughing. "Oh, Wesley. You will never change, will you?"

He was fairly sure that wasn't a compliment. He also knew that as much as he wanted to be different, there were some things about himself that were stuck to his personality like glue."Do you need me to change?"

To his surprise, Liesl seemed to think about that for a moment. At last, she shrugged. "I'm not sure about that, either." Looking away, she murmured, "Maybe I'm the one who needs to be changing."

Liesl was talking about changing. How could that be? She was confident, bright, and beautiful. Those were three of the things that had drawn him to her in the first place. It was both stunning and dismaying that she was thinking about changing at all.

When she continued to merely stand in front of him, not chattering like usual—not even telling him what to do—Wesley knew he couldn't take it anymore.

Reaching out, he curved his hand around her own. To his relief, she didn't pull her hand from his. Instead, she clung like he was her lifeline. What in the world was going on? "Liesl, talk to me. Why are you out walking by yourself?"

"I don't see why that is any of your business, Wesley."

He knew she was irritated with him, but he didn't think things between them were over. Were they?

Focusing on the fact that she still hadn't pulled away, he rubbed his thumb along her knuckles. She had on fluffy white gloves and likely couldn't feel it, but he'd couldn't help himself. He wanted to be close to her, even in that small way. "It's my business because I care about you, of course. Now, what is wrong? Are you still upset about my behavior?"

"*Nee.*" On its heels, she shook her head, like she was frustrated. "I mean, yes, I am still upset about your behavior, but at this moment, it has more to do with Roland."

"Who?"

"Roland Hochstetler. You know. I go over there sometimes and help him with his daughter, Lilly."

"Is that where you were? What happened? Was he mean to you? Wait, he was, wasn't he?"

"He was upset about me talking to Lilly about the Pinery."

"Why would that upset him so?"

"Oh, Wesley, it's a long story and one I'm not too interested in repeating at the moment. All you need to know is that my *mamm* has acquired some free tickets for Saturday night. If you'd like to join my family, you would be most welcome. If not, please let me know and I'll ask someone else."

"I would like to attend."

"I'll let you know right now that Jenny is going. You might have to close the market."

She'd thrown out her gauntlet. "I'll do it."

She raised her eyebrows but nodded. "All right then. I'll see you on Saturday evening."

"I'll look forward to it." Realizing he was still holding her hand, he turned his palm so their fingers could be linked. "I promise I'll be better."

At last, a smile lit her face, but it was far from a look of joy. Instead, it was barely a hint. "There's no need, Wesley. Life is what it is, *jah*? All we should do now is think about the season and other people. That's a better use of our time, I think." Slowly, she pulled her hand from his. "The bookmobile is stopping just a half mile from here today. I better hurry or I'll miss it."

"Do you want me to walk you there?"

"We both know you don't have time. Besides, I find that I'm in need of a break from men right now. I'd much rather read."

Though everything inside of him was protesting her departure, he knew that he deserved her attitude. Wesley turned and headed back to the market. Jenny and Ernie would no doubt tease him about coming back a few minutes early, but he didn't care.

He was starting to feel the Amish Market was his only constant and its success was the only thing he could control. Or that he was any good at.

Thanks to his hard work and Jenny's huge help, the store's profits were up by a full 8 percent over last year. It was a remarkable achievement and one to be proud of. His father would be mighty pleased—and relieved. Wesley was making a success of the Christmas season.

So why didn't it feel that way?

Chapter Twenty-Two

SHORTLY AFTER WESLEY RETURNED FROM his walk outside, looking somehow more stressed than before he'd left, Ernie found Jenny near the back of the store.

"Ah, there ya are, Jenny. I've been lookin' everywhere for you."

Since she'd been helping a young couple pick out an Amish-made high chair, and Ernie wasn't usually one to search her out for something he could do himself, Jenny looked at him curiously. "Is everything all right?"

He stuffed his hands in the front pockets of his baggy trousers. "*Jah*, but you're needed in the back room. I'll help these folks."

She'd been kneeling by two of the high chairs she'd pulled out, inspecting the legs for nicks. "I'm sorry about this," she said.

"Not a problem," the husband said. "We need a moment to decide on the colors anyway."

"Ernie can help you carry whichever one you prefer to your car." Climbing to her feet, she met Ernie's eyes.

"Cell phone," he mouthed.

She had a phone call? "*Danke*, Ernie," she whispered before heading to the staff's room.

Jenny had learned soon after she'd started working at the Amish Market that Wesley's bishop had given his family permission to have a cell phone at work. A business like the market needed to be able to get in touch with the numerous vendors and truck drivers who sold or delivered items.

Wesley made a point to rarely use the phone for personal calls, but he had encouraged her to write her parents with the Market's cell phone number and reassure them that they could use it if they felt the need.

Her parents must be calling now. Jenny quickened her step. Surely nothing bad had happened? *Nee*, they were probably just checking in.

The cell phone was sitting on the old circular dining table that Wesley had told her had once belonged to a great-uncle. "Hello?" she said quickly after picking up. "This is Jenny."

"Ah, Jenny," her father said. "What a nice treat to hear your pretty voice."

Some of her hope faded into worry as she heard her father's distinctive voice and not her mother's. Her mother was the chatty one. "It's gut to hear your voice, too, *Daed*. Is everything all right?"

His slight pause put her even more on edge. "As a matter of fact, everything ain't so *gut*. I called to let you know that your mother slipped on some ice and broke her wrist. She's in surgery now. Don'tcha worry, though."

Don't worry about Mamm being in surgery? "Hold on, *Daed.* You better back up. When did this happen? And what do you mean by surgery? I thought doctors just put a cast on broken bones."

"Calm down, now. Don't get yourself all riled up."

She pulled out a chair and sat down. "I'm as calm as anyone would be who has just received news that their mother is in surgery. *Daed*, please, tell me what happened. Is she going to be okay?"

"It's just a silly thing. She slipped on her way to the henhouse. It seemed she was chatting with Wilber, slipped on a patch of ice, and down she went!"

"What happened then? Did Wilber start barking?" Wilber was her parents' Australian Shepherd.

"We are blessed to have that *hund*, I tell you that."

"Indeed." She'd often joked with her parents that Wilber was smarter than most humans. "Were you around when *Mamm* fell?"

"I was inside sipping *kaffi* and reading the new issue of *The Budget*. Jenny, wouldn't you know? Wilber ran over to the house, went through his dog door, found me in the living room, and barked at me. I went running after him and then found your *mamm*. Isn't it amazing how smart he is?"

She was glad that Wilber had been so helpful, but it still pinched to realize that if not for that dog, her mother might have been lying on the cold ground waiting for quite a while. Her father tended to forget about the time when he was reading the paper. "I wish I had been there."

"Don't know why. There weren't anything you could've done, child."

"I could have at least gotten the eggs in the morning instead of *Mamm.*"

His voice lowered. "Ack. You know as well as I do that our Lord is in charge. Everything happens in His own way and in the right time. Doesn't do any good to second-guess accidents and whatnots."

"I guess you're right."

"*Nee*, I am right in this instance. Now, I'm calling not just to let you know about the accident but to see how you're faring. Your mother's been worried about you."

"I'm *gut.* I've been busy at the Market." She hoped the little bit of enthusiasm she'd tried to inject in her voice was filtering through.

"And otherwise?"

"I'm not sure what you mean."

"What about Wesley Raber? And young Liesl?"

She felt her cheeks heat. "They are fine, too."

"Jenny, are you spending time with Laura May and Liesl? Are you doing anything besides work? Are you taking time to enjoy life and the season a bit?"

She never could lie to her father. "Kind of."

He sighed. "Dear Jenny, you are my worker bee, and that's a fact. I've always been proud of the way you never shy away from a day's work, but even bees need to rest every now and then. Promise me that the entire Christmas season won't go by without you doing something fun or interesting."

"I won't."

"*Gut.* That's what Christmas is all about, you know."

Despite the seriousness of the conversation, Jenny giggled. "*Daed*, you're supposed to be telling me to ignore everything about Christmas except that it's about the birth of baby Jesus."

"Just because you spend time going sledding or ice skating or laughing with new friends doesn't mean you've forgotten about His birth. I feel sure and for certain that He would be the first to say that one can do both at the same time."

She chuckled again. "*Danke*, *Daed.*"

"You think I'm joking but I'm serious, Jenny."

"I understand."

"*Gut.* Now, I've got to go sit in the waiting room and get back to praying for the doctors and nurses." He paused. "If you don't hear from me, your mother is fine."

"What about you?"

"Don't worry about me or your mother." He paused. "You should not hurry home to help me and your *mamm*. Don't do it, girl."

Since she had just been thinking of looking at bus schedules, Jenny swallowed the lump in her throat. "I won't."

"*Gut*. Bye now."

He hung up before she could respond. Jenny closed her eyes and prayed for her parents and the medical personnel. Now that she'd done all that she could, she knew it was time to return to the shop and get back to work.

However, for the life of her, that was absolutely the last thing she wanted to do. She was even starting to feel like even standing up would take too much effort. So she sat.

The minutes passed. She heard the laughter of teenagers and a crying baby as a mother likely ushered it into the restroom. In the background, she was sure she could hear Wesley's steady, low tone. No doubt he was reassuring a customer that their wait was almost over and that they would be helped very soon. She'd certainly seen and heard him do that dozens of times.

At last she got to her feet and walked to the front counter where Ernie was standing next to Wesley and wrapping some cookie jars in paper.

"I'm sorry that took so long," she said in Pennsylvania Dutch.

Wesley shrugged off the apology like it wasn't necessary. "Ernie here told me you got an important phone call," he replied as he swiped a customer's credit card. "It was your father, *jah*?" After she nodded, he asked, "Is everything all right?"

"I think so," she said. If they had been alone, or if there weren't so much work to be done, Jenny would've shared the news about her mother's wrist and surgery. But that wasn't the case.

"Here you are, sir," he said as he handed his customer the credit card receipt and a pen. "Thank you for coming in."

The customer, a dapper-looking English man, smiled warmly. "You're welcome. You had everything I needed for my daughter."

"I'm glad to hear it," Wesley said with a smile.

Jenny knew that Wesley meant every word, too. This shop was not only in his family. It was in his blood. He cared about his customers, the merchandise, his vendors, everything.

"Would you mind taking over the cash register for a moment?" he asked. "I told Ernie he could have a break and I want to check some stock in the back."

"I don't mind at all. Take your time." She'd barely gotten the words out before the next customer set her basket of purchases on the counter.

Just as she finished ringing the woman up, Ernie said, "Jenny, you look worried. Was there a problem?"

"I'm afraid so. My mother broke her wrist and is in surgery."

Looking more concerned, he said, "You didn't want to speak to Wesley about that?"

"There was nothing he could do, ain't so? Besides, we both know where his heart is."

Ernie waited for her to help the next person, then said, "I'm not sure where you think his heart is resting, but it's not just on the shop."

"Of course." She hadn't meant to be rude. "It's with Liesl, too."

A hint of a smile played upon his lips. "Liesl wasn't who I was talking about, Jenny."

She froze and gaped at him.

But all Ernie did was chuckle and walk away.

Boy, talk about frustrating! She hated when people spoke in riddles. Now she was no doubt going to spend the next two hours wondering what Ernie had meant.

Or, rather, convincing herself that his comment had nothing to do with her.

Chapter Twenty-Three

WESLEY WAS A STRANGER IN his own home. Well, perhaps that might be a bit of an exaggeration. But as he sat at the kitchen table by himself, carelessly playing solitaire, and listening to nothing except for the growling of his stomach, he realized that nothing felt right. Nothing at all.

When he flipped over another card and realized that he'd lost his third game in a row, he tossed the cards in his hand on the table. Three of them skittered to the floor. Scowling at the fallen cards, he bent to pick them up, somehow managing to knock his head into the corner of the table as he did so.

Had there ever been a worse game than solitaire? He didn't think so.

Feeling even more peevish, Wesley straightened the messy pile, divided it into halves and shuffled. Then shuffled them again.

If he were a better man, a more gracious, giving man, he could blame the sense of unease on the fact that his parents were still in Kentucky. His father's near heart attack had been a terrible thing, and it was one that he never wanted repeated. Of course it had upset him.

But the root of his problem was that he was alone, and that he would likely be that way for some time. His siblings were busy with either *Mamm* and *Daed* or their own families. Next year, when his father was better, when he was back at the Market with *Mamm* and Wesley, things would be back to how they used to be. How they had always been.

Which meant that, although his parents would be around, he would be doing much the same thing as this year. Just the thought of that made him feel ill. If he didn't prioritize other things in his life, he would once again be alone.

Nee, it was more than that. He would once again have no *frau*, no *kinner*, no *haus* of his own to fix up and fuss over. He would have only a successful store that his parents and grandparents started.

Looking down at the cards in his hands, he grimaced. It was likely he'd also have plenty of time to lose games of solitaire, too.

The store was a legacy to be proud of, for sure and for certain. But was it his life's goal? He couldn't say that it had ever been. Something needed to change.

"Lord, I know that I haven't been as faithful as I should've been of late." He took a deep breath, and talked some more to Him, as had always been his way. "*Jah*, I know what you're thinking." Realizing that sounded cheeky, he added, "I mean, of course I don't know what You're thinking. Don't mean no offense. But what I'm trying to say is that though I've been freely asking for your help for *Daed*, and asking for You to be with all the doctors and nurses and such...I haven't been thanking you for my health or for all my many blessings."

Wesley cleared his throat, then at last said what was on his mind. "I also haven't been asking You for what I need most, which is guidance for my life. I need to learn how to balance work better." He chuckled. "I know what Jenny would say, too. She'd tell me that the first step to doing that would be to realize that things are out of whack." He smiled. "Oh, Lord. She is a right one, ain't so?"

Suddenly, he stilled as his words reverberated in his soul. Wesley could practically feel the Lord grinning ear to ear.

"That's it, isn't it? There's something about Jenny that I'm drawn to. She's the woman who's been on my mind. Not Liesl. She's the reason I haven't proposed to Liesl yet...and I'm not courting her like a man should. Liesl is my friend and I do love her...but she doesn't own my heart. It's Jenny who does."

Looking out to the night sky, he was pretty sure he caught sight of a shooting star. "Lord, you might've already intended to shoot that star there. But if you don't mind too much, I'm going to choose to take it as a sign from You."

The next morning, he was in better spirits. So much so that not even the change from a sunny, blue-sky day to a gray one filled with blowing snow could dampen his mood.

Jenny arrived just five minutes before he opened

the door for customers. "So sorry I'm late. I'm afraid everything that could've gone wrong this morning did."

His heart warmed at the sight of her. "No worries. I'm just glad you're here."

A look of confusion flooded her features before she smiled at him. "What has happened to you?"

"I'm afraid to ask what you are referring to."

"You're wearing a smile."

Wesley knew he had a lot of growing to do in the romance department, but he wasn't that bad. "I do smile, Jenny."

"I realize that. But...there is something different about you this morning." She waved her hand. "You don't seem as worried about everything. Actually, I'd even call you calm." Her eyes widened. "Wesley, did you receive some good news about your father? Is he doing much better?"

"Last I heard, he was. But that's not why I feel better." He paused, trying to think of the best way to describe his attitude adjustment. But since there was no way to do that, he opted to tell his tale the way it had happened. "I decided to have a chat with the Lord while I was playing solitaire last night."

"I see." Her eyes sparkled. "Is that something you and the Lord do together often?"

"Not exactly. I'm thinking that maybe I should, though."

"I didn't know He cared for card games," she teased.

He smiled back at her. "Don't know why you're so surprised. After all, He must like them, otherwise so many people wouldn't be whiling away their evenings playing them."

Her hand covered her mouth as she attempted to stifle a giggle. "You seem to have an answer for everything today."

"Not hardly. But sometimes, it seems so."

She tilted her head to one side. "I'll keep that in mind if I have any more problems this morning."

He loved when she did that. When she said the most benign comment but it held a whole other meaning. He especially loved it when her eyes were dancing.

"Jenny, sometimes you do the most adorable things," he blurted out.

Then he realized what he'd said out loud. And realized that, without even meaning to, he'd leaned closer to her. Close enough to kiss.

Before he could pull back and apologize, she turned away.

"You know, talk about being a terrible worker. I haven't even put my lunch or my purse away." The door chimed, signaling the arrival of the first customers. "And here we are, in the middle of the Christmas rush, too. I'm so sorry." She rushed down the aisle. Out of sight in a matter of seconds.

All before Wesley could say that he could care less about the Christmas rush.

Before he could say anything at all.

Chapter Twenty-Four

JENNY HAD NEVER BEEN SO happy to be in the small, rather cramped, staff room. Glad that the door was always kept closed, she practically tossed her things down on the linoleum floor and then leaned against one of the white walls.

Had that just really happened? One moment, she'd been teasing Wesley about his conversations with God. The next, they were standing too close together and he'd said that she looked adorable.

That hadn't even been the worst part. Wesley had stood close enough that she'd been sure he was about to kiss her. Right there, in the front of the store! And much to her shame, she'd wanted that kiss. Badly.

She'd stood there staring at him like a scared doe in the woods. Glanced at his lips. Wondered.

His gaze had heated. It was as if he'd known what she was thinking!

Twenty seconds later, he'd stepped back.

And then, right after whatever had just happened had happened, what had she done? Instead of putting them back on track. Instead of reminding them both about Liesl—about Liesl!—she'd scurried away like a frightened rabbit.

Jenny pressed her hands to her cheeks, which she was sure were flaming with embarrassment.

What on earth was the matter with her? It didn't matter what she thought or how she felt. The fact of the matter was that she knew what was right and what was wrong. What had almost happened was firmly in the "wrong" category. It was just too bad that her pulse was still racing and she felt almost giddy. Because it had been so, so long since she'd felt attractive. Or pretty. Or yes, even adorable.

Which she knew better to even think about. She was not sixteen. She was twenty-six years old. It had been years since she was adorable! Was she really so desperate for affection that she'd brazenly eaten up that compliment she'd had no business receiving in the first place?

Try as she might, Jenny couldn't think of a single reason for that.

Well, not beyond the fact that she feared she had a secret crush on Wesley. Although she would never do anything to hurt Liesl and never do anything to jeopardize their relationship…it was what it was.

Ruthlessly pushing all those feelings aside, she stuffed her lunch bag into the gas-powered refrigerator, straightened the ties of her *kapp* to lay neatly on her shoulders, and headed back to the store.

"Jenny! Ah, there you are," Ernie said, looking harried with half his shirt tail once again hanging down in the front of his pants. "Wesley told me to come find you."

"I'm sorry. I, uh, had to run into the restroom."

Ernie nodded. "*Jah.* I told him it was likely something like that."

"Where does Wesley want me?" And why did that suddenly feel like the absolutely wrong thing to say? "I mean, does he want me to help someone in particular?"

"Oh, *jah.* There's a couple over at the bakery who have a big order. Would you be able to help them?"

"Of course."

She hurried over to find not just one couple, but at least ten people, all staring into the bakery case like hungry dogs at the butcher shop. "Hello, everyone. I'm sorry to keep ya waiting."

A woman in the middle of the pack pointedly held up her arm. "Time might mean nothing to you, young lady, but we're on a tight schedule. The bus driver says we've got to get to Cincinnati by two."

"I understand." Quickly, she washed her hands, slipped on plastic gloves, and donned a thick white apron over her plum-colored dress. "How may I help you?" she asked the far more patient couple at the head of the line.

"We are wanting one of the Christmas cakes, a pecan pie, two dozen buttermilk cookies, and five glazed donuts, if you please."

Pulling out a sturdy brown-paper tote bag and a large baker's box, she opened the case and started to put the items they asked for in the box. "It's my pleasure."

The husband leaned a little closer. "Don't let Hazel back there bring you down. She complains about the sun shining. It's annoying."

Jenny wisely pretended not to hear the last remark as she handed the husband the bag holding the containers of cake and pie, and his wife the bakery box. After reminding them to pay at the main counter, she smiled at the next customer in line. "How might I help you?"

"Three apple turnovers. And one of those Christmas cakes with the poinsettia on top."

"Of course."

And so it continued. The customers were largely polite, she worked as efficiently as she could, and the time passed...all without having to say a word to Wesley.

Eventually the bus group left, Ernie left for his lunch break, and the store thinned out.

As if he'd been waiting for that very moment, Wesley walked to stand on the other side of the bakery counter. "Jenny, about earlier. I am sorry if I made you uncomfortable."

She was relieved he wasn't pretending that nothing had happened. "We can just forget about it." Would she be able to do that, though?

He rested his arms on the glass countertop. "May I be honest with you?"

"Of course." Actually, she was pretty sure they were being more honest with each other than they'd ever been.

His bright-blue eyes warmed. "I realized that my heart doesn't belong to Liesl. Last night, when I was chatting with the Lord, I realized there's a reason she and I haven't become engaged yet. It was because we weren't meant to be together. After being around you so much, I know now that He had someone else in mind for me."

Her heart beat harder.

His words were delicious. The type of thing that the young girl she used to be would have given anything to hear her boyfriend say.

Nee, they were the words that she knew Liesl yearned to hear Wesley say to her.

Which was exactly just how wrong both the feelings she'd been experiencing and the words he just said were. It didn't matter what she wanted or even how her heart felt.

What mattered was that she put a stop to it as soon as possible.

"*Nee*, Wesley, there's a far different reason why you and my niece haven't become engaged, and it has nothing to do with the Lord's will. It's because you haven't proposed."

He didn't even flinch. Instead, he leaned closer. "Don't you understand what I'm saying?" he murmured in a soft tone. "She is not the one."

"I understand that you are telling me all this and not her." When he gaped at her, she added, "Or do you not plan to actually tell her how you're feeling? Are you just simply going to let my niece sit at home and wonder what is going on? Are you content just to let her wait and hope that one day you will finally be honest about your feelings for her?"

Wesley straightened. "Of course not. Jenny, you know I would never hurt Liesl intentionally." His tone became more clipped. "I haven't meant to hurt her at all."

"But you have, yes?" Remembering the pain she'd felt from Jeremiah's breaking up with her, she said, "I can promise you this. Sometimes it doesn't matter what you mean to do, or what you want to do. What matters is what you actually do. And you are hurting her right now."

"I'll speak my mind soon."

"When? Tonight?"

"I can't tonight. You know that tonight is our big outing to the Pinery. I'm not going to ruin that event for her—or for her parents."

Jenny gasped. Oh, for heaven's sake. She'd forgotten all about it.

Then she realized that they'd drawn the attention of not only Ernie but of more than a few customers. Pasting a smile on her face, she said, "We need to get back to work."

"I know." He didn't move away, though. Instead, he said, "I'm not giving up. I want everything to work out between us."

Goose bumps trailed up her spine. He wasn't giving up. Wasn't giving up on them. With effort, she tamped down the burst of euphoria she was feeling. "I am sure it will all work out like it's supposed to."

Wesley searched her face, then nodded at last. "I better get to the counter."

"Of course."

She'd never been so glad to see another wave of shoppers enter the market. As far as she was concerned, she hoped it was the busiest afternoon yet. Anything would be better than to have another awkward conversation with Wesley.

That probably wasn't the way to be, but what could she do? It appeared she could only hold on for the ride.

Chapter Twenty-Five

"LIESL?"

"*Jah, Mamm*?" Liesl turned to look at her mother, who was standing in her doorway looking completely uncertain.

"You have a visitor."

The announcement couldn't have come at a better time. She'd been working on the fifth of the dozen bridesmaid dresses she'd been contracted for and was beginning to feel cross-eyed.

There was something about sewing twelve of the same exact dress that didn't set well with her. Even though Amish dresses were meant to be plain, she did like to add something special for each project, even if it was simply a particularly fine piece of fabric.

Feeling a bit rejuvenated, Liesl scooted her metal stool away from the treadle sewing machine. "Who's here, *Mamm*? Is it Wesley?" She chuckled before her mother had a chance to reply. "I'm joking. Of course I know it's not him. Wesley's not going to leave the shop this close to Christmas." Standing up, she shook out the skirt of her dress. "Is it Charity? She said she might be coming over with a Christmas gift this week. I made her a gift two weeks—"

"It is not Charity. It's Roland Hochstetler and his daughter, Lilly." Her mother gave her a pointed look. "They are waiting for you in the living room."

Roland was at her house!

"I'll be right out." Realizing that she probably looked like she'd been sitting behind a sewing machine all day, Liesl corrected herself. "I mean, I'll be out in five minutes."

Still not looking all that pleased, her mother nodded. "I'll let him know."

"Wait! Did you give offer him *kaffi* or tea?"

"*Nee*—"

"What about Lilly? She loves hot chocolate. Are you making any for her? And cookies. I bet she'd love one of those gingersnaps we made yesterday."

Her mother's eyebrows seemed to have climbed to new heights. "You seem to know a lot about their likes, Liesl. And I didn't realize you planned to entertain them." She lowered her voice. "Just how well do you know this Roland and his daughter?"

"Well enough to know they might like something warm to drink on a cold day, *Mamm*." She knew she sounded cheeky, but it was better than sharing just how well she knew Roland and Lilly right that minute. "I'll be right there."

"I'll see about those drinks, dear." Looking more bemused than upset, her mother walked into the hall.

The minute she did, Liesl hurried to the bathroom, examined her reflection, and took her precious few leftover minutes to smooth her hair, wash her hands, and smooth out her tangerine-colored dress. Maybe it was silly to go to such trouble when she and Roland had last parted on such fractious terms. But she couldn't seem to help herself. She was glad they were here.

When she entered the living room, she found her father sitting with Roland and Lilly. Lilly was giggling and Roland looked completely at ease.

Well, until he caught sight of her. The moment their eyes met, he got to his feet. "Liesl."

"Hello, Roland. I'm sorry I kept you waiting." Smiling more brightly, she added, "Hiya, Lilly."

"Hiya back!" Lilly hurried to her side and gave her midsection a hug. "*Daed* and I decided to visit you for a change!"

She bent down on one k*nee* and held her close. "Indeed, you did. And I am mighty thankful for it, too."

Her father leaned back in his chair just as her mother entered holding a tray of mugs and a plate of cookies. Immediately, he sat upright again. "Well now, isn't this a nice treat."

"*Danke* for doing this," Liesl said as she took the tray and placed it in the center of the coffee table.

Looking uncomfortable, Roland said, "I told your parents there was no need to go to so much trouble. We don't intend to stay long."

Her mother waved off his comment. "I told you that coffee and cookies are never any trouble. And neither is hot chocolate for sweet little girls."

Liesl carefully handed Lilly her cup before passing Roland his. Only then did she realize that there were three other cups on the tray. Her parents had decided to join them!

She was just about to send her mother a beseeching look when her father said, "Will you pass me a cup as well, Liesl?"

And now she was stuck. "Yes. Of course."

After making sure her father had his cup and two cookies, Liesl said, "Roland, Lilly is right. It is nice to have you here for a change. I hope you both are doing well?"

Roland glanced at his daughter, then the sweetest smile appeared on his face. "I think we're both doing better than just 'well' today. Aren't we, Lilly?"

"Uh-huh." She giggled before beaming at Liesl.

Liesl smiled. "Lilly, do you have a secret? If so, you have to tell me what it is." The little girl was practically bouncing up and down, she looked so excited.

"Should you tell Miss Liesl or shall I?" Roland asked.

"You, *Daed*." Her eyes were so bright they could light up a Christmas tree.

"All right then." He took a deep breath. "Liesl, Lilly and I wanted to tell you—and your family, too, of course—that we would be delighted to go with you to the Pinery this evening."

It was only then that he seemed to notice her parents' stunned expressions. "I mean, if you haven't already asked other people to take our place."

"Not at all," Liesl said quickly. "We would still be delighted to have your company. Wouldn't we, *Mamm* and *Daed*?'

"Of course. Delighted," *Mamm* said quickly.

"We're glad you both can make it," *Daed* added. Then, rather abruptly, her father stood up. "And now I think I'd better go check on the horses."

Roland stood up. "Thank you for the invitation, Armor."

"Of course. See you tonight."

Her mother suddenly got to her feet as well. "I think I'd better go check on the laundry. It doesn't wash itself, you know."

"I'll be down to help you soon, *Mamm*."

"No, no. You take your time. You've got a cup of coffee to drink and a plate of cookies, too."

Liesl looked down at her cup. She hadn't taken so much as a sip. Feeling awkward, she brought the cup to her lips. "That was a little strange, wasn't it?"

But instead of looking as mystified as she was, Roland looked contemplative. "I don't know. I think I understand where they're coming from. No doubt I would feel the same way."

"What do you mean?"

Lilly tugged on her father's arm. "*Jah*, what do you mean, *Daed*?"

He smiled. "Forgive me, child. You are such a good helper, I sometimes forget that every topic isn't for small ears."

Liesl stared at him until he met her gaze. But what she saw there silenced any questions she was eager to ask. Roland's eyes were filled with longing and regret—twin sentiments that tugged at her heart and made her wonder if she'd ever truly understand what had been on his mind.

She cleared her throat. "Lilly, have I told you that you can get caramel apples at the Pinery? And hot popcorn in containers that look like Christmas trees?"

"*Nee*. Do you think we might be able to get a caramel apple?"

"Of course! I can't let my best girl miss a treat like that."

Lilly beamed, causing Liesl to fall even deeper in love.

With the sweet little girl of course, not her father.

Perhaps one day she would believe that, too.

Chapter Twenty-Six

AFTER ALL THE COMMOTION, WORRIES, and stress, at last, the much-anticipated night had arrived. They were all going to the Pinery, and everyone at the Fisher house was beyond excited. Jenny had to admit that she was no exception. From the time she'd first arrived in Walden, almost every day had felt exactly the same. The days had been filled with chores and work, followed by more chores and early evenings.

Since her personal life was starting to feel like a knotted mess, Jenny couldn't wait to take a break from everything and simply relax and have fun.

They'd all decided to meet at the entrance at six o'clock sharp. At four forty-five, Jenny discovered what an undertaking that would be.

It turned out that things worked very differently when it came to schedules and excursions at her niece's house. Items for every extenuating circumstance had to be uncovered, inspected, and then neatly packed. Then came the decisions about what to wear. This took nearly as long as the packing.

"Armor, I still ain't sure that Snappy is the best horse for tonight," Laura May called out. "You know how he gets around other horses."

"*Jah*, but Snappy's been getting along better lately at church, don'tcha know?"

"*Nee*. Snappy tried to bite old Anson's mule two days ago when I was at the store. Anson wasn't happy about that."

Stunned by the way Laura May and Armor were chatting like they had nothing else to do, Jenny raised her eyes at Emma.

Emma shrugged and leaned against the wall.

"I think we should take Blacky," Laura May said. "He's got the better disposition. Plus, you know how he enjoys getting out in the evenings."

"He does, but it ain't like the Pinery is around the corner. Snappy is younger." Armor scratched his beard. "How old is he, again?"

"Hmm...maybe twelve? Is he twelve, Liesl?"

"He's likely thirteen by now. Let's go, *Daed*."

His eyes lit up. "Fine."

At long last, at five fifty, Jenny, her aunt and uncle, Liesl, and Emma all piled in the buggy—with Blacky hitched for the journey. Also in the buggy was an incredibly large canvas tote bag with snacks (even though they were all intending to go to the food carts for snacks), bandages, antibiotic ointment (because it seemed that rusty nails were always a possibility), additional gloves, scarves, and blankets in case they got into a snowdrift, and finally, two flashlights.

Jenny couldn't believe it all, which Liesl and Emma thought was mighty amusing.

"If you were here longer, you'd get used to it," Emma said.

"Are you two used to your mother preparing for an evening out like you were going into the wilderness?"

Liesl shrugged. "More or less. Of course, my worst fear is that I'll one day turn into my mother and think I need a huge supply of snack mix and granola bars every time I leave the house."

"Now I know who to go to for safety pins during family reunions," Jenny joked.

"You wouldn't believe the amount of things we have for a two-week trip. One would think we were permanently moving to the middle of nowhere," Emma said. "Worse, my parents always make us carry everything."

"You canna expect your parents to carry it all, right? Plus, you two are younger," Jenny teased.

Liesl lifted her chin. "That don't matter as much as you might think. Heavy is heavy. At least I told *Mamm* and *Daed* that I am not carrying that bag anywhere tonight." She lowered her voice. "No way do I want Roland and Lilly to see me looking like a vagabond."

Jenny noticed that Liesl had mentioned Roland instead of Wesley. She thought that was notable, but certainly wasn't going to say a word about it. "I did notice that the tote was left in the buggy."

"When push comes to shove, my parents want to have a good a time as much as any of us," she added with a grin. "Now they can say that they've done all they could for us to be prepared."

"And it's only a short walk away, anyway," Jenny finished with a smile.

"Exactly."

She and Liesl had lagged behind Liesl's parents. Emma had seen two of her girlfriends from school and asked to walk with them. They had about twenty or thirty yards to get to the meeting space. Even from the distance, Jenny could see that there were already a lot of people there. Many of them seemed to also have chosen the front entrance as a meeting spot.

Jenny also noticed that while Liesl seemed excited, she didn't seem like her usual chatty self. "Liesl, are you worried about tonight?"

"Hmm? Oh, *nee*."

"Are you sure?"

She pursed her lips together before sighing. "I fear I'm having some growing pains. They're catching up with me tonight."

"Growing pains? What hurts? Your legs?"

"Oh, not pains with my body. Pains with my emotions." She pressed a mittened hand on her heart. "And with my heart."

"Do you want to talk about it?" Jenny stopped. "You know I'm always happy to listen."

Liesl glanced at her in surprise before shaking her head. "*Danke*, but there's nothing to say. Nothing worth saying out loud, anyway."

"Are you sure?"

"Very. Oh! Look at all the lights!"

When Jenny got her first good look at the Pinery celebration, she finally understood why everyone had been talking about it nonstop.

The whole scene looked like something out of a storybook. Scores of green pines had been draped in white lights. Lanterns hung from some oaks and maples. The orange glow from the candles nestled inside of each added another layer of beauty. At the front of the entrance was a huge sign decorated with bright-red bows and emblazoned with the words *The Pinery Merry Christmas*.

At a small building just to the right of the sign, someone dressed up like Santa Claus was selling tickets. Christmas music flowed out of speakers, and in a large pen off to the side stood six or seven reindeer.

Jenny couldn't help but gasp. "This is all so beautiful."

"It is, isn't it? While of course I enjoy Christmas Day, this event comes a close second. I think it's magical here."

"I didn't imagine that this place would be so fancy! It seems to have everything."

Liesl giggled. "You haven't even entered it yet. Prepare yourself. Some of the trees and decorations are absolutely stunning."

Jenny scanned the crowd, but she could only find Wesley. He was standing with three or four other Amish men and seemed relaxed and happy. One of the men surrounding him clapped him on the back and he laughed. She couldn't look away. Every other time she'd seen him, he'd been focused on work—or calling on Liesl. This was a new, carefree version of the man she'd been coming to know so well. He looked younger, more handsome, and was quicker to smile. This Wesley was captivating...so much so, she was having a hard time looking away from him.

"He seems in good spirits."

"He does, doesn't he?" Liesl mused. "Of course, with the way Lilly is practically bouncing up and down on her heels, it would be impossible to be in anything but a good mood."

What? Jenny darted a sidelong glance at Liesl. "I was referring to Wesley, Liesl. Are you speaking about Roland?"

This time Liesl drew to a quick stop. "Wesley's already here, too?"

"He's standing with the group of men by the ticket booth."

She scanned the crowd. "I see him." She smiled and gave a little wave before facing Jenny again. "Oh my stars. Do you think he saw me looking at Roland and not him?"

Now Jenny was *really* confused. "I don't think so, but even if he did, what does it matter? I mean, Roland is just a friend, right?"

"I'm not sure," Liesl said after a pause. "I'm really not sure at all."

Noticing how flushed she was, Jenny whispered, "Liesl, you look a bit stressed. Are you sure you're doing okay?"

"I will be if..." Her voice drifted off before she seemed to come to a decision. "Jenny, will you please do me a favor? Would you please try to spend some time with Wesley tonight?"

Oh my. "I don't mind that at all, but why?"

"I don't want Roland and Lilly to feel like they are the odd ones out."

"We'll all be in one big group. And your parents will be nearby, too. Everything is going to work out just fine," Jenny said.

"I sure hope so." Liesl sighed dramatically. "If it

doesn't, I'm going to have a whole lot of people upset with me."

They arrived at the group just in time to see Liesl's parents shake Roland's hand and give Lilly hugs. Her father shook Wesley's hand as well and performed an introduction, though it was obvious that Roland and Wesley knew each other.

"Ah, here they are," Laura May said with a relieved look on her face. "Girls, I was beginning to wonder if you'd ever get here."

"Sorry, it's my fault," Jenny said. "I kept asking Liesl questions."

"I watched you both approach. You seemed as if you were having a serious conversation," Wesley said.

Liesl smiled. "We were. It was all about what food we should sample first." *Good answer*, Jenny thought.

"What did you two decide on?"

Jenny said, "We decided to let Lilly tell us what to do."

"Let's get caramel apples!"

The group of them laughed. "Lead the way, kids," Armor said. "Laura May and I will follow along."

Jenny was sure she would be doing the very same thing.

Chapter Twenty-Seven

WITHIN A FEW MINUTES AFTER arriving, Wesley decided that the Pinery Christmas event was a good example of how descriptions of some events can never completely do them justice.

He and his family rarely took part in events during the holiday season. His parents had always avoided the Pinery because it was a secular attraction. Wesley had followed suit, though he'd known many, many Amish who attended the event year after year. He realized now that calling it too secular had been just an excuse to work more.

Now, as he looked around with wide eyes, Wesley regretted all the times he'd elected to stay late at the store instead. To put it simply, the Pinery event was amazing. Lights of all colors decorated almost every feature. The wooden cutouts were charming instead of garish, the decorated trees were beautiful, and the numerous assorted food trucks and carts were sure to make even the most careful dieter indulge. Even the silly Christmas music, which usually wore on his patience after an hour or more, seemed more jubilant than any that he recalled.

But perhaps the problem was that he'd never walked through the lit gravel walkways the way he was that evening, with Liesl clinging to his arm. All right, maybe that was a bit of an exaggeration. But from the moment they started walking, she'd curved one mittened glove near his elbow and smiled up at him.

It was both a surprise—and a dream come true. He'd spent many, many evenings imagining the whole community seeing beautiful, vivacious Liesl Fisher walking on his arm.

And now it was happening.

He did his best to keep his steps small and his pace slow. Liesl wasn't exactly a slow walker, but she seemed determined to examine every decorated tree and painted wooden sign or figurine nestled among the flashy forest.

She'd also insisted they stop at the first food cart and get some hot chocolate for the two of them—but for Roland and his daughter, Lilly, too.

Roland had seemed uncomfortable. Wesley had been, too, especially since Liesl wouldn't let him pay for the drinks. But he soon forgot about the awkward occasion when Lilly smiled and gazed at Liesl as if she were a princess in a fairy tale.

"That Lilly sure is cute, ain't so?" he asked Liesl.

"Oh, *jah.* She's like this all the time, too. She is curious and interested in most everything around. I always learn something new when I'm with her."

Wesley was slightly taken aback. "You know a lot about her. Do you see Lilly very often?"

"Oh, every now and then," she said in an airy, un-Liesl-like tone. "Only when my schedule allows."

"I see." Of course he didn't, but what could he say? After taking a first sip of his drink, he looked for Jenny and found she was walking next to Liesl's mother. "We didn't get her a hot chocolate. Let me go see if she or your parents would like some."

"That's nice of you. I'll go see if Lilly needs any help."

Wesley couldn't imagine that the child would need help sipping a drink but he let that pass.

Jenny smiled as he approached. "Hiya, Wesley. This place is lovely, isn't it?"

"It truly is." He held up his cup. "I came to see if I could get the three of you something to drink."

"None for me," said Armor. "But you ladies ought to enjoy it."

"It's not necessary that you pay for ours," Jenny said when Wesley pulled out his wallet.

"It's my pleasure—and the least I can do."

Her cheeks pinkened while Liesl's mother chuckled. "You always were a charmer, Wesley. I can't refuse you now."

Turning, he walked to the small line and waited his turn. A few seconds later, Jenny joined him.

"Jenny, did you need something? I would've been happy to get it for you."

"*Nee.* I just didn't want to make you wait alone."

"I don't mind. Besides, this is my fault. I should've thought about the three of you when Liesl was buying the first round."

"You don't need to explain yourself. I've been in the midst of Hurricane Liesl a time or two. Once she gets her mind made up about something, she's nearly impossible to ignore."

He laughed. "I never thought of Liesl being like a storm, but your description isn't entirely wrong."

"She's always been that way." Remembering the way Liesl had been so intent on playing school when they were young, she shrugged. "I don't think she tries to be a force of nature. She just is."

"I think it's cute. I always have. I don't know why she would want to change."

Jenny smiled at him. "That's good to hear. Some extended members have suggested that she's a mite too bossy." Remembering how her mother had reacted to Jenny's decision to come to Walden to help her out, she added, "Even my parents from time to time."

"Even you, too?" he asked before ordering two drinks.

"*Nee*. Never me. I prefer to think of her as enthusiastic—and even encouraging. There have been times in my life when I've needed a bit of a prod from time to time."

He grinned. "Indeed. Now, what about you?"

For the first time during their conversation, Jenny looked unsure. "What about me?"

"How would all those extended family members describe you?"

She looked taken aback. "I couldn't say. Perhaps more on the quiet and steady side?" She sipped from her drink. "I've always been the type who blends into the background."

He reckoned she was a lot of things. But a person who blended into the background? No—not even a little.

"For what it's worth, I don't think you blend in at all. I noticed you from the moment you walked into the store."

Her eyes flared for a moment, as if she was attempting to figure out how to process that statement. "I'll take that as a compliment."

"You should." He wanted to mention how pleasing her features were. How beautiful her eyes were. And her skin...how it looked as if the Lord Himself had given her skin an extra dose of cream to make it more luminous.

But even more importantly, how much he appreciated her company, and how it just felt right whenever they were together.

"Now, if I had to share my thoughts, it's only fair that you do the same thing. How do you think other people think of you?"

Hating to bring up his weaknesses to her, Wesley groaned. "I should've expected this."

"Of course you should've. If I have to share, then you do, too." She wagged a finger. "Don't change the subject, either, because I'm not gonna let you get out of this."

"Fine." Thinking of all the comments he'd heard from time to time from Liesl, Ernie, his parents—even his sisters—he struggled with how to be honest without making himself sound completely without merit.

Well, there was the fact that his family appreciated that he worked so much. And the customers at the shop had complimented him for going above and beyond. "I'm a good worker, I suppose." Of course, as soon as he'd said the words, he wished he could take them back. Maybe he should've said friendly instead?

Jenny looked nonplused. "Pardon me?"

"I'm pretty certain that's how most people see me." He shrugged. "I guess that's not too good, is it?"

"It would be if it was the truth. I think you're more than a good worker at the Amish Market."

He was dying to ask her in what way did she see him as more. But again, it felt demanding and petty.

Looking around, he realized that the rest of their group was nowhere to be found. "Where did everyone go?"

"Hmm?" Jenny turned around, then looked just as surprised as he was. "I guess they got tired of waiting on us. Which way do you think everyone went?"

They walked down the main path, this time not gazing at the decorations as much as the various people scattered everywhere. Then, of course, they saw Flora. She strode up to them.

"There you two are!"

Stopping abruptly, Wesley rested a hand on Jenny's arm, almost as if he was attempting to shield her from a vicious hunter. "Were you looking for us?"

"Me, not so much. But the rest of your group wandered by a full ten minutes ago."

Jenny frowned. "I really didn't think we were that far behind."

"Don't worry. We'll catch up," he said to Jenny before turning back to Flora. "Any chance you know where they went?" The question was a rhetoric one, of course. Flora knew where everyone went at all times.

"I do." She pointed to a white wooden sign with the words TREE MAZE spelled out in bold red and green letters. "They went into the tree maze, of course."

The Pinery liked to brag that they had the biggest

Christmas tree maze in the Midwest. He wasn't sure if that was the truth or not. But it didn't matter. What did matter was that the maze was mighty big and tricky, and people had been known to get lost in it for hours. He hated it.

With a feeling of doom, he said, "Any idea which way they went, Flora?"

"Sorry, no. Soon after your group walked by I caught sight of the Schmidt triplets. They were getting into trouble as always."

"*Danke* anyway." After telling Flora their goodbyes, Wesley led Jenny over to the maze's entrance. An *Englischer* wearing a green felt suit and hat greeted them from his stool. "Ready to give the maze a try?"

"Actually, we're just looking for some friends of ours," Jenny said. "Did you happen to notice a group of five, including a cute little blond girl?"

"What do you think?"

Jenny blinked. "I don't know. That's why I'm asking you."

"Miss, I've been sitting here for the last five hours and must have given maze tickets to several hundred people already. I couldn't tell you if I've seen your friends or not."

"I guess he has a point," Jenny murmured.

"There's a good fifteen people lining up behind you lovebirds. Do you want to go in or not?"

Making a decision, Wesley nodded. "We do."

"Five dollars each."

"It's not included in the admission price?" Jenny asked.

"Obviously not."

"Fine. Here," Wesley said as he pulled out a ten-dollar bill.

Looking happier now that he was paid, the elf said, "Want a timer? You can get entered to see how long it takes you."

Wesley knew he wouldn't win any race that involved this maze. "Thanks, but no."

"Give me your hands, then." After they held out their hands and the elf stamped them, they walked to the entrance. Unfortunately, it was made up of three entrances.

"What's going on?" Jenny asked. "You're acting as if you're about to enter a cemetery or something."

"I just don't like navigating this maze." He wrinkled his nose. "I'm not good at it, and that drives me crazy."

Jenny smiled. "Let me guess. You're not a fan of corn mazes, either?"

"You guessed right." Feeling a little embarrassed, he added, "Don't worry, though. I'm sure I'll get us out of here all right. It just might not be very quickly."

Jenny raised her chin. "You're in luck then, because I happen to be great at mazes."

"Is that a fact?"

"Oh, *jah*." Jenny's eyes looked almost as bright as the twinkling lights surrounding them. "I went to the corn maze every October in Middlefield. I have a lot of practice."

Intrigued by this new bit of information, Wesley grinned. "I hope you are. One of us needs to be." He waved a hand. "All right, Jenny. You lead the way. Do you want to go left, straight, or right?"

"Left."

In they went. Almost immediately, everything seemed darker. There were no overhead lights—only the lights on the trees. They could hear the faint sounds of other couples talking and giggling.

"Oh!" Jenny said. "It is beautiful in here, isn't it?"

"It is."

"I like how there's snow on the ground and cute little wooden cutouts of animals among all the trees."

Jenny was definitely acting like the proverbial kid in the candy store. "It is pretty."

She nudged him with her shoulder as they squeezed through a narrow section. "Cheer up, Wesley. We'll get through the maze in no time, we'll find Liesl and the rest of our group on the other side, and everything will be *wonderful-gut* again."

"You're right. Everything will be just fine. Perfect."

Strange how he was starting to think that being stuck in the maze for a full hour didn't sound like a great hardship after all.

Chapter Twenty-Eight

As far as Jenny was concerned, the Pinery not only looked beautiful, but smelled good, too. As they wandered down the bark-covered paths, she detected the scent of fragrant pine, fresh snow, warm caramel...and Wesley.

If she was being honest, she was aware of Wesley most of all. She'd realized on about the second or third day of work that Wesley favored a rosemary-pine type of soap that was sold in the market. It blended with his natural scent and was distinctive and appealing.

Here in the dark Christmas tree maze, where they were forced to walk so closely together, Jenny was ashamed by how much she liked it, too.

Dwelling on her niece's boyfriend's soap wasn't a good thing. But then again, she reckoned that thinking about how she wasn't *really* all that good at mazes wasn't something she wanted to fixate on, either. Bragging was a sin. She imagined bragging in a lie was even worse.

But what could she have done? Wesley had looked

so blue and depressed. She'd needed some way to make him smile. Right at that moment, she probably would've said almost anything to keep him from leaving. Wesley had, indeed, looked relieved when she had told him that she was skilled at finding her way through giant mazes. Jenny said a small prayer, asking the Lord to maybe give her a helping hand in the maze department.

Five minutes passed. When they came to a giant snowman made out of Styrofoam, wearing an old-fashioned woman's coat, Wesley turned to her. "Which way?"

She had no idea. "Left again."

He frowned. "Really?" When she nodded, he shrugged. "Well, all right."

They turned left, practically ran into a pair of teenagers kissing under a large sprig of mistletoe, and hurried on by.

When they were a few more yards beyond the couple, Wesley chuckled. "I was tempted to tell them that the mistletoe wasn't real."

Jenny had been so intent on giving the teenagers privacy, she hadn't noticed. "You don't think it was?"

"Nope. It was plastic. One of my vendors tried to get me to sell it the first year I became the manager of the shop. I told him in no uncertain terms that such a thing wouldn't do."

"You might have told them about the dangers of fake mistletoe, but I have an idea that they would pay you no mind."

"You think?"

She giggled. "Oh, Wesley. No one kisses under

mistletoe because they think it's the real thing. They kiss because they're looking for an excuse to kiss."

"I reckon you're right." Something about his sidelong glance made her feel fluttery inside.

"I know I am." She might not be an expert on outdoor mazes, but she knew a thing or two about longing to kiss someone.

As they continued to meander down the paths, half listening to the Christmas carols that were playing overhead, Wesley said, "I just realized that I sound pretty unromantic."

"About?"

"Kissing under the mistletoe."

She couldn't resist teasing him. "Really, because you only think of mistletoe in terms of stock for your store?"

"Okay, I sounded very unromantic."

Unable to help herself, she stared at his lips. "Not everyone yearns for stolen kisses, I suppose." Of course, the second she said the words, she wished she could take them back. It was too bold. No, it was too close to what she was imagining.

"Did you?" he blurted.

"Me?" she squeaked. "Um, I don't know."

"You never gave your ex-boyfriend a kiss?"

She hadn't even been thinking about Jeremiah. "That sounds awfully personal, Wesley."

"Sorry. It's just that I just started wondering why I never tried to sneak a kiss with Liesl. Do you think she sees that as a problem?" His voice turned more intent. "Has she ever told you that?"

"We've never spoken about anything like that." And he should not be talking to her about that.

"What would you think?"

Oh, no way was she going to go down that path. "I think we should turn right now."

"Fine." He waved a hand for her to turn. "So, what do you think?"

She was feeling so flustered now. Flustered and confused. Because while she'd thought she had been in love with Jeremiah, she'd never wanted him to sneak kisses...or anything else.

"I think that a lot of courting couples have shared kisses and there's nothing wrong with that. I mean, if a couple is in love, one would like to show it in a number of ways. Kisses and um, other things are a way to show that love."

"I've never thought a few stolen kisses was terrible, either." He chuckled. "Once when my brother Paul was courting Jenna, I found them kissing in the barn. I was so shocked to see them, I yelped."

"Uh-oh. I'm sure he didn't appreciate that."

"Not at all. Paul told me to go away and keep my mouth shut."

Jenny chuckled. "Did you keep the secret?"

"I did, especially after he warned me that one day I'd be doing the same thing."

"Sneaking kisses in a barn?" she whispered. They were walking so slowly they were almost stopped.

"*Nee.* Kissing a girl I was courting because I couldn't help myself." His voice lowered, turned husky. "Because I didn't want to do anything but taste her lips. Feel her in my arms. Because I'd want to kiss her more than breathe."

Jenny stopped and stared at him. They were standing close to each other. So close that she wasn't even thinking about the rosemary-pine soap scent and had moved right on to noticing the flecks of gold intermingling with the blue in his eyes.

He was staring at her intently. "Jenny," he whispered.

She lifted her chin. Parted her lips. They were so close, all he would have to do to kiss her would be to lean down just a little bit. Wrap an arm around her shoulders. Pull her closer.

All it would take was just a few inches for their lips to touch.

"Jenny," he said again, this time hardly more than a whisper as one of his hands curved around her waist.

She wrapped her hand around his bicep. Her pulse skittered a little faster. There was no doubt about it, she wanted to be closer. Wanted to experience this first, lovely kiss.

"Bill, no!"

"I promise, Janine, this is the way!"

The exclamations, followed by a burst of laughter, tore them apart.

Jenny gasped as an older couple appeared around the corner.

The woman took one look at her and Wesley and pressed her palms to her cheeks. "Oops! I'm sorry we interrupted you two. We've been trying to get out of this maze for the last forty-five minutes."

As she and Wesley gaped, the couple kept talking.

"We've been walking in circles and circles," the man added. "It's getting ridiculous."

His wife grinned. "I'm afraid we've become slap-happy. Don't worry, we'll leave you alone as soon as we can figure out how to get out of here."

"You weren't interrupting anything," Wesley said. "We were just debating about which way to go as well."

Jenny nodded.

The older pair didn't look like they believed his words even for one minute. And who could blame them? Jenny was breathing so hard, one would think she'd just completed a race.

And as for Wesley? Even in the dim light it was easy to see that he was having a difficult time pretending they hadn't been doing anything other than debating whether to turn right or left.

Realizing she was still standing rather close to him, Jenny backed up another step. "This maze is rather challenging. Do you have any advice about which paths not to take?"

The woman shook her head. "I couldn't even tell you which paths were the right ones! Even all the Christmas trees have started to look the same."

"Other than to watch out for a pair of triplets who act like hooligans, not a bit," the man said. "Honestly, I'm so turned around, I can't remember where we've already been."

"We started telling each other that they probably send out search parties before they close for the night. At least we won't freeze."

Wesley smiled. "I've been thanking the Lord for good boots."

"Well, I suppose we had better continue on," the woman said with obvious reluctance. "I suppose I should be glad that I have my FitBit on. Do you Amish kids ever use them?"

"I'm afraid not," Jenny said. Smiling faintly, she added, "I know what they are, though. I hope you get lots of steps."

"I've already hit twelve thousand for the day. That's a silver lining."

"Indeed." Jenny smiled again as the couple wandered down another path. After their footsteps faded, she looked at Wesley. "I hope they are right and that search parties do come out to rescue the stragglers."

"It won't come to that. I won't let that happen," Wesley promised. "Let's go that way," he announced, just before he started off again.

Jenny followed, but she didn't understand how he could promise they would make it out, and she also didn't understand what he was thinking.

All she did know was that something between them had changed and there was no way they were ever going to be able to go back.

She also wasn't sure if she wanted them to.

Chapter Twenty-Nine

"WHAT ARE WE GONNA DO next?" Lilly asked Liesl.

Chuckling at the dot of caramel on Lilly's cheek, Liesl wiped it off as she replied. "I'm not sure. We have to see what the rest of our group wants to do. It will be something fun, though."

Lilly nodded as she took another tiny bite.

Thinking it was going to take Lilly several hours to finish that apple at the rate she was going, Liesl exchanged a smile with Roland.

They'd been out of the maze for thirty minutes and were currently sitting on a bench helping Lilly eat her caramel apple while they waited for Wesley and Jenny to arrive. Liesl's parents told her they were going to listen to a bell choir with some friends of theirs and they'd meet Liesl, Roland, Lilly, Jenny, and Wesley at closing time.

Liesl had promised to relay the message to the others. But so far Wesley and Jenny were nowhere to be found. She was getting a little worried about them.

"What do you think happened?" Roland asked. He'd been eyeing the exit of the maze for the last ten minutes. "Do you think we missed them when we walked over to the apple cart?"

"I don't think so. Wesley has told me that he's gotten lost in corn mazes before. Once for almost an hour." She chuckled. "There's a chance that might have happened."

Roland's eyebrows lifted. "Really? I think it only took us fifteen minutes."

He was right about that. He probably would've exited even quicker if she hadn't asked him to slow down. "You seem to have a gift for walking through mazes, Roland," she teased. "It was like you knew every turn and corner."

Looking embarrassed, he took the apple from his daughter's hands. "Have you had enough?"

She nodded. "It's a big apple."

He took a large bite and then grinned. "It's tasty, though."

Pointing to a group of a half-dozen rabbits in a pen just a few yards away, Lilly said, "Can I go look at the bunnies, *Daed*?"

"Do you promise to stay right there?" When Lilly nodded, he said, "Go look at the buns, then."

Once Lilly was watching the rabbits with a few other children, Liesl turned back to their topic. Roland was avoiding her question! Something was starting to feel fishy. "How is it that you seemed to know every turn and corner in this maze?"

"I didn't know every turn and corner."

"You knew most of them."

"Would you care for a bite of this apple?"

"*Danke*, but *nee*. Roland, what do you know that you aren't telling me?"

He averted his eyes. "Nothing of importance..."

"Roland, have you already been to the Pinery this year?"

"I have, but not in the way you're thinking. They needed volunteers to help design and build this year's maze. I happened to be one of the men they chose."

She crossed her arms over her chest. "And you didn't think to tell me?" She really had been amazed by how easily he'd navigated the tree-lined corridors. Suddenly remembering the money he'd paid, she moaned. "You paid ten dollars for us to walk through it, too."

"You had your heart set on the maze. I didn't want to disappoint you."

"I hate that you wasted your money, though. You should've told me to go without you."

Leaning closer, he placed two fingers under her chin. Carefully he pressed, forcing her eyes to meet his. "Don't. I wanted to go in the maze with you. I enjoyed it."

"Really?"

"Really. Besides, I wanted to make you smile." Lowering his voice, he murmured, "I know it's wrong, but making you happy is one of my most favorite things to do."

She thought she knew what he meant. But she was so afraid that she was misreading him. Misreading everything about what she thought they were. "Why do you think it's wrong to make me happy?"

He looked pained. "Don't make me say it, Liesl."

"Why?"

"Because if I say the words out loud, I won't be able to take them back."

He was older. He'd already been married. He had a child to care for and to see to. Perhaps all of that meant Roland was wiser and she should follow his lead. But she was tired of doing that. Tired of listening to what everyone else thought she should say and do.

So even though she wasn't even sure about what she wanted in her future, Liesl did know that she wanted someone who wanted her, too. There was something in Roland's eyes to make her believe that he did want her in his life. That was why she gathered her courage and spoke from her heart.

"Maybe I won't want you to take them back, Roland."

He blinked. Obviously, she'd taken him by surprise. "Do you know what you're saying?"

She nodded. "You may think I'm ditzy and childish but I'm not."

"I don't think you're either of those things."

"Then, if I can be brave enough to ask you to say the words...could you be brave enough to say them to me?"

His expression softened. "You, Liesl, never cease to amaze me. You look so perfectly angelic, but there is a steel inside of you that is a sight to behold. It never fails to take my breath away."

His words were so sweet and honest, she felt her insides warm. Would Roland actually tell her that he cared about her? If he told her that his intentions were true...that he wanted her in his life, and in Lilly's life...then she would tell Wesley that her heart and her future belonged someplace else. She'd tell that to Jenny. And to her parents.

And look any nosy gossips at church or in her circle in the eye and dare them to say a word.

"All right then. This isn't the place where I planned to do this, and it certainly ain't the way I planned to tell you it, either. But I suppose the Lord enjoys laughing at all our good intentions."

He took a deep breath and leaned closer. "Liesl, the truth of the matter is that I never did need any more jackets, pants, or shirts. Lilly never needed so many dresses. The only reason I ordered all of that was because I needed a reason to see more of you."

"You wouldn't have had to make up reasons." She chuckled, thinking of all the money he'd given her. "I would've come over just to see you and Lilly."

"I didn't know that. Maybe I was afraid to hope." He lowered his voice. "You see, Liesl, from the moment we first ran into each other at the market, I knew there was something about you that I wanted in my life." He shook his head. "*Nee*, that I needed in my life." He took a breath, and a new warmth entered his eyes. "Liesl, you see, the truth is that I—"

"We did it!"

Liesl turned to face the excited couple who'd just burst out of the exit. They were English, wearing jeans and sweaters with reindeer on them. The woman had silver hair cut in a bob and the man was almost bald.

But their exuberance was adorable.

As Lilly trotted back to join them, Roland stood up. "You got through the maze, then?"

"We did," the man said. "And it only took Janine and me one hour, fifteen minutes and five thousand steps."

"I'm going to go get a hot fudge sundae," Janine declared. "I've earned it."

Liesl giggled. "I reckon that is true. Enjoy the treat."

"Thanks." Just as she was about to turn away, the woman glanced at them a little more closely. "Oh, dear." Looking embarrassed, she said, "Bill, I think we did it again. I'm so sorry, you two."

Liesl had no idea what the woman was referring to. After glancing at Roland, who shrugged, she murmured, "What are you sorry about?"

"Interrupting you two lovebirds." Looking at her husband, Janine frowned. "First we practically pounced on a kissing couple in the middle of the maze, and now, here we did it again with the pair of you."

Bill chuckled. "We're like bulls in a china shop. Knocking into folks here and there and causing damage."

"Not hardly," Roland said. "We were not kissing."

Liesl thought Roland looked affronted that the Englishers would even think he'd be kissing her out in public. She felt her cheeks heat. Hopefully he would never know that she would have loved to have shared a sweet kiss with him.

"Of course you weren't doing anything of the sort," Janine said.

"Yes. This was my bad." Bill stepped closer to his wife. "Well, I better go get my girl that sundae. She won't forget about that!"

His wife winked. "I didn't walk fifteen thousand steps for nothing. Merry Christmas!"

Lilly giggled. "Merry Christmas!" she chirped before returning to the rabbits' pen.

Liesl waved a hand. "Merry Christmas to you both as well."

"*Jah.* Merry Christmas," Roland murmured.

As they wandered off, once again recounting their harrowing experience through the Pinery tree maze to a group of teenagers, Liesl chuckled. "I don't think they've ever met a stranger. They're quite a pair, aren't they?"

"*Jah.* They are, indeed." Roland scanned her face, then averted his eyes again.

"We're alone again. Do you want to finish what you were about to say?"

"Liesl, I think it would be best if we finished this conversation another time. I don't think I can take another sudden interruption like that."

She didn't want that at all, but what could she say? "All right. It would be awful if we got interrupted again. Besides, I'm sure Wesley and Jenny will be popping out any minute."

"If I hadn't been so frazzled, I would've asked if they'd seen them in the maze. Then we could've figured out where they were."

After hearing about how Janine and Bill had interrupted another couple in an embrace, Liesl smiled. "If they had seen them, it would've been quite the coincidence. We'll have to try to ask them if we think about it."

"Liesl, maybe me and Lilly could come over to see you at your house one day soon. Lilly could draw some pictures or maybe sit with your sister Emma for a spell...and then we could finally have that talk."

"I'd like that very much. I'm sure Emma wouldn't mind entertaining Lilly, either."

"*Danke.* Looks like we've got a plan then." His eyebrows raised. "And...it also looks like we have Jenny and Wesley back, too."

Liesl stood up. She tried to look excited, but inside she was really wishing that Jenny and Wesley had stayed lost for a little while longer.

Now that they were back, she realized everything was about to change all over again.

Chapter Thirty

ROLAND HAD LONG AGO LEARNED that cows, horses, and pigs didn't care what season, year, or day it was. All that mattered to them was that their morning meal came at six without fail. Usually, Roland thought their six o'clock feeding time was a fair trade. In return for the milk, the transportation, and the sustenance they provided, he got up before the sun, said his prayers, and then joined the animals in the barn. But that didn't mean that sometimes he really would've appreciated another hour of sleep.

This was one of those days.

It was snowing, the air was bitter cold, and he was still reeling from the previous night's events. He and Lilly had returned home close to nine. After making sure his dear daughter washed her face, brushed her teeth, and said her prayers, thirty minutes had passed.

After that, it might as well have been two in the afternoon, because he was wide-eyed. He stayed that way for hours. As the clock continued to tick, he paced, he fretted, he thought about things to say, and he thought about things he wished he had said hours previously.

Only after midnight did he fall into an ex*haus*ted slumber, fueled by memories of the ten precious minutes when he'd almost tossed aside everything that was responsible, right, and proper—and kissed Liesl in full view at the Pinery.

The noisy arrival of Bill and Janine had helped him come to his senses. But Roland wasn't sure if the couple's appearance had been a blessing or a curse. There was a part of him that regretted not knowing how Liesl felt in his arms...especially since he realized that she, too, at last had been eager to give into temptation.

His donkey Velma stuck her nose out when he opened the barn doors. As usual, her somewhat wonky expression and the hopeful look in her eyes made him smile. He'd rescued Velma after learning she'd been neglected and essentially abandoned at a nearby farm. From the moment he'd pressed his palm to her face and kissed her dry, chapped nose, he'd known they needed each other. Velma was affectionate and rather smart. She'd also gotten him through many a difficult day after his Tricia's death.

"Hiya, Velma. Good morning to ya."

Velma snorted and blew out a burst of air.

He laughed. "I hear ya. I wish the sun was out as well. The snow and gray skies might mean a white Christmas, but it also means a lot of trouble." Walking to the feed, he pulled out a good amount of hay and a cupful of oats. Then he pulled a treat from his pocket. "Brought you a carrot, too."

Velma leaned her head farther out of the stall and

nudged his shoulder with her nose."Patience is a virtue, donkey."

But still he handed the carrot to her and grinned when she took an eager chomp. When she finished her treat, he refreshed Velma's water and gave her some gentle rubs.

Then he then moved on to Pig, his three-year-old sow. Truth be told, she should've been a ham dinner by now. Unfortunately, Lilly was as fond of the animal as he was of Velma. The only difference, he supposed, was that Lilly had stayed true to his edict that pigs shouldn't be given names. Lilly had solved that problem by calling her Pig.

Pig had repaid the favor by following his daughter around the yard in the spring and summer—and conveniently ignoring the occasional hog that he brought home to butcher once a year.

He fed Pig and then chatted with Bitsy as he milked her. He gave his horse, Star, half an apple after cleaning out his stall. The hard work felt good, and visiting with the animals helped to settle his mind. By the time he finished he was almost certain he was more at peace with what had almost happened with Liesl.

Walking back to the house, he looked up at the heavy clouds dusting the earth with fluffy flakes. "Thank you, Lord, for giving me this morning—and for helping the animals provide me with some comfort. Your will be done."

When he entered the kitchen, Lilly was sitting at the table drinking a glass of orange juice. She'd gotten herself dressed—everything except for fastening the three buttons on the back of her dress. Her hair was in disarray down her back, and she looked sleepy and so very young. Before he knew it, she would be much older and likely not waiting on him to start her day. His heart clenched at the thought.

"Hiya, *Daed.*"

"*Gut matin* to you, too." Walking behind her, he smoothed the collar of her dress and then fastened the buttons. "What are you doing up so early this morning?"

She shrugged. "I kept thinking about all the Christmas trees and Liesl. I got too excited to sleep anymore."

He washed his hands and poured himself a cup of coffee. "Did you enjoy your night at the Pinery then?"

Her eyes sparkled. "Oh, *jah.* The trees were so pretty."

"I thought so, too."

"And Liesl is so pretty, too."

"Indeed she is. As are you, child. You're pretty, both inside and out."

Lilly nodded, swinging her legs as she continued to chatter like a magpie. "Liesl stayed with us a lot, too. Even when you said she might want to be with Wesley."

Why had he even put such thoughts into her head? "All of us are friends. It wouldn't be seemly for her to only keep company with one or two people at a time." As he prepared her hot chocolate, Roland mentally rolled his eyes. He sounded as pious and full of himself as an elderly spinster.

"Do you think Liesl is gonna come over today? If she does, I'm going to see if she wants to meet Pig. She hasn't met her yet."

He couldn't help but chuckle. "I don't know if Liesl is going to be too interested in meeting your sow."

"But do you think she'll come over anyway?"

"I don't think so."

"How come?"

"Because it is snowy outside, and she is a busy woman." And she was no doubt waiting for him to come calling.

"Liesl can't be that busy. Not if she had time to go to the Pinery last night. Ain't so?"

Trading her empty glass with her mug of hot chocolate, he murmured, "We don't know all Liesl does during her week."

"I know she sews a lot," Lilly countered. "She's made us lots of clothes."

"Indeed." Remembering his confession about ordering items just to see her again, Roland took a long sip of coffee.

"I might make Liesl two pictures for Christmas. I want to draw her one of the Pinery last night with the sparkly trees."

"She will like that, I am sure."

"What are you going to give Liesl?"

"For Christmas? Well, I don't rightly know. She and I might not exchange gifts."

He didn't have to give Liesl anything...except the truth about how he felt for her.

Lilly shot him an incredulous look that was so like Tricia's, it took his breath away. "*Daed*, you're supposed to give a Christmas gift to people you care about. That's a rule."

"Who says?"

"Aunt Esther."

Aunt Esther was Tricia's opinionated older sister. "Aunt Esther doesn't know everything."

"I know. But she does know more about Christmas presents than you, *Daed.* Aunt Esther makes everyone fruitcakes, you know."

"I haven't forgotten about those cakes." Every one of her fruitcakes was dense, filled with abnormally colored pieces of fruit, and smelled faintly of brandy. Tricia had buried one in the backyard the first year they were married, and when he'd discovered it in May it was still intact.

She smiled. "See? You have to give Liesl a gift."

"I'll think about it. Now, let's feed you some breakfast, then you may go see Pig."

She sighed. "All right."

"Eggs?"

"*Jah.*" When he paused, she got to her feet. "I'll help with breakfast."

"There's my daughter," he teased. "I knew she was lurking there somewhere."

"I was always here, *Daed.* It's just that sometimes I don't always want to be exactly the same. Sometimes I want to be different." She opened the middle drawer next to the oven and pulled out forks and napkins.

"Is that right?"

She nodded as she carefully placed the silverware on the table. "Uh-huh. I don't know why, but sometimes when I wake up, I think about things differently than I used to."

He had often felt the same way. There had been many days after Tricia's death when he'd wondered if he'd ever recover. Now, more often than not, he discovered the pain that he'd once worn like a shield between him and the rest of the world had gone missing.

"You, my dear girl, have gotten very wise," he said as he scrambled four eggs in a mixing bowl. "Get out the bread for toast."

She stood up a little straighter as she opened another drawer and pulled out a loaf of bread. "I'm getting older every day."

Roland tried hard not to chuckle because he didn't want to hurt her feelings, but it was hard. "Indeed, child. I fear that is the case for all of us. Now, do you want bacon, too?"

"*Jah.*" Lilly sat down with a sigh. "I sure wish Liesl wasn't so busy today."

He wished that, too. But unlike his little girl, he knew what he needed to do. It was time to stop worrying about the what-ifs and start moving forward. One step at a time.

He needed to call on Liesl very, very soon...and at last tell her what was in his heart.

Chapter Thirty-One

"It's crunch time, son," Wesley's father said over the phone. "You've got no time to take breaks, *jah*?"

Wesley shifted the cell phone to his other ear as he attempted to keep his temper in check. Only because he admired and respected his father so much did he refrain from pointing out the obvious fact that this was not his first Christmas season at Raber's Amish Market.

Or the fact that he'd been bearing the weight of the store's success on his shoulders while working ten- and twelve-hour days for weeks and had received very little in the form of gratitude or even acknowledgment.

Instead he bit his tongue and replied in the way his father expected. "I understand."

"Much of our year's success depends on these last few days, Wesley."

That wasn't exactly true. Historically, the bulk of their customers' shopping was done the first two weeks in December, not just days from Christmas.

But no matter how many times Wesley had told his father that, he'd pushed aside the facts like Wesley was a young know-it-all pup. If his father had been in good health and standing in front of him, he probably would've pointed out his opinion yet again.

But he wasn't.

When Wesley stayed silent, his father paused, then went down another conversational tangent. "So, how's your help doing? Is Ernie pulling his weight?"

"He is, *Daed.* He is a *gut* man, and I'm glad he's put in so many hours."

"*Gut.*" His father continued. "He was acting like his hip was bothering him in October, but I told him to just visit the chiropractor. Now, what about that woman you hired? What was her name again?"

"The woman's name is Jenny and she's doing very well. Everyone at the shop loves her. I'm going to hate to see her go." For so many reasons besides her work at the shop.

Thinking about her bright smile, easygoing sense of humor, and her innate sweetness, Wesley realized it didn't matter to him if Jenny never worked at the Amish Market again. He just wanted her to stay in his life.

"Really?" His father's voice held a new note of interest. "If she's that good of an employee, maybe you could hire her to continue on. I wouldn't mind taking more time off in January." Before Wesley could respond, his father corrected himself. "*Nee,* maybe in May, when it gets busy again. We don't want to ruin all our Christmas profits, you know. Unless you think she might work just ten hours a week? I reckon her help might be worth that much." He snapped his fingers. "I know! Tell her that you canna pay her as much because it's our slow season. I imagine a young girl will agree to that."

Wesley gritted his teeth, annoyed with the way his father still refused to change any of his mindsets with the times. "*Daed*, Jenny is worth a decent salary. She's worth being hired on full time for the same salary." Realizing his voice had risen, Wesley took a deep breath. "But that ain't the point. Jenny ain't going to be available in May because she's gonna be at her real job. She's a nanny for a rich Englisher family."

"You should still talk to her about it, son. Remember, it doesn't pay to be hesitant when it comes to good help. One canna read other people's minds for them. Don't forget that I've got a lot more experience than you have."

"I haven't forgotten."

Another wave of disappointment surged through him.

Wesley loved his father dearly. Nothing would make him happier than to learn that his heart was doing better and that the doctors were sure he was going to live for many, many years to come. But that didn't mean he wanted to be talked down for the rest of his life.

Feeling his jaw clench, Wesley stood up, paced the small confines of the office, and reminded himself that this wasn't the time to express his feelings.

"So, you'll speak to her?"

"*Nee*. I promise, there's no point in pressing Jenny. She's a woman who knows her mind and it is made up."

Hearing his words, his stomach sank. He wished

she wanted something different. He wished he could ask her to give up her exciting life with the Anderson family and stay with him in Walden.

"Wesley, you are misunderstanding me. I want you to ask her. I am not suggesting it."

Enough was enough. "*Daed*, I love you and I appreciate your advice and experience on many things. However, in this case, you are wrong."

And there it was. He'd flat-out told his father he was wrong.

Sitting alone in his office, he closed his eyes. Hadn't he just told himself mere seconds ago to hold his tongue? He'd just begun a battle that wasn't going to be easily ended.

"It sounds like you've become cheeky this December. Have you forgotten who you are talkin' to?"

Wesley could practically see the irritated expression on his father's face. He clenched his hands. Counted to three.

"I'm waiting for an answer, Wesley."

And...all of his good intentions flew out the window. He had to do it. Even though it might not be the right moment, it was absolutely time for him to stand up for himself.

"I think the question should be if you have forgotten who you're talking to, *Daed*. I'm twenty-six years old. I've been working at the market since I was twelve. I've been managing the books and finances for the last four years. I've also been running the store all on my own for the last month. I do not need you to tell me what to do from Paul's *haus* in Kentucky, and I really don't need you to talk down to me like this.

Like…like I'm nothing more than a foolish teen with a chip on his shoulder."

Unable to stop the words that seemed to be pouring out of his mouth like water, he added, "*Daed*, why can't you simply say that you know I'm doing my best? Why is it so hard for you to even acknowledge that?"

"Is that how you really feel?"

Wesley rolled his eyes. "I wouldn't have said it if I didn't mean it."

"It sounds like I better get back home quickly then."

"What are you going to do? Take over the last four days?" he asked sarcastically.

"Maybe I need to talk to this Jenny and see if she'd like to work for me, because I'm going to need a new assistant."

He was going to need a new assistant. Wesley could hardly believe his ears. The words hurt.

Standing back up, he said, "Have you just fired me, *Daed*?"

There was a significant pause.

"One of us has to be in charge, Wesley. If you don't want to follow my directions—and you're going to go and spend your evenings out at the Pinery instead of working on the store—it's obvious that the person in charge should not be you."

Tears filled his eyes. Oh, he knew that half of what his father was saying was bluster and pride. But it was awful to realize that his father could throw out that suggestion so easily without any regard for his feelings.

Wesley deserved more than that. Taking care to

speak both quietly and calmly, he said, "I'll finish out the season but then I'll find another job after Christmas Day. Goodbye, *Daed*."

His father didn't even have the grace to tell him goodbye. He simply hung up.

Hung up after breaking his heart.

Wesley could hear lots of chatter outside his closed office door. Undoubtedly either Ernie or Jenny could use a hand. But he was so stunned by what had just happened, he couldn't seem to make himself move. Had his disagreement with his father really turned into him leaving his family's store?

When the store's cell phone rang again, he glanced at the screen and sighed. "Hello?"

"Wesley, it's me," *Mamm* said. "What in the world happened with you and your father?"

He really didn't want to go there but he supposed he didn't have a choice. "I think you know, *Mamm*. When I told *Daed* that I didn't want to take his advice he got upset."

"He said you quit."

"I did, after he told me that he was going to replace me." Even though it was petty, he added, "*Nee*, he said he was going to look for another assistant."

Her voice turned an octave higher. "What? Oh, Wesley. I'm sorry. But you have to know that he didn't mean anything by that."

"*Daed* sounded serious."

"He's sick and bored. I imagine he just felt like taking out his frustrations on you." She made a little tsking noise. "You know what he's like. Just turn the other cheek."

Just like he always had. "*Mamm*, I love you. I love

Daed, too. I'm also sorry he's sick, and I've been praying for his recovery." He drew a deep breath. "But him saying things like that ain't okay with me. Not after all these years of practically living for this store." Thinking about how he'd given up so many other things in order to work, something shifted inside of him. "Maybe *Daed* is right, *Mamm.* Maybe some things do need to change around here."

"Oh, dear." Sounding more aggrieved, she added, "I promise I'll talk to him. I'm sure Paul will, too."

Wesley knew those talks wouldn't mean much. His father would cool off and then both he and his mother would pretend the whole conversation had never happened. "All I want is for him to feel better, *Mamm.* Anyway, I need to go. We've got a store full of people. I canna argue with you about this."

"Then don't argue. Just agree with me not to do anything until we get back and speak in person."

Though he was his father's son, and a part of him wanted nothing better than to win the argument, he also knew his mother had a good point. "Fine. I won't do anything...but I really do have to go."

"Wesley, please try to understand how hard this situation is for him."

"I do understand. But I fear both of you are refusing to understand my point of view. Now, I really do need to go, *Mamm.* Go relax, all right?"

"All right. I love you."

"I love you, too. Don't worry."

After he hung up, he deposited the cell phone back in a drawer and walked out his office door. Two girls were waiting in line to the use the restroom, a pair of English men were looking at the Care and Share baskets—the baskets made by people in the community who needed extra assistance—with looks of confusion, and there had to be almost forty customers in the store.

Behind the counter, Jenny was calmly ringing up customers like a pro. Just as if she'd been doing it as long as he had. As if she sensed that he was nearby, she lifted her head and smiled at him.

He stared at her. She was lovely and bright. She'd instantly made him feel better, just by looking his way. Feeling his frayed nerves settle, he smiled back.

"Wesley, just the person I was looking for," Saul Freeman said. "Come help me decide which desk and chair to buy for my daughter."

"For Anna?" Wesley asked as he followed him to the back of the store, where all the handmade furniture was on display.

"Oh, for sure," Saul said with a smile. "Now that her *kinner* are growing up, she wants to be a writer. She needs a desk to do that."

Wesley smiled at him. "That's wonderful that you are helping her make her dream come true."

"Everyone has dreams, *jah*?" he said as he wove his way through a row of dressers and dining tables. "I told *mei* Anna that dreams are all well and good, but sometimes one needs to also find a way to make the dreams a reality."

"That's good advice." Thinking that he needed to take that advice for himself, too, Wesley stopped in front of one of the newer desks in their inventory. It was whitewashed and delicate, with five total drawers. "What do you think of this one?"

Saul ran a hand over the top. "Well, now. It is a pretty thing."

"It's made of solid maple and then stained white. The craftsman went over the stain three times."

"Maple's a good wood. Hard, not soft like pine." He opened the drawers and smiled when they glided easily. "How much are you charging me for it?"

When Wesley told him, he whistled low. "That seems kind of high, Wes."

"You're right. It isn't cheap, but it's not cheap furniture, either."

He folded his arms over his chest. "What will you give me if I take this off your hands?"

Wesley mimicked the man's pose. "I'll give you the desk that you're paying for."

"What about the chair?" He pointed to the matching chair that sported an ivory cushion.

The chair was a perfect match and was as finely crafted as the desk. "The chair is four hundred, Saul."

"*Nee*, I want it for free."

Against his will, Wesley remembered watching his father have dozens of conversations over the years. When he was younger, he had been confused by why his *daed* had enjoyed the bargaining so much. Later, he'd been irritated that people tried to take advantage of him because it was Amish-run.

It was only later that he'd learned the delicate give-and-take that went into every negotiating conversation. For some customers, it was as necessary to complete the purchase as to touch and feel the piece of furniture.

Wesley put on his best regretful expression. "Well, now, here's the deal, Saul. Arnold Freeman made this set over in Winot. I know for a fact that he paid good money to the Kinsingers over in Charm for the maple. That's good, quality wood, you know."

Saul grunted. "Kinsingers are good folk."

"Indeed. Arnold only uses the best." Wesley sighed. "Then it took him another four months to make this desk from start to finish. And another two to make the chair. Frannie in Berlin found the velvety fabric and made the cushion. Arnold had to pay her for her services, too." He waved a hand. "So, the way I see it, when you are asking for the chair for free, you're really saying that you don't believe that either Arnold or Miss Frannie needs to get paid. You're saying that their hard work ain't worth much to you at all."

Saul's eyes widened. "That's not what I'm saying at all. I only meant to inform you that this chair isn't cheap and the desk is almost double what I intended to pay."

"Well, what I'm saying is that I don't feel good about jilting Arnold out of a fair price because you don't want to buy a beautiful, solid maple handmade desk and matching chair, so Anna can pursue her dream." He let that stew there a bit, then added, "Now, if you'd rather, you can head over to New Philly. The store there has some particleboard pieces made somewhere overseas."

"There's nothing wrong with buying something made overseas, Wesley."

"I didn't say there was. I hope Anna will enjoy pursuing her dreams on it, too."

Just as he turned away, Saul yelped, "Wesley, halt."

He turned back. "*Jah*?"

"I can't go getting my sweet girl just any old desk. She needs this one." He sighed. "And the matching chair. Any chance I can get them before Christmas?"

"Of course. I'll be glad to set that up and deliver it to you with a driver if needed. I feel Anna's gonna love it."

"You drive a hard bargain but a good one, Wesley. It's no wonder everyone thinks the world of you."

The compliment felt good—though it was now very obvious that not "everyone" did think the world of the way he ran the store. Pushing that pain aside, he held out his hand. "It's a pleasure doing business with ya, Saul. I appreciate you shopping at the market."

Chapter Thity-Two

WANTING TO SEE AND HEAR what happened next, Jenny kept close while Wesley finished up Saul's transaction. She rearranged and dusted a display of beeswax candles on the front table while she listened to Wesley keep up a chatter with the customer about his family, his daughter's writing, and his holiday plans.

For his part, Saul looked both shell-shocked and pleased to be getting so much personal attention. By the time he buttoned back up his coat, wished her a merry Christmas, and walked out the door, Jenny was sure that Saul believed he had gotten the finest desk in the area for his daughter.

She'd been quite impressed with the natural ease in which Wesley handled both the man and the sale. While she rang up several customers, Jenny noticed that Wesley looked pleased as punch for about two minutes, then walked over and helped a couple interested in some Amish cookbooks.

Later, when they were alone, she walked toward him with a wide smile.

"Uh-oh," he said. "What have I done to deserve that grin?"

"Oh, probably a couple of things...but I'm smiling because of the way you talked Saul into that desk. I didn't know you could be so sneaky."

Wesley looked slightly offended. "I'm not sneaky. All I did was point out the truth."

"I think you did a little bit more than that."

"All right, fine. I guess I did do some fast talking. But I really did only point out the truth the way I saw it. The craftsmen deserved a fair price."

"I'll be sure to watch myself next time I buy something here."

"Of course I'm not going to drive a hard bargain with ya." Looking concerned, he added, "Is there something you need? You need only to ask."

"There isn't anything I need at all. I was joking." When she smiled at him, he returned it, then looked away. Almost like he was embarrassed.

There was something going on with him. "Wesley, what is it?"

"I think we need to talk."

She looked around the store. Since it was near four o'clock, it had thinned out. None of the customers inside needed help. They seemed to be simply enjoying a few minutes of looking around the market. Jenny smiled. "I'm listening."

"I don't mean now, Jenny. We need to talk when we're alone. When, no one is rushing us."

"After everyone leaves, then?" The doors would close at five o'clock sharp.

Wesley froze, then finally nodded. "*Jah.* Today, as soon as all the customers leave."

"It's a date." To her dismay, he looked even more sick to his stomach. "I'm gonna go see if I can move any of these folks along. Do you mind staying at the counter?"

"Of course not." Moving to the spot behind the counter, she noticed a few scuff marks on the fine wood. She bent down, pulled out a can of furniture polish and a cloth and wiped it away. Then, still at loose ends, she continued polishing the wood.

As she rubbed, her mind spun. What did he want to talk about? Had she done something wrong at the shop? Jenny mentally reviewed the day's work, but nothing came to mind. Could it be about something more personal?

"Miss, is everything all right?"

Jenny blinked—and realized she'd been absently rubbing the same spot on the counter for several minutes. "Of course," she told the kindly faced Amish woman wearing glasses. "It's, ah, simply been a long day."

"I imagine so, though every day is starting to feel long. This morning I was tempted to put my feet up on the coffee table and do nothing but read."

Jenny shrugged. "Wesley has told me that it gets like this every year."

"I reckon he's right about that." A line formed between her brows. "Sometimes I wonder why even we Amish make Christmas into something more than celebrating the birth of Jesus."

Jenny knew what she meant. A lot of Amish liked to believe that they were above all the commercialism that the general population bought into during the holiday season. She supposed for the most part they were, but the temptation to do just a little more than the year before was strong. She'd felt it herself.

"I suppose we're all only human," she said at last. "It's nice to plan a special meal or purchase a small gift for people we love."

"And, perhaps, allow ourselves to be tired, too." The woman placed a wicker shopping basket on the counter. "I'll take these, dear, then I'll get out of your hair. Your workday is almost over, ain't so?"

Jenny smiled just as she realized Wesley was standing nearby and had no doubt heard the exchange. Worried that he might have thought she was complaining, she winced. No doubt her face was flaming.

Hurriedly, she rang up the woman's purchases. "Yes, but I don't mind being here." Feeling even more awkward, she added, "Did you hear that it might snow soon? I would love that."

"I've heard the same thing. My Gus says he can feel it coming in his bones," she added as she handed Jenny several bills. "A white Christmas will be a blessing, indeed."

"*Jah.*" After she counted out the change, she walked around the counter and handed the woman her bagged items. "Merry Christmas."

"And to you as well, dear."

Still feeling Wesley's eyes on her, Jenny hurried back around the counter, willing the last forty minutes of the day to fly by. As far as she was concerned, this talk Wesley was planning couldn't come soon enough. Anything would be better than waiting and wondering.

After the last customer came and went, the front door was locked, and he'd carefully put all the deli meats and cheeses back into the walk-in refrigerator, Wesley knew it was time to talk with Jenny. He couldn't put it off any longer.

For the last hour, he'd been practicing his speech, weighing the pros and cons of what to say as he'd helped the remaining customers. So far his mind had come up with very little that either made a lot of sense or conveyed what he was feeling. More than once, he'd closed his eyes and had asked the Lord why He hadn't given him a more glib tongue or even a more romantic nature.

Of course, God didn't give everyone all the gifts one wanted. Only what was needed. He'd given Wesley many other qualities that helped him be an asset to his parents and run the store well.

However, there were times when Wesley yearned for just a little bit more divine help. There had to have been a dozen other places to have one of the most important conversations of his life than the store. He really should've known better.

"Wesley, would you still like to have our talk?"

"*Jah.*" He looked around. The break room wasn't a good spot. Neither was anywhere near the counter. "Let's go sit down on some of the chairs that are for sale."

"All right." Looking confused, she took a chair and folded her hands neatly in her lap.

He sat down, saying a quick prayer as he did.

A second passed. Then two. He mentally tried out various ways to begin. Nothing sounded very good.

When Jenny began to worry her bottom lip, Wesley knew there was nothing to do but blurt out the truth and face the consequences later. "Jenny, there's no other way to say this. I don't want you to leave after Christmas."

"Pardon me?"

Instead of going back and trying to phrase things in a better, sweeter way, he continued on his script. "Do you have to work for the Anderson family? Is that where your heart is?"

She took her time replying. "I like the Andersons and I enjoy watching their *kinner.* I love Annabeth and Parker. I know they love me, too. But I couldn't say that being the Anderson's nanny is where my heart lies."

Her words sounded positive. "Then you'll consider staying here in Walden?"

"For how long?" Her dark-brown eyes looked so pretty when they were shining, "Wesley, do you know?"

"Hmm. Well, I suppose, however long you would like."

Jenny studied him for a second, seeming to be searching for something in his expression. Whether she found it or not, he didn't know. However, he could see there was something new in her eyes when she finally answered. "You've taken me by surprise. I thought I had done something wrong."

"What could you have done wrong? You've been a wonderful employee." Of course, the moment the words were out of his mouth, he ached to take them back. She was so much more than an employee to him. Truth be told, he didn't know if she had ever been just an employee to him.

When she met his eyes again, Wesley realized that he'd just messed up in a big way. Her expression looked carefully blank.

"Was that all you wanted, Wesley?"

"*Nee.*" Frustrated with himself, he stood up. "No, Jenny. I'm saying this all wrong. To be honest, this wasn't what I wanted to say at all." He studied her again. Saw that she was staring back at him. Waiting.

It was time. For better or worse, it was time to tell her his feelings. "I think I've fallen in love with you."

She inhaled sharply. "Wesley, are you serious?"

Still on his feet, too dismayed by his lack of timing to do anything but pace, he nodded. "I couldn't be more serious if I tried."

"What about Liesl? Do you love her, too?"

He paused, made himself face her, then blurted out, "I do love Liesl, but not like my love for you. It's different."

"I see."

"Do you?" He waved a hand in the air. "Because I don't see anything at all. Jenny, I didn't mean for this to happen. I thought Liesl and I were meant to be together. I really do love her, but the things I feel for her are more about friendship. Familial. Not in a romantic sense. Not in a husband-and-wife kind of way."

Jenny's eyebrows rose and she studied him for a long moment. And then, to his complete surprise, she started crying.

He rushed to her side. "I'm sorry. I really am the

worst at speaking from my heart. For some reason everything I mean to say gets convoluted and turned around by the time it gets to my mouth. This is the worst example by far."

When she covered her face with her hands, he added desperately, "Please. Just ignore what I said. Maybe in time we'll even be able to forget this ever happened."

"I don't think that's possible."

He wished he could kick himself. How could he mess one of the most important conversations of his life so badly? "Jenny, it's okay. I'm so sorry I upset you. I promise, I won't mention it again."

"I'm not upset about you loving me, Wesley."

"You're not?"

"Oh, *nee*." At last she met his eyes. "I love you, too. I love you back."

Pure relief filled him. He felt like standing up and cheering or waving a celebratory fist in the air. He settled for grinning like a fool. "That's wonderful. *Wunderbar*."

A small smile lit her face before it faded again. "You're right. It is...but how can we be happy? Our love is going to break Liesl's heart."

And just like that, reality came crashing down. "Which is going to break our hearts, too," he whispered as he stepped closer. He didn't know whether to grasp her hand, pull her into his arms—or put more distance between them.

Then it didn't matter, because Jenny got to her feet and headed to the break room like hounds were chasing her.

Wesley let her go and simply stared. How could

one of the sweetest moments of his life also turn out to be one of the most painful?

It surely didn't seem fair.

Chapter Thirty-Three

SURROUNDED BY TEN COMPLETED BRIDESMAID dresses, Liesl frowned at the two she still needed to pin and sew. When she'd gotten the contract, she'd accepted it immediately, and had even gone so far as to tell Mary Weaver that getting them done before Christmas would be no problem. She'd even believed that she would enjoy such a project.

She had not. She didn't like making the same exact dress over and over. Plus, there was something about having to make a dozen bridesmaid dresses for yet another wedding that wasn't hers. Every time she folded a finished dress, it felt like fate was laughing at her.

Like she was destined to always be a bridesmaid instead of the bride.

Still in no hurry to finish bridesmaid dress number eleven, Liesl got to her feet and looked out the window. Was Wesley ever going to propose? And if he did, what would she say?

"Daughter, it is one o'clock," her mother said from the sewing room's doorway.

She turned toward her. "I know."

"If you know, then you likely remember that you said you would help me with the widows' and orphans' baskets today." She raised one eyebrow and paused.

Her mother had a special way of staring at her and Emma when she was particularly put out with one of them. She and her sister were well used to it—but that didn't mean it was very easy to accept.

"I meant to help. I'm sorry I didn't get to it." She held up the piece of dark-green fabric she'd been fashioning into a dress for the last few hours. "I got sidetracked by this dress."

"That doesn't do me much good, though, does it?" *Mamm* replied. "Or the widows and orphans."

"No, it does not. I am sorry." Tired of both the green dresses and her mother's needling, she straightened some of the bright-orange fabric squares she'd been cutting out for Lilly's Christmas quilt. She couldn't help but smile at them. Some squares were plain orange, others had jaunty-looking lions, tigers, and giraffes on them. So cute.

Mamm folded her arms over her chest. "Who are you making that quilt for?"

"Lilly."

"You're making a quilt for Roland's daughter?"

"*Jah, Mamm.*" Hadn't she just said that?

"Liesl, practically every week you make that child something new. Don't you think that's too much?"

"*Nee.*" She fiddled with some of the squares again. "Besides, I don't make new things for Lilly every week."

"Does she really need so many clothes and such?"

Though she loved her mother dearly, when it came to Lilly and Roland, Liesl didn't really care what other people thought. All she cared about was her feelings for them. And Roland's and Lilly's feelings for her, she supposed.

But of course she couldn't say such things. "Everyone enjoys new dresses and quilts from time to time, *Mamm.*"

"Daughter, you know what I mean."

Annoyed, Liesl pushed her chair back from the table. "I'm sorry, but I don't. You didn't complain when I made you a new Christmas dress two weeks ago, and we both know that you don't need any new clothes."

Her mother frowned. "Liesl, I think you and I need to have a talk."

"All right, but I'm pretty busy right now. I still have lots of bridesmaid dresses to make." Talking with *Mamm* about Roland and Lilly was absolutely not something she wanted to do. Especially since she knew she was likely going to spout off a lot of things that her mother would find fault with.

"I don't think this can wait. I think we need to have it right now." She sat down in the metal card table chair that some of Liesl's clients used whenever they were getting measured. "Liesl, there is no other way to say it…You are treating Roland and his daughter with far too much familiarity."

Liesl sat down on her sewing chair. "I am not. He and I are friends."

"There is friendship, and then there is something more. You two are too close."

She didn't think so. "It doesn't really matter if you

think we are too close or not. I care for Roland and his daughter, *Mamm*. I can't pretend I don't."

"Liesl, do not play word games with me. You know what I am talking about. Your feelings for this man are becoming very obvious." She tapped her foot. "I also don't think you are thinking about Lilly."

"Of course I am! You are acting as if there is something wrong with having a close relationship with her. She's a sweet little girl who lost her mother. She needs me."

"She needs someone, but not you."

Liesl gasped. "Mother!"

"Liesl, don't you understand what I'm trying to tell you? Lilly is going to think that you want to be her mother."

"Maybe I do," Liesl retorted before she could stop herself.

Mamm inhaled sharply, just as Emma entered the room.

"I wondered where the two of you were." As if she felt the tension in the room, she frowned. "What is going on?"

"Nothing that concerns you," *Mamm* said. "Give your sister and me some privacy, if you please."

"*Nee*, she can stay," Liesl said.

"Liesl—"

"Mother, if you insist on sharing your opinions, then I might as well hear other people's viewpoints, too. Turning to her sister, she added, "You could probably give us some valuable insight, Emma."

"I can?" Looking delighted, Emma pulled up another folding chair. "What are you discussing?"

While their mother fumed, Liesl said, "*Mamm* says

I have an unnatural attachment to Roland's daughter, Lilly."

Emma raised her eyebrows. "I don't think that is the case at all," she said.

Liesl relaxed. Even though it was prideful, she lifted her chin a bit. "See, *Mamm*? You are just imagining things."

Their mother did look a bit disconcerted. "I'm surprised to hear you say that, Emma. We've talked about how hard it will be for Lilly to accept a new mother one day—and now it will be even harder if she begins to think of Liesl as a possibility."

"That's where you're wrong, *Mamm*," Emma said as she turned to look Liesl in the eye. "See, I don't think Liesl has an unnatural attachment to Roland, because it's obvious that she's in love with him. I'm fairly sure that Roland feels the same way about her."

Their mother leaned her head back. "This just keeps getting worse and worse," she muttered.

"I canna believe you said that!" Liesl chided.

"It's true, right? I mean, of course Lilly is going to want you to be her mother one day, because you and her father love each other."

"Out of the mouths of babes," her mother murmured.

Liesl felt like sticking out her tongue at Emma but displayed her maturity by doing nothing of the sort. Instead, she pulled herself up straight and said, extremely haughtily, "Wesley Raber is my boyfriend."

Her mother and sister exchanged glances but said nothing. Which, she supposed said everything that needed to be said.

Getting to her feet, she said, "I am twenty-two

years old. I have a job and I've helped around this house all my life. I think you both need to respect the fact that my, um, courting practices are my business."

"I respect it all right," Emma murmured. "I think it's *wonderful-gut* that you have not one but two men who are smitten with your charms. I just wish you'd give one of them up so the rest of the single women in the area can have a chance."

Mamm raised her eyebrows. "What do you have to say to that, child?"

Emma's words were hitting too close to home and her mother's concerns were making her uncomfortable. "I...I'm sorry but I just remembered I have an appointment," Liesl said.

"Are you sure you don't have bridesmaid dresses and a quilt to make?" *Mamm* asked in a sweet tone.

This was impossible. She hurried to the door. "Sorry, but I'm about to be late. I promise I'll work on the baskets for the widows and orphans this evening, Mother."

"No need for you to worry about them," Emma said as she walked to stand beside her. "I'll finish them today."

"*Danke.*"

Emma's expression softened. "I think it's time I started doing more around here. Don't you?"

Liesl hugged her. "I wouldn't change a thing about you," she whispered.

"I feel the same way, sister. Don't worry about *Mamm*," she whispered back. "I'll calm her down. Just keep your chin up. I have a feeling our Lord is watching out for you even now."

"I hope so. I need His help." When they parted, she said, "I think it's time I left. Like I said, I'll be home in a few hours."

"All right, but watch the weather now," *Mamm* warned. "Snow is on the way."

"*Danke, Mamm.*"

She couldn't get out of the house fast enough. She picked up her tote bag and purse. Then, after at last putting on a black bonnet over her *kapp*, her warmest black cloak, and sturdiest boots, she walked out. If the snow came, so be it. Walking in the snow would be a whole lot easier than discussing her feelings about Roland and Wesley with her mother.

Instead of wandering about alone, Liesl decided to visit Ruth. The elderly lady was a dear. Because she lived so far away, Liesl didn't have the time to visit her as often as she would have liked to do. The long walk there did her a world of good. It cleared her head and lifted her spirits.

Unfortunately, she stayed there too long. After sharing tea with Ruth, Liesl had cleaned her kitchen and made her a simple meal of soup and a sandwich. Then, when Ruth had asked, Liesl had helped her straighten up her bedroom and bathroom, too.

Three hours had passed by the time she'd left, and much had changed with the weather. Thick, wet snowflakes had begun to fall, covering everything almost immediately.

Thirty minutes after that, a buggy going in the opposite direction stopped for her. "You want a ride?" the man asked.

Liesl might have considered it if the man hadn't been a stranger. "*Nee.* I don't have too far to go." She'd waved, then kept walking.

The snow got heavier. Soon she was trudging through several inches of white powder.

Thirty minutes later it became even more difficult to see. It was the type of snowstorm that her grandfather would've called a *bad'un*, and he would've been right. The snowflakes were large and were coming down fast. So fast, they were sticking to her nose and eyelashes. With the way the sky was darkening, she was sure it wasn't going to stop anytime soon.

Which meant that her walk was going to be very long.

Never one to worry too much about things she couldn't control, Liesl started making to-do lists for the evening. Ten minutes later, she moved on to a mental pro-and-con list about Wesley and Roland.

It wasn't very fair. She knew that. After all, it wasn't like Wesley had ever proposed. And as for Roland, even though there was absolutely something between them—and it was so obvious that even Lilly was aware of it—he hadn't exactly offered her a long-term relationship, either.

But she was a woman who prided herself on making decisions and getting what she wanted. It wasn't her best trait, but it seemed to be so ingrained in her that she couldn't help it. She figured if the Lord had been disappointed in her, He would've made sure there were enough obstacles in her life to make her realize that she needed to change her ways.

After swiping the remains of a melted snowflake from her eye, she said, "Here is why Roland is the right man for me. He is patient with me and doesn't seem to get upset or bothered when I make suggestions. He also is a *wonderful-gut* father to Lilly. That is a mighty good quality."

Feeling pleased with herself, she continued. "Roland is also handsome." A lifetime of farming had given him muscles on top of muscles. Whenever she was near him, Liesl felt small and petite. One time she'd even told him that. He'd responded by chuckling. *If I make you feel small and petite, it's because you are, Liesl. You are small, petite, and pretty. There's no doubt about that.*

"I know I'm not supposed to care about looks, Lord, but I think it does matter a little bit. After all, I would want to think the man I plan to be married to for a lifetime is attractive."

She sighed, just thinking about how much she liked his pale-blue eyes and dark hair with the flecks of gray in it.

Roland also has his own home, and he keeps it tidy and clean. I wouldn't have to spend all my days picking up after him. I like his *haus*, too."

Feeling guilty, she blurted out, "I'm sure Wesley could have his own home if he wasn't so busy with the store."

Wesley.

She sighed. "Wesley is a *gut* man, too, Lord. I am aware of that. He works really hard in his store and cares about its success."

Liesl nodded. "He is also good-looking, with his blond hair and blue eyes. And while he isn't as tall or as muscular as Roland, it does seem he is in good shape." Realizing that she hadn't thought a whole lot about his muscles in quite a while, she sputtered, "I mean, a lot of other girls say that Wesley is in good shape."

But...shouldn't she have been thinking about his looks more often? Shouldn't she be wanting to spend all her time with Wesley? And shouldn't he be wanting to spend all his extra time with her?

Realizing that her face was damp, she drew to a stop and pulled off one of her gloves. Boy, the snow must have really started to come down faster than she'd realized. She couldn't think of another reason why her face could be so wet. With the side of one of her hands, she wiped her eyes and cheeks, then pulled her glove back on.

She was getting cold. Gazing down the road, she looked for a familiar landmark. When she spied the outline of the Hochstetlers' new barn with its shiny green metal roof, she figured she had almost another hour of walking to get home. Her heart sank. She wasn't just cold, but her feet were hurting and she was tired, too.

"Why are you so stubborn, Liesl?" she asked herself. "If you hadn't been so sure that your mother was wrong, you could've stayed home and finished those stupid bridesmaid dresses. Instead, you left in a huff and now are likely going to catch a cold right before Christmas!"

It would serve her right if she had a bright-red nose on Christmas Day.

Determined to stop worrying and make progress, she increased her pace. Ignored the way the muscles in her thighs screamed in protest. "You are a young woman in good shape. Just walk, Liesl. Think about Wesley."

Ah, yes. She'd been thinking all about the things she enjoyed about her longtime beau.

"Everyone expects us to get married," she said. "He's been my beau since we were teenagers. All this time, we've been waiting to get old enough to marry and start our family. It's what I've planned on, for sure and for certain."

Unfortunately, as that thought settled in, all she felt was dismay. A lifetime with Wesley would be more of the same. Always coming second and third to both the store and his family's needs. Christmas season wouldn't be a time of joy and anticipation but work and ex*haus*tion. Why, last year when she and Emma had visited his family late in the afternoon on Christmas Day, everyone was half asleep.

Wesley had been so tired he'd hardly noticed that she'd spent weeks making him a new comforter and pillow shams for his bed. He'd just set them in a pile and yawned. She'd been disappointed in his response. Worse, she'd been disappointed in herself, since she had continually hoped that things would change. That things would be different than they'd been the year before.

Or the year before that.

"*Gott*, I know You are watching over me right now and I'm grateful that You are keeping me safe. But could You also give me some sort of sign about what I should do? I really need Your help, you see."

Of course she didn't hear His voice, but she was so

tired of walking through the snow that she pretended she was listening for it.

Then, in the distance, she heard the faint sound of sleigh bells. She shook her head slightly. Was she now so addled that her ears were ringing?

Minutes later the bells were loud enough for her to turn around.

There, racing toward her, was a black gelding pulling a black sleigh. It was gliding through the snow in a way that only perfectly run sleighs could.

Just as she moved to the side of the road, a familiar voice called out. "Liesl! Liesl, halt!"

"*Jah*?" she called out, staring hard into the distance.

"Liesl, it's me. Roland!"

Roland was approaching in his sleigh. Just minutes after she'd asked the Lord for a sign, He had given her Roland.

"I'm so glad you're here." Of course, he couldn't hear her, but she smiled and waved so he would know how happy she was.

After his horse stopped and Roland set the brake, he climbed out. "Liesl, look at your boots! They're fairly covered in snow. So is your cloak, too. I'm so glad I found you. I was so worried."

There were a hundred questions in her head. How had he known she was out walking? Where was Lilly? But all she could seem to do was stare at him.

And start crying.

His relieved expression turned to worry. "Liesl? Liesl, what is the matter?" He reached out. Ran his hands up and down her arms. "Are you hurt?"

Still unable to talk, she shook her head. And then

she did what she'd secretly been wanting to do for years. She launched herself into his arms.

Immediately, he pulled her into a warm embrace. "Shh, it's okay. I've got ya."

"I know you do," she said at last. "I know and I'm so grateful."

Chapter Thirty-Four

ROLAND WAS WORRIED ABOUT LIESL. She'd been crying in his arms for five minutes, clinging to him the entire time. Every time he had attempted to move away, she'd gripped him harder. Roland had felt so concerned, he gave up trying to coax Liesl to get into the sleigh. Instead, he opened his thick wool coat and pulled the ends around her. She was so slight, much of the covering wrapped around her body. It was a futile effort to shield her from the cold and snow but it seemed to help a bit. Little by little, the worst of her tears seemed to abate.

It was only when Taco whickered and stomped his hoof that Liesl seemed to realize what had been happening.

She pulled away. "I'm sorry." Swiping a hand on her face, she frowned. "I got you all wet!" She ran a hand down his chest, ineffectually trying to dry the tears with her wool glove. "I really am sorry, Roland."

"No need for apologies. I'm not sorry at all."

"No?"

"No. I've had quite a day. I fear I needed a hug as well."

She hiccupped. "Is a hug what I was doing?" She chuckled softly. "I feel like I was doing nothing but clinging to you like a vine."

"Like I said, it was no trouble. I was eager to pull you into my arms as well. Now, however, it is time that we got you in the sleigh. At least for Taco's sake, *jah*?"

She blinked at his horse, who was staring at them both with a disgruntled expression. "I'm sorry, Taco. I'm sure you are chilly."

Taco pawed at the dirt and blew out a snort.

Liesl laughed.

Roland decided his old horse would get an extra bit of oats for that. Wrapping one hand around her waist and the other around her elbow, he helped her onto the sleigh's bench and wrapped her in one of the quilts he'd hastily pulled out of the linen closet when he'd learned that Liesl was likely walking alone in the storm.

"*Danke*, Roland."

"Of course." He got on the other side and situated the second quilt around his lap. After releasing the brake, he snapped the reins. Taco didn't need any more encouragement and pulled forward. "*Gut gaul*, good horse," he murmured. "Let's head on home now. We've got to get our Liesl home."

One of her eyebrows lifted. "*Our* Liesl?"

He'd had a slip of a tongue. Stomach sinking, he murmured, "Sorry. It's just an expression. I didn't mean anything by it."

"You didn't?"

Confused, he glanced her way. Tried not to stare into her green eyes. "Why am I getting the feeling that you're funning me?"

"I'm not." She paused. "Maybe it's more of a feeling that I would like you to mean something by it." When he remained silent, her voice turned more sure of itself. "Did you, Roland?" she pressed. "Do you ever think of me as 'your Liesl'? Because if you did, I would like to know."

She would like to know.

Did she, really? What if she was serious? What if he really did tell her the truth? What if he told her that everything from the first moment she walked on his front steps to the moment she stepped out the door were his favorite parts of the week?

What if he admitted that there had never been a day when he hadn't hated to see her go? What if he revealed that he often counted the days until he saw her again?

What would she do then?

As Taco *clip-clopped* along and Liesl snuggled under the quilt next to him, Roland played the guessing game with himself some more. What if he told her that Lilly felt the same way? What would she say then? Would she say she felt the same things…or would she reveal that she never thought of him as anything but a friend? Or worse, just another job?

He racked his mind, turning over each reply, weighing and balancing it between hoping that she'd be pleased and fearing that he would embarrass both himself and her.

It was too much to contemplate. "Liesl, I don't think now is the best time to discuss that."

"Why not? We're alone." Her eyes widened. "Where is Lilly, by the way?"

"I was over at *mei* friend Robert's *haus* when he came home. As soon he told me that a young woman with golden hair and green eyes was out walking by herself, I dropped her off at my sister's and hurried to try to find you."

"Truly?" She smiled at him softly. "I didn't know you had a sister."

"I, too, have a family, Liesl." He kept his voice light so it didn't seem he was chiding her.

She rolled her eyes. "Obviously. What is this sister's name?"

"June."

"That's a pretty name. I always fancied being named a month of the year."

He chuckled. "The things you say. For the record, I think the name Liesl suits you."

"What is June like? Is Lilly close to her?"

Once again, it felt like he was walking on eggshells. He didn't like to talk about June because most things he had to say about her felt harsh and maybe even unsympathetic. So, like the coward he was becoming, he prevaricated once again. "Have you ever heard Lilly talk about her aunt June?"

"I haven't."

The wind blew a gust of snow across the road. Though the plexiglass windshield and the doors kept out most of the elements, a few brave flakes found their way onto their skin. "I think you have your answer there," he said lightly. "And keep the quilt over you. It's chilly out and your cloak and legs are likely soaked."

"I'm fine, Roland. Don't treat me like a child. I promise, I am not."

"I don't think of you as a child."

"What a roller coaster of a conversation we're having!" she declared with a chuckle. "Roland, I'm cold, I think I'm soaked from head to toe from melting snow, and I'm recovering from crying like a babe. But here I am, laughing. Only you could make me feel so much better."

"You make more of my actions than is needed."

"I don't think so. I think maybe I haven't made enough of them."

Once again, her words floated over him like a welcome warm breeze. It was obvious that he could either continue to worry and fret and hesitate...or be brave like her and at last tell her what was in his heart. It was likely Taco would deliver them to her house within ten minutes.

Like Christmas, that point was coming soon whether he was ready for it or not.

"I love you," he blurted out.

"What did you just say?"

It was on the tip of his tongue to say that he had misspoke. But he couldn't. Some things were simply too important. He knew now that no matter what happened, she needed to know how he felt. No, he needed to say what was in his heart, at long last.

"Liesl, I know you are younger and could have any man you choose, whether it is Wesley Raber or some other man in the county. I know that I have been married, and life with me comes with a little girl. I know that life with a farmer isn't easy. My livelihood depends on the land, and the land is a fickle boss. There are many days when I am away from the *haus* from sunrise until sunset."

"Roland, I love Lilly."

That sounded promising. "Lilly loves you, too. But I'm wise enough to know that a little four-year-old girl is much easier to love than a farmer like me."

"Roland, I also happen to realize that you are older, have been married before, and are a farmer." Her eyes warmed. "I might be younger than you, but I'm not oblivious."

He swallowed. What was she saying? "Are you saying you aren't upset by my feelings?"

"Not at all." Smiling, she said, "Roland, I've always thought that I was pretty good at sharing my feelings with other people, but I seem to be as tongue-tied as you."

It felt as if a pile of rocks had suddenly just lodged themselves on top of his chest. He was having trouble breathing. "Liesl, what are you trying to tell me?"

"That I feel the same as you. I love you, too, Roland."

He blinked. Her answer was more beautiful, no, more *everything* than he'd ever expected."That's *gut*," he said at last.

When she smiled, he reached for her hand. His hands were worn and rough, hers were covered in soft, rather useless white fuzzy gloves. But having her hand in his?

It was perfect.

Taco increased his pace as he pulled the sled to the top of the hill. At the crest, her house came into sight. Taco snorted and increased his pace as they slid down.

"We're almost there," he murmured. "We're almost at your home."

Looking down at their linked fingers, Liesl sighed. "I wish that wasn't the case."

Roland squeezed her hand gently. He couldn't agree more.

Chapter Thirty-Five

Christmas Eve

It was a Fisher family tradition to have Cincinnati chili on Christmas Eve. Supposedly, the origin came from Liesl's great-grandfather, who'd spent a few weeks one summer with a friend in Cincinnati. The story went that this great-grandfather had become such a fan of the chili served on spaghetti noodles that he'd asked for it one Christmas Eve when he'd been sick with pneumonia. Liesl's great-grandmother, caring woman that she was, had frantically gone to an Englisher's house and called this friend. He, in turn, had driven to Walden through a terrible snowstorm, and together they'd made the creation. Great-grandfather Ezra had taken two bites and immediately felt better.

And so the tradition stuck.

Jenny's branch of the family had always thought the entire story was a bit farfetched and outlandish. She, for one, didn't think there were any healing properties to the stuff. And since they always had turkey on Christmas Eve, she found the idea of eating bowls of spaghetti, chili, onions, and shredded cheddar cheese off-putting. Jenny didn't even particularly enjoy the unusual chili, which was flavored with a bit of both chocolate powder and cinnamon.

However, since she was a Fisher guest, she pretended to look forward to the meal.

It was what was going to happen afterward that she was dreading.

After several lengthy conversations weighing the pros and cons of waiting to talk to Liesl about Jenny and his newfound love, Wesley had decided to break the news to her after supper. Jenny had said that December twenty-sixth would be soon enough.

Wesley had disagreed. "No good will come out of putting something like this off, Jen," he'd said quietly. "It's not like I'm going to pretend to be eager to marry Liesl when it's you who has my heart."

Wesley had elected to share the bombshell about telling Liesl during a lull in the shop's final open day. Jenny had been so shocked—after all, they'd just shared that they loved each other—she'd merely gaped at him.

He'd taken her silence to mean that she agreed with him completely.

Now, as she worked in the kitchen with Emma and Laura May, Jenny was a nervous wreck. She'd been having trouble following their conversations. So much so, Emma had even asked if she was getting sick.

Jenny had been so uncomfortable, she'd almost said she was worried that she was coming down with something.

But of course she hadn't done that.

At least she and Emma were working on the actual Christmas supper instead of Christmas Eve's chili. The supper was going to be *wonderful-gut*, too, with turkey, stuffing, all the sides, and both a chocolate peppermint cake and a pecan pie.

"I'm glad you're making the stuffing, Jenny," she said. "I hate chopping all the vegetables for it."

"I feel the same way about you making the cake. I'm not a very good baker."

"Liesl is the best baker in our family." Emma frowned. "I'm not sure why she has to make all those fancy gingerbread men and women for tonight's supper. It seems like a waste of time, don't you think?" Raising her voice, she called out to Liesl, who was working in the second kitchen, known to some as a butler's pantry, "Liesl, why are ya making gingerbread men, anyway?"

"I'm making them for Lilly, Emma!" Liesl replied. "I told you she and Roland are coming tonight."

Emma wrinkled her brow. "Why are they, anyway? You never said."

"Because I invited them!" Liesl called out. "And you know why. Roland saved me when I was out walking."

"You shouldn't have been out walking in the first place!"

"You are going to give me a headache, girls," their mother chided. "Stop yelling at each other from across two rooms."

"We're not yelling, *Mamm*," Emma called out. "We're conversing between two rooms."

"While working hard," Liesl added in a loud voice.

"Oh, brother," their mother muttered, loudly enough for Jenny to hear from her corner of the room.

Jenny chuckled. Laura May might not agree, but she and her girls were as alike as a trio of noisy goats. "You Fisher women are a handful, for sure and for certain."

Emma grinned. "I reckon that the Kurtz branch has a few foibles or two."

"Indeed. All eight of us *kinner* can be a handful at times," Jenny agreed as she rinsed off two more stalks of celery and set to chopping. "We're full of flaws, without a doubt."

"At least you don't eat chili and noodles on Christmas Eve," Emma whispered.

"You don't like it, either?" *Oops!* Had she actually said that out loud?

Emma shook her head. "The only person in the family who really likes it is Liesl. Even my father stares at the bowl like it's a stomachache waiting to happen."

Still talking under her breath, Jenny said, "Why do you all have it, then?"

"Tradition. We like to stick to things."

"I guess there's something to be said for that."

Emma lowered her voice. "Don't tell anyone, but I think there's something to be said for throwing out the old and bringing in the new, too."

Jenny gulped. That saying felt a little bit too close to home.

Four hours later, when they were all sitting at the Fishers' beautiful table with steaming bowls of chili in front of them, Jenny had to admit that the Fisher family certainly were fans of tradition.

"Let us bow our heads and give thanks," Armor said quietly.

Together, the eight of them did just that. Then, after everyone was finished, they passed bowls of shredded cheese and onions around the table and dug into the meal.

It was obvious that the dish was brand-new for Roland and his daughter. Little Lilly's eyes grew big at the sight of it, Roland simply appeared skeptical. However, when Lilly proclaimed that it was *mighty gut* after one experimental bite, some of the tension in the room dissipated.

Jenny was glad about that. From the time Wesley had walked through the door, she'd been doing her best not to meet his gaze. She was afraid if she dared to look his way too much her cheeks would heat and everyone in the room would be able to read her mind and know that she was keeping a secret.

Whenever she did seem to catch Wesley's eyes, it was obvious that he, too, was trying not to do anything that might seem out of the norm. He was polite to her, cordial to Roland and Lilly, and teased Emma about the Sunday singings she'd been recently attending.

Jenny could have been mistaken, but Liesl and Roland also seemed rather quiet. Roland talked to her father about farming while Liesl didn't seem inclined to chat with anyone besides little Lilly.

After the long supper was over, Laura May shooed them all out of the kitchen. "Armor and I will do the dishes tonight. Go sit down with your guests. I'll bring in dessert and coffee in an hour or so."

"*Danke, Mamm,*" Liesl said. When her parents were out of the room, she asked Emma quietly, "Would you please read a story to Lilly for a few minutes?"

"Sure, but is everything okay?" Emma asked.

"I hope so," Liesl said. "*Danke*, Em."

Emma cajoled Lilly to go up to her room to read a Christmas story, leaving only the four of them in the room. Jenny joined Liesl on the sofa while the two men each sat on a chair.

After a few seconds passed, Wesley rested his elbows on his k*nee*s and spoke. "For the last two days I've been praying about how to say something, but I fear even the Lord knows that there isn't any good way to do this."

"Do what?" Roland asked.

"To say that as much as I care about Liesl, I realize that I don't love her. Not in the romantic sense at least."

Liesl gaped. "You truly don't love me, Wesley?"

Wesley shook his head. "I love you as a friend, but not as a beau. I…I feel terrible about it."

"I…I see."

Jenny could feel tears gathering in her eyes. "I'm sorry, Liesl."

Liesl turned to Jenny. "For what?"

"What she means is that I'm sorry," Wesley said. "You see, what I'm trying to say—and once again doing a poor job of explaining myself—is that I've fallen in love with Jenny and I aim to marry her."

Jenny closed her eyes briefly. She loved Wesley,

too. But he sure did not have a way with words. Not at all.

Liesl's hands were clenched together so tightly, her knuckles were white. "Jenny, is this true?"

"I'm afraid so," she replied. "For the last couple of years, I've been rather depressed. I couldn't figure out why the Lord had decided that Jeremiah and I didn't suit. More importantly, I didn't understand why I was more upset about being unmarried than upset about breaking up with him." Meeting Wesley's eyes, she added, "Now, of course, I realize that He was waiting for Wesley and me to have the right time."

"I see," said Liesl.

This response from the normally chatty and vibrant Liesl felt like a slap to the face.

But maybe she deserved it?

"Liesl, I don't know what to say. Maybe there isn't anything to say except that I'm sorry. I hope one day you'll forgive me."

"This isn't Jenny's fault. It's all mine," Wesley added. "I'm sorry for the timing but I didn't want to wait until December twenty-sixth. That didn't seem right, either."

Liesl exchanged glances with Roland and then said, "I agree."

Just as Jenny breathed a sigh of relief, Roland chuckled.

Wesley looked horrified. "Roland, I'm sorry, but this really isn't the time for jokes."

"Wesley and Jenny, if you two are feeling uncomfortable, I'm afraid it's no less than how I am feeling at the moment." He rubbed his palms on his legs. "You see, I had wanted to discuss some things tonight as well." He took a deep breath. "While the two of you were falling in love in spite of your best intentions, I was doing that, too."

"As was I," Liesl added with a smile. "Wesley, Jenny, you two weren't the only ones to fall in love despite their best intentions. You see, Roland and I are in love, too."

Jenny felt as if someone could knock her over with a feather. "Liesl, are you serious?"

"Oh, yes. I wouldn't joke about love."

Wesley frowned at Roland. "You love Liesl."

"I love her with all my heart."

"Liesl, maybe you should think about things for a spell," Jenny said. "I mean, you don't have to say such things just to make us feel better."

Without hardly missing a beat, her niece declared, "I promise, Jenny. I love you very much, but I wouldn't fall in love with Roland just to ease your guilt."

Stunned silence followed her remark.

And then everyone burst into laughter.

It felt so good to laugh, too. For the last twenty-four hours, Jenny had worried and fretted so much, it seemed like the stress just kept piling on itself. Now that everything was out in the open, and Liesl and Roland's secrets were out as well, Jenny felt better than she had in days. Glancing at Wesley, she saw he was wearing the same type of bemused expression that she was: bemusement mixed with relief. Liesl and Roland had the same expressions.

"What do we all do now?" Jenny asked. "Liesl, should we tell your parents?"

Liesl shook her head. "I'd rather not. There is someone else we need to talk to first. Right, Roland?"

Oh, Jenny thought. *How sweet!*

He nodded as he stood up. "Let's do it now, though, Liesl. I can assure you that she's gonna be very happy."

They walked together to Emma's room, where she'd taken Lilly to read a book.

When they were alone, Wesley joined Jenny on the sofa. "How long do you think we have solemnity?"

Jenny laughed and lifted a shoulder. "I couldn't guess. They said they'd come back in an hour, but if they know that Liesl and Roland have gone upstairs together they might pop in sooner."

"I better do this quickly, then," Wesley said.

He leaned in close and kissed her, so very sweetly, on the lips. When he lifted his head, he gazed into her eyes. "Are you all right now?"

His kiss had been lovely. Lovely enough that she was eager for more. But she also wanted something else. A memory to cling to years from now. A memory to one day share with their children and grandchildren.

So, feeling a little bit like she had stars in her eyes, she shook her head.

Immediately concern replaced his pleased expression. "*Nee*?"

"We just announced our engagement, but I never got the proper proposal. I'd like it, please." She held her breath. Was she being presumptuous?

But then she spied something in his eyes. Tenderness. As if he loved that she needed this moment to be pulled from her dreams.

All humor faded from his expression. In its place was a new solemnity. Wesley knelt on one knee on the floor. "I love you, Jenny. Though I canna say life with me is always going to be easy, I can promise that I'll do my best to make it a happy one. I know you'll make me happy."

Near tears, she clasped his hand. "I know you will. You already have made me that way." That was the truth, too.

He got to his feet and then pulled her to hers. "I think I kissed you properly."

Jenny curved her hands around his neck, leaned close and kissed him with all the love and passion that had been bottled up inside her for years.

The door opened. And a gasp was heard.

"What is going on?" Laura May asked. "Wait. Wesley! Are you kissing Jenny?"

Wesley looked into Jenny's eyes and smiled. "I am. It's all right, though. You see, she's just consented to be my wife."

Abruptly, the door closed. Through the wood, Jenny and Wesley could hear Laura May say to Armor, "I think it's time we found Liesl. We should do it as soon as possible, too. There are strange things going on around here."

As their footsteps faded, Jenny chuckled. "I don't know what to do now. Should I go attempt to explain things better?"

"*Nee.* The only thing you should do is kiss me again."

Since Jenny couldn't argue with that, she stepped right back into his arms.

Chapter Thirty-Six

She was his. Beautiful, vibrant, happy, loving Liesl Fisher was going to be his wife. Roland could hardly believe it was true.

When Jenny and Wesley had said they wanted to speak with them, Roland had been worried that Wesley wanted to call him out about him spending so much time with his girl. Of course, he'd been more than ready to defend her honor—and to announce he was sure that he was the one for Liesl, not Wesley. He still was amazed that no one seemed upset about the outcomes.

God was so good. Only His will could have brought them all together without creating further tears or arguments.

Now he just had two more conversations to get through. The first was to Lilly, of course. He had no worries about how she would react.

The second might be a different story, however. Armor and Laura May Fisher might have a far different opinion about Liesl's new beau. Furthermore, they could protest so much that Liesl might even change her mind about spending the rest of her life with him and Lilly.

They could hear Emma reading a story out loud to Lilly in her room. He paused outside Emma's door, enjoying his little girl's giggles as Emma used different voices.

"Emma has a gift for storytelling," Liesl said. "She always has enjoyed reading out loud and using different voices for all the characters." She paused, tilting her head to one side. "Are you worried about interrupting them...or are you worried about how Lilly might react to our news?"

"I'm not worried about either. I was only thinking about my good fortune. Your love makes me happy, Liesl."

"*Gut.* I would hate it if my love made you sad," she teased.

"Far from it." He leaned close. "I am already looking forward to the day when I can pull you into my arms every time you say you love me."

She chuckled. "If that happened, we might not get anything done."

Oh, they would. He could imagine exactly what he'd do with her when she was his wife and they had private moments together. "I think we should have a long honeymoon."

"Really?"

"Absolutely."

"Hmm."

"Let's go talk with Lilly now."

Apprehension shone in her eyes. "I hope she's not going to be upset."

Roland wasn't sure about a lot of things in life,

but he was sure about how his daughter was going to react to the news. "She won't. I promise," he added as he opened the door.

Emma was sitting on the floor with Lilly in her lap. Emma had a picture book in both of her hands and Lilly was gazing at the open page intently.

"Hiya, *Daed*!" Lilly chirped.

"Hello, Lilipad. Have you been enjoying Emma's storybooks?"

"Uh-huh. She is just like the librarian. Emma's a really *gut* book reader."

Liesl giggled. "I've told her the same thing many times."

"It's something I enjoy doing," Emma said as she looked up from the book. "So, are you two all done with your private discussion?"

Liesl chuckled. "We are. But now I'm afraid Roland and I need to speak to Lilly for a few minutes without you."

Her sister raised her eyebrows as she helped Lilly climb out of her lap. "Now where should I go?"

"I think you can go anywhere you want. Jenny and Wesley are downstairs in the hearth room."

"Fine." Her sister looked a bit put out, but who could blame her?

"I'm sorry for all the moving around," he said. "It couldn't be helped, though."

Looking from him to Liesl, Emma smiled. "I think you're right about that."

After the door closed behind her, Liesl sat on the end of Emma's bed. "Want to sit here with me, Lilly? Your father and I have something to talk to you about."

His little girl scampered to her feet, then climbed up on the bed. Seconds later, Lilly was leaning on Liesl's side and staring up at Roland with wide eyes.

For a split second, panic set in as he thought about all the times she'd done the same thing with Tricia. Of course, she'd been just a tiny thing back then, and Tricia had been so frail. He'd watched them many a time with an aching heart, wishing he could grant a miracle and save his wife. Then there were the memories of him holding his daughter and feeling like he was failing her on so many levels.

And then Liesl had come into their lives, and everything had changed.

"Roland?" Liesl prodded. "Do you know what you want to say? Or perhaps you'd like me to leave also?"

"*Nee,*" he said quickly. "I mean, yes, I do know what I want to say." Feeling too far apart, he gestured to the small space left on the bed. "Do you ladies mind if I join you?"

"Of course not." Liesl scooted another five or six inches to the other side of the twin bed.

He sat down with a sigh. And realized that he needed to stop worrying so much and simply share their news.

"Lilly, I asked Liesl to marry me and she said yes. She's going to be my wife and your new *mamm.*"

Lilly's eyes widened. "Liesl wants to be my mommy?" she asked in a whisper.

All the love she'd been feeling for this tiny girl poured into her voice. "I do. I want to be your mommy so much." When Lilly continued to stare at her, she added, "I want to live with you and your Daddy...if that is okay with you?"

Lilly smiled but looked hesitant. Roland knew she needed reassurance. Maybe they all did. "Lilly, I loved your Mommy very much and I know you did, too. But like I've said before, the Lord loved her as well and took her up to heaven."

"I know. She's happy up in heaven and she watches over us."

"*Jah.* That's right. But here's the thing. Just because we loved your *mamm* doesn't mean we canna also love Liesl, too."

"I want you to be *mei mamm,*" Lilly said to Liesl.

"Oh, Lilly," Liesl murmured as she pulled her into her arms. "I know you loved your Mommy very much. I'm sure you always will. But if I could be your new mom? Well, that would be a blessing, indeed. You've made me so happy."

Roland wrapped his arms around both of them and pressed closed his eyes and silently added a word to Tricia. *Thank you for watching over us. I'll never forget you, and I'll make sure Lilly never forgets you or your love for her. You will always have a special place in our hearts.*

Standing up, he held out both hands. "Now it's time to make one more announcement."

As Lilly took one hand and Liesl took his other, she looked at him curiously. "To whom?"

"Your parents, of course."

Looking like she was about to head into battle, Liesl nodded. "Yes. Let's go get this over with. I have no doubt that they're very curious about what is going on around here."

"It is a strange Christmas Eve, for sure and for

certain. First we eat Cincinnati chili, and now everyone is announcing engagements."

"I'm half expecting pigs to start flying," Liesl quipped.

"I'm sorry, but pigs canna fly, Liesl," Lilly said. "Only birds can do that." She wrinkled her nose. "And sometimes bats."

"But not pigs? Are you sure?" she teased.

"I'm verra sure." Looking very serious, she added, "I think *mei daed* and I have a lot to teach you about living on the farm."

"I have a feeling you're right." Reaching for Lilly's hand, Liesl added, "It's a good thing that I have you to teach me so much."

Lilly nodded. "Don't worry. I know a lot."

Roland chuckled as they walked down the stairs... only to see Wesley, Jenny, Emma, and Liesl's parents all staring up at them.

"We were just about to come get you," Laura May said.

"There's no need. Everything is fine now," Liesl said. "I'm going to marry Roland, Lilly is good with it, and she's also going to teach me about taking care of pigs on a farm."

Her father blinked. "It sounds like everything is all taken care of."

"All except for one thing," her mother said.

"What is that, *Mamm*?" Liesl asked.

Her mother kneeled down and held open her arms, "Would it be possible to get a hug from my new granddaughter?"

That question was answered when Lilly launched herself into Laura May's arms.

Her mother's eyes closed as she held Lilly tight.

Chapter Thirty-Seven

Christmas Day

Wesley had woken up before sunrise, at five o'clock on the dot. After feeding the horse and gathering eggs, he made a pot of coffee and sat on the front porch. The snow that had come two days previously still lay on the ground, but the temperature had risen slightly. The clouds had dissipated as well.

It was going to be a beautiful Christmas Day.

Still dressed in his coat, hat, and heavy boots, he was warm as toast. He sipped his coffee and thought about all that had happened in just a few short weeks. First his father's illness, then their extended visit to Kentucky, and how overwhelmed he felt.

Soon after, he'd missed his date with Liesl at the Pinery and felt her disappointment in him. But it seemed everything happened for a reason. If he hadn't forgotten his date, Liesl would have never reached out to her Aunt Jenny.

Then Jenny had been his age instead of the far older woman he'd imagined. No, she'd been far more than he'd ever imagined, just as Liesl started spending time at the Hostetler house and had found a new romance as well.

And now? Well, now everything was so different than he'd ever dreamed was possible. He shook his head. The Lord truly did work in mysterious ways, and that was a bit of an understatement.

Wesley was sipping his second cup of coffee when a van pulled into the drive. Startled, he walked down to greet the driver, thinking it was likely he was lost, when a back passenger door opened and his parents and his brother Paul came out.

He stared at them in shock. Paul looked as he always did, like an older version of Wesley. He was in a dark-blue shirt and holding his coat. Their parents, on the other hand, were dressed in their traveling clothes. His mother was wearing both a black bonnet and a black cloak over her dress, and his father's salt-and-pepper beard stood out against his black hat and coat. However, beyond the somber outer garments, a fresh glow of happiness seemed to radiate from them.

He felt frozen in place as they smiled.

"Wesley! You're here to greet us! How did you know we were coming back today?"

"I didn't. I came out to enjoy the sunrise." He walked to greet them. "What a blessing, though. *Daed*, you're looking much better." He hesitated for just a moment, then gave him a hug.

"To my surprise, you're looking better, too," his *daed* said. "I have to say I'm surprised you're even awake. Usually we're all ex*haus*ted on Christmas Day."

"The store did so well this season, I kept it closed

on Christmas Eve, too. I think we should do that in the future."

His father frowned. "We'll need to discuss this, son. That isn't how we've always done things."

"I know it isn't, but I don't think being closed is wrong. I looked at the last three years' receipts, *Daed.*"

"But still—"

"Ignore him, Wesley," his mother interjected. She stepped forward and hugged him tight. "I think taking an extra day sounds like the best idea I've heard all week—besides joining our driver for an early-morning Christmas surprise."

Wesley grinned at her. "Thank you for that, and for coming home early. I couldn't ask for a better Christmas present. Now, all of you, tell me more. How did you come to be here? No one said a word when I called a few days ago."

"Doug is our neighbor, two doors to the east. When Jenna and I were over yesterday, delivering a Christmas basket, Doug mentioned that he was going to be traveling up north to see his grandparents. One thing led to another and we decided to join him."

"What are the chances?" *Mamm* asked.

Wesley walked to the van and helped Paul and Doug remove the rest of his parents' things. "Thanks for bringing my family home," he said to Doug as they shook hands.

"You're welcome, but it was my pleasure. I was glad for the company."

"Would you like to step in for a cup of coffee or anything?"

"Thanks, but we had a pit stop at a convenience

store about an hour ago. I'm eager to knock on my grandparents' door."

"Of course you are. Safe travels and Merry Christmas."

"Merry Christmas to all of you."

After another round of handshakes and Christmas wishes, Doug went on his way and the four of them stood on the porch together. The morning sun cast a bright glow over the snow-covered fields of their neighbor's house, making the snow look like bright, shiny crystals. It was a glorious sunrise for a glorious morning.

Beside him, his brother and parents seemed to be thinking the same thing. Each wore a contented expression. Little by little their bodies eased.

"I canna lie. I'm so glad to be home," *Mamm* said as she loosened the strings of her bonnet. "There's no other place like this farm. At least, not for me."

"I'm glad you all are here, too." He hugged his mother one more time. "Come on, let's get you inside. There's lots of coffee and lots of baked goods from neighbors and customers. You all can snack for days."

"I was hoping you'd say that," Paul said as he strode right in.

Daed smiled. "I guess life did continue on if everyone still brought over treats." Regret filled his father's blue eyes as he looked directly at him. "Wesley, I'm sorry if I didn't sound grateful."

His words were good to hear but unnecessary. "There's nothing to apologize about," Wesley said. "It's like you've told me again and again: Look at the positive instead of the negative. I know you were worried about the shop."

"*Jah*, but I was also worried about you."

"What?"

"It's true," *Mamm* said. "Hardly a day went by without your father fretting that his heart problems might have put too much on your shoulders."

"I'm not going to lie. There were a couple of days when I would've given a lot for the two of you to be in charge and allow me to sit back and relax. But there were also several moments when I was grateful to manage things on my own."

His father chuckled. "And maybe to not have two pairs of eyes watching every move you made."

Wesley winked. "Or commenting on those moves, too." Looking at his father in the eye, Wesley added, "*Daed*, nothing matters as much as your health. I'm very glad you are better."

"I'm glad, too." Their eyes met, once again conveying not only their love, but also the acceptance that their relationship had shifted—for the better, too. Wesley's father slapped his hands on the front of his thighs as he obviously tried to control the surge of emotion he was feeling. "Now, let's talk about something important now. Did Ethel Rosen make her sour cream coffee cake?"

"She did. Flora made cinnamon rolls, too."

"I canna wait to have a plate of each," *Daed* said as he led the way inside. "I'm starving."

"*Nee*, Able. You may have a small plate of one of those treats."

His father frowned. "Beth Ann, that's hardly fair."

"It's more than fair," Paul interjected. "We heard

the same things you did at the doctor's appointment. You have to change your ways."

Wesley frowned. "What doctor's appointment? I thought you all were resting."

"I was. Your father didn't rest as much as he should've and had a little scare."

"What kind of scare?"

"It was nothing," *Daed* groused. "They're making mountains out of molehills."

"His blood pressure spiked, he got light-headed, and his doctor almost put him right back in the hospital," Paul said.

Even their usually even-keeled mother looked shaken. "He just about gave me a heart attack."

"I don't like to hear about that. And that's a pretty bad joke, *Mamm*."

"Sorry, dear."

"I learned my lesson. Enough fussing, now."

As their parents continued to fuss, Wesley turned to his brother. "Are you staying for a few days?"

"I was planning to, if you're okay with it, of course."

"Of course I am. It will be good to have a chance to catch up."

Motioning toward their father with a nod, Paul said, "I'm looking forward to that as well. And I can also fill you in about our father's new treatment program."

Their mother stepped closer. "We also can't wait to hear the latest about you and Liesl." She clasped her hands together. "Do you finally have some news for us?"

"I do, though you'd better hold on to your hats,

because I have a feeling my news is nothing that you expected."

His mother frowned. "Is something wrong, Wes?"

"No. Actually, I think many things are very right."

Paul slapped him on the back. "Wesley, you never change, do you? Even when you were a little boy, you always drew out every story."

"This one actually does need to be drawn out. A lot of things have happened while *Mamm* and *Daed* have been gone."

"I sure hope it is good," their father said as he walked toward them. "I could use some good news."

"Please say it's *gut* news," his *mamm* said.

Wesley thought about that for a full minute then nodded. "It's such good news, I'd actually describe it as *wunderbar*."

Chapter Thirty-Eight

Late on Christmas night, long after they'd seen both Roland and Lilly and Wesley—and his parents and brother—Jenny was sitting on Liesl's bed and sipping peppermint hot chocolate.

"Remember when you used to sneak this to me when I was a little girl?" Liesl asked.

Jenny chuckled. "I could never forget. Those were some of my favorite Christmas memories."

"I was always worried you were going to get into trouble." After taking another sip, she added, "Back then, I was sure that the worst thing in the world would be to get caught drinking hot chocolate in my room."

"That's what childhood is for. Innocence is a wonderful thing."

Liesl met her gaze. "Our lives are about to change again. We're about to both be married."

"Maybe one day we'll be sitting together and sharing stories about married life," Jenny mused. Smiling at her niece, she added, "And you can even tell me stories about being a mom."

"I canna believe I'm going to be a mother before you will," Liesl exclaimed. "Though, I have to admit that I kind of like that I'll be able to give you a bit of advice from time to time instead of always the other way around."

"I'm going to love that," Jenny said.

Jenny yearned to ask if Liesl was being completely truthful about not minding that she and Wesley had fallen in love, but she knew better than to bring it up again. Asking those things might be perceived as not valuing what Liesl had with Roland. Then there was also the possibility of an unexpected reply. What if Liesl did say that she was bothered by Jenny's relationship with Wesley?

There was nothing she would be willing to do. As much as Jenny loved her sweet niece, she loved Wesley, too. She also wanted—no, needed—to have the relationship that she'd always dreamed about.

Liesl asked, "Are you sure you're going to leave tomorrow?"

"I'm afraid so. I've got a lot to tell my parents," Jenny said. "My phone call to them was a bit of a shock."

Liesl giggled. "I bet!"

Jenny chuckled as she recalled the few seconds of stunned silence that had greeted her after she'd shared her news. Then, of course, they'd had dozens of questions…too many to answer quickly or succinctly.

"My parents said they trusted me and wanted me to be happy, but that doesn't mean that their patience is infinite. I can't explain things properly from a shanty phone."

"*Nee*, I don't suppose you can. I'll miss you,

though, especially since we found love at the same time. We'll always have that bond, won't we?"

"Always."

Sitting side by side on Liesl's pink comforter, they gazed out the windows at the stars, each lost in her own thoughts.

"Hey, Jenny?" she said after a while.

"*Jah*?"

"I am really glad you came here. As crazy as everything has been, I sure wouldn't have wanted to go through it with anyone else but you."

"I feel the same way." Reaching for Liesl's hand, she held it between hers and squeezed gently. "Merry Christmas."

"Merry Christmas to you. I hope every Christmas will be as wonderful as this one."

"If it was a little more peaceful, I wouldn't mind that."

"Agreed. All right. Let's promise each other that next year's Christmas will be far more peaceful."

Jenny wisely kept her mouth closed. If she'd learned anything this year, it was that Christmas wishes and promises didn't promise a stress-free holiday.

Instead, she smiled. "Instead of wishing for something next year, let's just give thanks for the blessings we've received."

"I can do that."

Jenny could too. Leaning back, she looked out the window and simply smiled.

After all, it was Christmas. The most wonderful day of the year.

The End

Cincinnati-Style Chili

A Hallmark Original Recipe

In *Christmas at the Amish Market*, Liesl and her family eat Cincinnati-style chili every Christmas Eve. It's an unexpected tradition…but in this story about people discovering what their hearts truly want, almost nothing is expected! For any chilly day, our chili recipe is the perfect comfort food.

Prep Time: 30 minutes
Cook Time: 60 minutes
Serves: 5

INGREDIENTS

- 4 tablespoons vegetable oil
- 2 medium onions, chopped
- 1 cup celery, finely diced

- 2 green peppers, chopped
- 4 garlic cloves, minced
- 1-pound ground sirloin
- 1-pound ground pork
- 5 cups canned tomatoes
- 2 teaspoons ground cumin seed
- 4 tablespoons chili powder
- 1 teaspoon ground cinnamon
- 1/2 teaspoon ground cardamom
- 1 bay leaf
- 1 tablespoon cocoa
- 1/4 teaspoon ground allspice
- 1 tablespoon Worcestershire
- 1 (15 ounce) can tomato sauce

PREPARATION

1. Heat the oil in a large dutch oven over medium heat.
2. Add the onion, celery, pepper and garlic. Sauté 10 minutes.
3. Add the beef and pork and brown for 10 minutes or until you no longer see pink.
4. Add the remaining ingredients and bring to a boil.
5. Reduce heat and simmer, uncovered, for 1 hour; stirring occasionally.

Thanks so much for reading *Christmas at the Amish Market*. We hope you enjoyed it!

You might like these other books
from Hallmark Publishing:

An Amish Flower Farm
Wrapped Up in Christmas
On Christmas Avenue
Christmas Charms
A Simple Wedding

For information about our new releases and exclusive offers, sign up for our free newsletter at hallmarkchannel.com/hallmark-publishing-newsletter

You can also connect with us here:

Facebook.com/HallmarkPublishing

Twitter.com/HallmarkPublish

About the Author

Shelley Shepard Gray lives in southern Ohio and writes full time. A busy wife and mother of two, she spends her days writing and keeping track of her two teenagers. Her two dogs keep her company when she writes in her basement.

Shelley enjoys writing about the Amish and visits Amish communities in Adams and Holmes counties several times a year. When not spending time with her family or writing, she serves on several committees in her church. She also bakes a lot, loves coconut cream pie, and will hardly ever pull weeds, mow the yard, or drive in the snow.

Shelley also spends a lot of time online! Please visit her website, www.shelleyshepardgray.com, to find out her latest news...or become her friend on Facebook.

Turn the page for a sneak peek of

An Amish Flower Farm

An uplifting romance from Hallmark Publishing

MINDY STEELE

Chapter One

BELINDA FACE WITH HER SHORT blue sleeve and stepped out onto the porch with her family. The blue van that had come to transport her parents skidded to a stop in front of them, stirring up a plume of white gravelly dust into the air.

On any normal Saturday evening, Belinda would've been in her flower garden, singing old hymns or daydreaming about a life far different than the one she had been given. But since they'd heard the answering machine message with *Aenti* Irene's pleas for help, nothing about this day was normal.

Belinda had wanted to go with her parents to Kentucky to tend to her grandfather, Saul Graber. Dawdi was losing his battle with cancer...but her presence was needed here at home, in Havenlee, Indiana. Without their parents, each of the three siblings would have their hands full managing the family greenhouse business at the peak of the season.

Belinda would make hanging baskets and tend to the family's large gardens alone. Tabitha would continue selling their goods at the Amish market in town five days a week without Mamm to help her. And Mica would handle the farm and produce auctions, without Daed to guide him.

Belinda glanced over her shoulder as their mammi, Mollie Bender, limped outside to join them. Even her maternal grandmother would have to do more managing the house, despite the way her hip troubled her.

A short, pudgy man exited the van and began helping Daed load his and their mother's things. Belinda ducked into the shadow of her lofty brother, Mica, becoming invisible—a maneuver she had mastered in her growing years anytime unfamiliar faces drew near. He barely noticed her using him as a human shield anymore.

Her childhood unease—shyness, Mamm called it— stemmed from the port wine birthmark on her left cheek. She'd been stared at and heckled over it far too many times over the years. While she was no child anymore, interactions with strangers could make that unease surge again. The man offered a hello to each of them, sending a shudder through her.

Mamm offered up the last suitcase as they all joined her at the van. Belinda knew her mother would not be at ease until she was at Dawdi's side, willing

him to defeat the odds. And Mamm's will was nothing to scoff at. At fifty, Hattie Graber had hardly a grey hair marring her auburn locks, but Belinda could see a prominent one doing its best to slip out from under her *kapp*. She reached over and tucked the wandering An Amish Summer Farm strand back into submission. Hattie took a breath, forced a smile, and gazed over her children.

"Is Dawdi really giving up on taking treatments?"

Belinda whispered to Mamm. She was unsure how she'd feel about the answer, whatever it might be. She'd heard Mica and his friend Ivan whispering days ago that the treatments only prolonged the inevitable, that they made their grandfather sicker too. How could medicine make one feel worse than the disease? She didn't want him to feel worse, but neither did she want him to go on to glory.

Mamm took in an irritable breath. "Stubborn, that's what Saul Graber is. He thinks he can tell *Gott* when. Well, I have a thing to say about that." Belinda didn't doubt that for one minute. Her mother was certainly the most stubborn of the Graber and Bender lot.

"Your dawdi should not give up and refuse the help the doctors are trying to give," Mamm continued. "Where is his faith now?" She shook her head and knuckled away her tears.

Belinda closed her eyes and squeezed Mamm's shoulders. Her mother was the strongest person she knew, and here she was breaking down. They had all seen their share of loss, but it was one of those things a person never adjusted to. Death was cruel and robbing, and certain.

"Hattie. It's time." Mollie's voice broke the building tension.

Hattie nodded, straightening out any wrinkles of her dress that a few wayward emotions might have caused, regaining her composure. Belinda wished she could do more. But if Dawdi decided he was done with treatments, tired from trips to the clinic and the weakness that ravaged him...then, sadly, all she could do was pray.

Mamm and Daed explained to each sibling what

they expected in their absence. Meanwhile, Mammi shuffled behind them to the open side van door. Her limp was growing more painful-looking every day. Stubborn ran as thick as winter sap in her bloodline; a new hip would have given her less grief than this old one, but she refused to consider it.

Belinda buried herself in the farewell hug her father offered. His pale blue eyes were rimmed in red, but his arms were as strong and safe as they had been all her life, and he stood upright with a bearing that said he never doubted himself. Belinda had inherited Melvin Graber's eyes, but none of his self-assurance.

A damp late May breeze tickled the hairs on her lower arms, stirring a shiver. Rain-scented air mingled with the fragrance of a moist earth that would give her flower gardens the nourishment they needed to spring forth. Even thinking about her flowers and the joy they always brought her couldn't make this dreadful evening any better. She understood plenty about life and death at twenty-three, and the possibility she might never see her dawdi again, or hear his raspy voice sharing stories, broke her heart.

"We will call each afternoon and leave a message on the phone machine, if..." Daed began, his voice choked with emotion. Mica stepped forward and touched his shoulder. They no longer stood eye to eye, Mica having long ago surpassed Daed's height. In the absence of their parents, Mica would be head of the household, so Belinda knew Daed would worry little as he faced what the days ahead would require of him. Mica was responsible, levelheaded, and always did what needed done.

"Don't worry, Daed. Have faith and trust His will,"

Mica said solemnly. Daed looked up at Mica, visibly grateful that his teachings hadn't fallen on deaf ears.

"Take care of your Mammi and your *schwesters*," Melvin instructed, as if it needed to be said.

Tabitha threw two willowy arms around him tightly. They were very close, Daed and Tabitha, alike in many ways. Belinda didn't envy them that, for her parents loved them equally, but it was clear, the nearness between them; just as clear as it was that her brother and mother shared something tight-knit, too, which always made her feel like the fifth wheel. Belinda was the quiet one, and in a house with so many talkers, it often separated her from the pack.

Mammi Mollie patted her arm again, as if reading Belinda's mind. Her parents loved her, but it was her grandmother who evened out the unbalance. Mammi didn't pity her, like Daed, nor push her, like Mamm.

Her parents climbed into the middle seats of the van. "We cannot know how long we will be." Mamm poked her head out to see each of them clearly. Crickets chimed in, as if only now remembering they had a duty to perform. "Remember the things I have told you." Her mossy green eyes arrowed into Belinda's. "You have worked hard; don't waste all that effort. I know those gardens are going to be beautiful." She was speaking of the extra garden rows Daed had gifted his daughter to grow more flowers to sell, adding extra income for her family and herself. Belinda nodded, her face turning red.

She never should've told her family about her hope to have a flower farm someday. Mamm thought selling her flowers, freshly cut, was such a grand idea that they spent all winter planning for the right seeds to add market value to what had once been Belinda's hobby.

"Now Hattie, be on with ya. I'll see to them," Mammi Mollie said. "I might have all three married off before you return," she added, never one to let things get overly serious.

Tabitha chuckled at Mammi's playfulness. Mica suppressed a grin. Talk of marriage was never far from their mother's thoughts. It must be hard having three *kinner* full grown, and not a one even contemplating courting while all her friends were already bouncing *bopplin* on their knees. In this, the three siblings were equal. Having two stubborn children was just as much a burden as having one who feared speaking to others.

After a final farewell, Belinda and her siblings watched the van speed down the drive and onto the pavement. Across the street, Belinda caught a movement, and noticed Adam Hostetler, their neighbor, exiting his barn. He cast a long shadow across the field. At this hour on a Saturday night, Belinda would've expected him to be out courting Susanne Zook, as he usually did. She hoped all was well on his side of the road.

"She's gonna drag Dawdi into treatments against his will," Tabitha said to no one in particular, eyes fixed on the van racing down the asphalt.

"*Jah*," Mammi Mollie agreed. "Hattie always was a determined one."

"And we'll have at least four messages a day on our answering machine," Belinda added, pulling her gaze away from the barn across the way and the man who, oddly enough, was still standing there, gawking at them.

Mammi chuckled. "*Mei dochder* is thorough. She gets that from her daed."

Mica stepped in line with them as the van turned the bend from Mulberry Lane onto Whitley.

"What did she whisper to you?" Tabitha elbowed Mica gently. His smile came easily.

"She told me to find a worthy *maedel* before she gets back," Mica said, as the red of the van's brake lights disappeared. Belinda smiled. That wasn't a lot of time for Mica to find a suitable young woman. "Even with so much going on, she is still trying to get us married off."

"She asked me to *please* smile at Colby Plank next time he smiles at me." Tabitha shook her head. Belinda knew Colby Plank would not be receiving any smiles from her sister. Despite his owning his own cabinet shop, little about him appealed to Tabitha.

"The good Lord sends what is needed when it's time, Mica. And"—Mammi Mollie turned to Tabitha—"don't be smiling at a Plank if you can help it, dear. I don't want *kinner* running around here looking starved. Those Planks can eat all day and never gain a pound. You will work your fingers to the bone for nothing." Tabitha laughed and promised she would never smile at Colby Plank, not ever.

It was a wonder their mother hadn't taken on full matchmaking meddling to ensure a marriage in the family. Well, she'd have to depend on Mica and Tabitha for that. If God wanted Belinda to have a family of her own, then he wouldn't have marked her as he had. Belinda sighed—and then set aside the care. Life was what it was, and who was she to challenge it?

"She told me to sell my flowers," Belinda muttered. Going to town, facing strangers, and striking deals was out of the question. When it appeared Adam was strolling their way, Belinda reached for her cheek. The ugly mark had driven her to live in the shadows, keeping her head down, careful to never draw attention to herself. It was the perfect defense to protect her heart... and maybe, if she was being totally honest, her pride, too.

She wasn't naïve. She knew that some thought her strange, given her quiet nature and timidity. But she couldn't change who she was or how she reacted. Talking to others meant letting them focus on her ugliness, and just the thought of that nauseated her.

Adam reached the pavement separating their family farms, locking eyes with her. At this distance she couldn't tell if he looked concerned or simply nosy, and she didn't care. She wanted no part of his curiosity, and skedaddled off toward her gardens.

Belinda wanted to be alone in the one place she always found solace. She didn't want to be stared at by her neighbor...and no one needed to see her cry for the grandfather she might never speak to again.

Adam Hostetler could tell something was wrong this evening when he returned home. As soon as his horse was settled into pasture, he'd glanced across the road and witnessed Hattie and Melvin Graber climbing into a van. It was awfully late in the day to need a driver for something simple like shopping in the next town over, so it must be something more urgent. Everyone knew Belinda's grandfather from Kentucky had been ill for some time. Since Adam's father had been in a terrible accident a month ago, he knew what it was like to worry over family. Adam whispered a quick prayer for the neighbor family before stepping out of the shadows.

If there was one thing his recent breakup had taught him, it was that he needed to be more present in the lives of others and less consumed with his own—currently disheveled—life. And that meant reaching out to those around him. The Grabers had been his neighbors for years. A normal man would walk over to offer comfort or concern. See that all was well. When he walked toward them, he didn't fail to notice how Belinda—just a couple of years younger than his own age of twenty-five—made a quick retreat, tucking herself under the shadow of her brother. Mica had always shielded her like a faithful dog standing guard over a kitten with no *mudder*.

When Adam reached the pavement, his gaze locked with Belinda's. For more years than Adam wanted to admit, she'd been the secret object of his affection. At one time, he'd hoped she would grow out of her shyness and finally welcome his attentions. He'd waited for years and watched for subtle signs from her, but she never gave them. Just as well, really. All that foolish hoping was behind him, now that he knew the female species better. He would steer clear, never to be made a fool of again.

Adam hadn't given Belinda a close look in years,

and the distance between them was preventing him from getting a closer look now. But that habit of hers still lingered: She jerked her hand up and covered her cheek. Her eyes widened as he closed the distance. Before Adam made it to the gravel drive, she pivoted and scurried from the lawn, around the house, and out of sight.

Yes, change was inevitable; his current life was proof of that. Still, some things never changed. Belinda Graber would always be the girl who ran from him. Proof she was still as smart as she had been in school.

Mica ushered his remaining family indoors, not noticing Adam's quiet approach. Just as well. Adam shook his head and turned back to his own house and the late supper he knew awaited him. He hoped all on that side of the road was all right. If not, tomorrow was Church Sunday. If news was to be learned, he would know then. Nothing went unnoticed in Havenlee.